THE DEVIL'S SPAWN

By

David C. Brown

ISBN: 978-0-9997994-4-4
BISAC code: FIC028010

Cover Design: Mark R. Hayes
Editing: Michele Schiavone, Ph.D.

Previously Published Works:
Concrete Girl
Serendipity Hollow
Gap Hollow
The Trashman's Daughter
Donnelly's War
Boilermaker
Caroom Raid
Nitro Wild
The Spur

♠ Scott Depot, WV ♠

The Devil's Spawn

Chapter 1

Captain Alexander Belcher an army captain in command of a special force recon squad waited at a corner table in the North Warf Saloon. For the preceding four months, Al and his squad had been hunting down Ichneumon snipers who were trying to sabotage the railroad spur construction effort in the Erie Valley by murdering the workers. The squad had successfully eliminated the threat and were in River Point enjoying a brief break as they awaited the next assignment.

Al had decided to take advantage of the break to check out an opportunity at the sleazy waterfront bar. It was one of several saloons along the navigable rivers around River Point, a town in the Zircon Empire's western territories. The grimy violent establishment was no place for unwary or fastidious folks but a convenient meeting place for persons with felonious activities to discuss.

So far, his past side deals had attracted zero interest on the part of the authorities. This one was a bit more complex than ignoring a wagon load of untaxed whiskey, but potentially quite profitable. Matias Niino, owner of the Blind Owl saloon in New Hamburg had suggested he meet with Larry, an elderly felon who traded in assorted contraband items. He had to laugh at that "suggested" thought. Like he would dare ignore a request from that young harpy and lose access to the Niino factor and hawala services.

Matias wanted Al's opinion on the quality of the furs the trader had for sale. If they were silver otter pelts, the type she wanted, she would pay twelve-hundred D-marks for them. She had proven trustworthy in past deals and Al liked to stay in her family's good graces.

One thing Al had learned, whiskey was an essential lubricant for arriving at a satisfactory understanding in one of these illicit negotiations. He had purchased a sealed bottle of Simpson corn whiskey to avoid drinking the North Warf's concoction sold as house whiskey and risking his eyesight. Pouring a shot, he waited for Larry to return from his trip to the outside urinal.

After several more minutes and another glance at his pocket watch, Al wondered what could be delaying the man and looked about the noisy room to see if he had stopped at another table. No sign of the trader, but he spotted that wary brown mouse. The busy little creature had been venturing out on quick trips to harvest crumbs from a corn muffin smashed on the floor under the neighboring table. Suddenly it dashed into its hole in the wall and a moment later the peddler returned. They resumed haggling over price.

"You think I'm crazy, but those silver otters have attacked people," Larry said, addressing Al's earlier skepticism before the privy break. "They're smart creatures. Last winter three trappers never returned from checking their trap lines. Some wonder if the otters got them."

"Otters! You cannot be serious. More likely the gators or poachers got them." Just how inebriated was this character, Al wondered while watching the man help himself to the whiskey and after topping off his glass, not replacing the cork.

"Don't let that cork fall on the floor," he cautioned the man.

"Never were problems with them in the past," the trader said, while making a half-assed attempt to stick the cork back in the bottle

2

before taking a sip of whiskey. In that, the man was different from most of the bar's regulars who usually bolted their shots of whiskey.

"Neither apparently were the otters," Al answered, shaking his head at the man's ludicrous assertion of homicidal otters and recalling the playful cat sized animals he had seen in French Creek. "Your assertion an otter could kill a full-grown man is absurd."

The trader ignored Al's point, took another sip of whiskey, and renewed his pitch on why the furs were scarce and bound to explode in value. "Believe what you want, sonny. It's a fact the otters have the trappers leery about entering that swamp." Al rejected the veracity of that fact but refrained from commenting to speed up the negotiations. The old man added. "That's why along with those foolish new hunting laws these pelts are a good deal, there won't be any more to be had."

Al had some sympathy for the animals' plight. The otter's winter white fur was beautiful and much in demand in the empire's capital. The complication, one he did not understand, was many in the Wapiti and Clovis territories revered the semiaquatic weasel. If the Wapiti police discovered the skins, they would arrest the person possessing the pelts along with seizing the contraband. Al considered most laws, especially hunting laws, guidelines, not absolute rules. He did not kill the otters and if he did not do the deal, someone else would, and besides not doing the deal would not resurrect the unfortunate animals. However, if he delivered the furs to Matias, her twelve hundred D-marks would certainly resuscitate his savings.

"I might be inclined to buy the pelts, but I need to inspect them and ask where you, ah, acquired them. You're not claiming to have trapped the animals and just traveled thousand kilometers from the Uneeda swamp through hostile territory?" The man lacked sangfroid. After shaking his head for a moment, he started buttoning

3

the duffle bag containing the illicit furs and muttered, "If you're going to be like that . . . ,"

Al did not want the apprehensive trafficker to walk away and dropped several gold coins on the table. The distinct clank of heavy coins caught Larry's attention. After a moment and a glance around the room, he sat back and answered.

"I found this bag in one of the wagons abandoned by the retreating Ichneumons across from the Hickory Ridge fort. I wanted fifty gold D-marks a pelt, or two hundred and fifty for the five skins."

Loud happy cheering from a group of rivermen seated around one of the saloon's heavy oak tables caught Al's attention as he considered Larry's offer. The group had enticed, paid more likely he reckoned, one of the Warf's skinny young whores to dance naked on their table. A wretched sight: between disease, drugs, and abuse the girl was unlikely to reach her twentieth birthday. She was one of the thousands of homeless children the brutal endless war still littered the territories with. He had been one of them twenty years ago. Slavers working for Donnelly, a local warlord and those evil Ichneumons had raided his family's goat farm. His father and mother both died fighting them. The slavers raped and murdered his sister. They spared him because a neighbor, a York bootlegger, had needed a goat herder and purchased Al from the raiders. He was four years old.

Watching the young whore, he felt sad, but that was life. Some survive, many do not, but her fate was irrelevant to the pending matter. He inspected Larry's duffel bag on the floor. The black canvas bag had the Ichneumon military golden serpent logo and looked authentic. The alien army had nearly captured River Point this summer but was now in retreat down the Erie Valley. The man's story was believable, so maybe the real owner would not come looking for the pelts.

4

"Let's slip into the back room where I can inspect them." Al figured he was not the first person to discuss a violation of law in that room. He turned up the wick of the room's lamp to better watch the trader unroll the furs. They were much larger than he expected and had been properly prepared. The furs were soft and odor free.

"Throw in the bag and I'll pay the two hundred."

He paid the two hundred gold coins and later left for his room at the fort. The freight office had closed hours ago, and he needed sleep. The cry of pain from the alley grabbed his attention. He was three blocks from the saloon and had been thinking about his face-to-face meeting with the general tomorrow.

The alley was dark. Al was tired, feeling the effects of one too many shots of whiskey and, carrying a bag of illicit furs, he did not need police trouble. Still, he could see a large person several meters down the alley slapping a smaller thin person who cried, "That's all he paid me, I swear."

"Fu*king bitch, no way they only paid you twenty D-marks," the large man said in a low harsh voice. "Now give me the money, or I'll break your arm."

The pimp, at least that was Al's thoughts, followed his threat with two more slaps that sent the person, a female, he had decided, stumbling, and then falling to the alley pavement. Nothing but trouble would come from getting involved, but Al despised unfair fights, especially when a woman was involved. A large brute of a man who enjoyed a brawl, though he would claim otherwise, Al jogged into the alley and yelled, "Asshole, leave her be."

The man had stepped forward to kick the woman, but the warning caused him to snap around to see who had shouted. In a raspy loud voice, the man spoke. "She's a thieving whore who

5

cheated me. She's getting what's owed her, now f**k off like a good soldier before I hurt you too."

Al slung the bag with the furs into the thug, knocking him down. He followed with several solid kicks to stop the pimp's loud cursing and threats that might attract the night watch. Retrieving his canvas bag, he checked on the trembling girl who stood there with her hands clasped. She appeared terrified of him.

"Please, officer, don't hurt him," she mumbled while edging away from Al.

"Why are you still standing there, get out of here, go," he told her, making a skedaddle motion with his hand that sent her dashing away down the alley as the thug struggled to stand.

He had recognized the pimp's victim. She was the skinny girl who had been dancing on the table earlier in the saloon. The lack of illumination and the man's hood hid his features except for his goatee and that he was shorter than him. The thug realized his inquisitor seriously outclassed him in brawniness.

"I don't want any trouble with the army. She's gone. I'm leaving," the thug said as he cautiously edged away.

If the ass wanted to slitter off that suited Al, but he waited to make sure the thug did not pursue the girl. At the alley entrance man bolted and ran off in the direction of the saloon, opposite of where the girl went. The thug felt safe enough to pause and deliver a threat over his shoulder. "Asshole, I'll get you for this."

Al ignored him and left the dismal place and continued to his room. That tame pair of the old messenger ravens abandoned by the Ichneumon army ignored him as he passed them perched on the mess hall's trash can. The door to reach his quarters over the fort's rear stables was just across the alleyway from the mess hall rear dock. He did not spot any of the normally bold rats that foraged in the fort's garbage. The large birds must have made had the rodents wary.

Back in his cramped room above the fort's stables, Al thought that with a bit of luck, he should soon have another thousand D-marks to add to his savings. His account's current paltry balance of three thousand D-marks was a long way from his goal of a half-million in savings by the time he was forty. He was already twenty-four, in four years he had managed to save only a few thousand. He needed some big deals if he were to have any hope of reaching his goal of financial independence. Weary of being dirt poor, he hoped the new army assignment would offer better opportunities, like in the Uneeda goldfields.

Al's life as the bootlegger's slave and goat herder had lasted two years. York Anthracite Coal and the bootlegger had a falling out over double billing for cheese and milk supplies to the mine. The man who owned Al knew coal mines always needed breaker boys and by then he suspected his young goat herder was allowing two of the neighbor women to milk the goats in exchange for meals. He decided to deal with both problems and offered his young goatherder to the mine to settle the overbilling matter. Al spent the next three years breaking lumps of coal and picking rocks out of coal. Already big for his age, he was toughened by the work.

Then the new Zircon emperor, Wolfgang Schnabel, abolished slavery throughout the empire along with requiring the territories to provide all children a free basic education. The coal company begrudgingly complied. Al's mother had been a teacher and in the process of teaching him basic math and reading when the raiders murdered her. As a result of having some prior knowledge, he benefited from the required lessons. His grades bought him to the attention of the mine's chief engineer, Marc Wistrich who was looking for a goffer to help around the office. By Al's twelfth birthday the engineers had him helping with their survey calculations needed to draw the mine maps when they did not have him carrying survey equipment or cleaning the office.

Near his sixteenth birthday Al got in a fight with the mine owner's adult son over a girl, a fight that put the son in the hospital with a broken jaw and other injuries. Al had a choice, join the army or jail. He joined the army. To his surprise, he adapted well to the medieval mindset of the Zircon army and applied for and passed the Officer Candidate School program. He never ran from a fight and the army value that lack of sense.

General Markel, the commander of the Zircon territorial forces, was visiting the River Point fort, Al's station for the last two years. The general had called a 6am assembly on the fort's parade ground to inform his men on the status of the army's campaign to eliminate the Ichneumon presence in the entire Erie Valley and retake Port Delta.

Al was eager to learn if his squad would receive a new independent task or be reintegrated into the 88th Mountain Division ranks. After the meeting, the general and his aides such as Colonel Caprivi would meet with select unit commanders and give them their special assignments. He hoped a call would come.

The Zircon commander, General Markel, a clean-shaven, muscular man with dark thick hair, cut short, wore the same gray-green Wehrmacht combat uniform as Al's, except it was new, unstained, and not tattered. He would guess the general's age at around mid-thirties, a decade or so older than he was. They were both around 185 centimeters in height and weighed about ninety kilograms. Both were OCS graduates and both men had strong voices that carried well.

After the small military band played the stirring "Call to the Colors" tune the general told the several hundred soldiers that Emperor Schnabel and the free people of the empire were proud of the army's efforts to eliminate the scourge of slavery and Ichneumons from the western territories and rivers. To loud cheers he told the men of the recent battle that the army won recently that freed the important river town of Westport, known as the gateway to the gold fields. He then told them that two of the navy's new super battleships would join the army for a final drive on the Ichneumon stronghold at Port Delta.

"One more great push, men, for our beloved emperor. We will deliver the entire Erie Valley from the northern icefields to the Iapetus Ocean to human control," the general shouted to the cheering crowd and the band played "Hail to the Emperor."

One of Colonel Caprivi's messengers, a lieutenant, found Al by the fort's south gate an hour later haggling with an old Clovis woman street peddler who sold various sweets and candy. He wanted a twelve-count box of Beckman chocolate bars. She did not have one in her pushcart and was telling Al to check tomorrow. She would be sure to have one if he would agree to her price. The lieutenant interrupted their friendly haggling and told Al the colonel wanted him to report, now, to the general's office. That was what he had hoped for and told the woman he would look for her tomorrow. If she had come to her senses on the price, he might buy two boxes.

"Sonny boy, the price will not be lower tomorrow," she answered with a laugh and a shake of her head as she watched him jog off with the lieutenant.

The stone temple the Ichneumons had built in the fort for their sacrifices to the Sun God now served as the general's office. The creatures had occupied the area over a half century, until the Wapiti rebels had won the fort during the Donnelly troubles. They had turned it over to their ally, the Zircons as part of the agreement to become an independent territory in the Zircon empire instead of part of an enlarged Guderian Territory.

Chapter 2

About the time Al was going to the meeting with General Markel, the Ichneumon general in command of the Erie Army and the fort at Port Delta, General Paget, was boarding a large battleship anchored in the Iapetus Ocean near the Erie River's delta. Emperor Ratakonda had abruptly summoned him to a meeting, and he was nervous as any sane person would be.

Paget realized with a start that the old and shriveled bald Ichneumon male with alert clear golden eyes who greeted him was the emperor. The man had aged since Paget's last audience three years ago when the emperor had promoted him to head the Erie Army command. The public pictures of Emperor Ratakonda always depicted a vigorous large man with a stern mien.

"General Paget, I know you are a busy man and will keep this meeting sort," the emperor said in a pleasant voice while motioning for him to take the left chair.

The meeting was in the admiral's plush private quarters behind the battleship's bridge. The admiral was not in attendance. The rear door opened and Prince Cherukuru, rumored successor to Ratakonda, entered and asked Paget in a mocking voice, "Lost any more forts since Westport?"

The prince was a simpleton and Paget made the effort to not take offense and answered, "No my lord."

"Nephew, let us focus on the reason for calling the meeting," the emperor said. "The Zircon navy's two new battleships are steaming toward Delta. They will arrive off Delta in five days and have orders to blockade the Erie. Another Zircon fleet will deliver soldiers that will land near Delta and lay siege to the fort while

General Markel is to make a major push down the Erie to take Fenwick."

This was about what Paget's command had been expecting as the emperor added. "I am not too worried about the enemy's battleships. Fools command them. Our navy will focus on the enemy troop transports. My question to you is, can you hold Fenwick?"

"I will or die in Fenwick trying." Paget answered.

The prince started to say something, but his uncle cut him off with a hand signal and spoke. "I am not interested in last stand nonsense. I want the Zircon western army eliminated, and if that involves retreating, do it. Just do not lose the Erie River and our fort at Delta."

Paget understood, it was his battle to win however he thought best, but only victory would save his life. He had no problem with that, thought the old emperor showed good sense giving him free range and not trying to direct the action from a distance.

Later over dinner before disembarking, Prince Cherukuru addressed his and the Sun God Church's concern about the number of free humans in the Erie Valley. They thought Paget needed to remind his men the Empire's long-term goal was eliminating all free humans from the Erie Valley and western territories.

"If the person is not a slave or one of us, he should be shot on sight. I hear the humans are running free in the western territories. The old-womanish fool in charge of Uneeda, Colonel Kropp, is still doing business with them. I want to put backbone in the Uneeda command by putting Colonel Gupta in charge. He will put Uneeda right, give my cousin, Lieutenant Halona some help."

Paget knew the colonel was a hard merciless killer. The Sun God Church's genocide policy was a strategic mistake, but his opinion counted for nothing. The Clovis and Wapiti massacres had united the natives against the Ichneumons and made them allies of the

Zircon Empire. Other than that concern, he thought the world would be a better place if the only humans were slaves. He assured the prince he would provide Colonel Gupta safe passage to Uneeda and all requested support.

Al had to wait in the hallway about an half hour before General Markel's aide, a one-armed captain came to escort him into the commander's office.

"Captain Belcher, you look well," General Markel said from behind a paper-cluttered old wooden desk, before adding. "I compliment you and your crew on a job well done. I made the emperor aware of your squad's vital role in the successful completion of the spur railroad."

The kind words surprised Al. He had expected the colonel to instruct him on the reason for the meeting, not send him to the general's office. He and the colonel had never clicked, but he liked his commander.

Other than brief thanks for the compliment to his men, Al resisted the urge to talk as he watched the general search among the documents scattered on his desk. Instead, he wondered if the general and the colonel genuinely appreciated just how determined and capable those enemy snipers were. Four of his men, good soldiers, died in three ambushes during that four-month period the squad hunted down the seven Ichneumon snipers. The enemy wounded Al during two of those ambushes. The man found what he was looking for under his coffee mug. Smiling the general said.

"This assignment is perfect for your squad. They deserve a break. The Imperial Intelligence Service has requested the army contact their agent, Hans Maxim, in Uneeda. He works for the Bergdorf mining company. They have not heard from him in the two months since he requested a transfer. I want you and your squad to travel there and recon the area."

That task sounded easy enough to Al as the general added, "I need to know whether the Ichneumons still control the area or if the Oztec tribes revolted and seized the mine. The IIS claims no gold has come into Westport for several months. Check on their agent and help him, but I need to know if he thinks occupation of Uneeda can wait until I have won control of Delta."

Frankly, thinking of his experience with agents of the Imperial Intelligence Service, better known as the IIS, he would be surprised if their agent had much useful information to offer the general. Al inferred his orders to mean Markel and the IIS were worried the Ichneumon army had found a way to slip the gold by the Zircon blockade at Westport, a city located by the confluence of the Erie and Uneeda Rivers.

The new mission pleased Al. He had read about Westport, an unruly decent sized river town five hundred kilometers down the Erie from River Point. For the last twenty years it served as the jumping off place to Uneeda for gold prospectors and miners until the Ichneumons closed all the rivers to humans. Al had envisioned going to the western gold fields after completing his six-year OCS obligation next year if he decided not to make the army his career. He believed where there was gold, surely there would be opportunities.

The fur peddler had added to his knowledge of the Uneeda River. The river was the outlet for Uneeda Lake in the high western mountains. It flowed east from the lake as a placid deep river until it cut through the escarpment that separated the grasslands from the swamp. There the river slowed and transformed into multiple ever-shifting channels and oxbows for three hundred kilometers. The area was a vast swamp and wilderness with tree-covered hammocks, sand bars, open water, and fields of tall reeds. Tannins from the swamp and reed beds gave the river water a light tea-like color by the time it reached the Erie. The Uneeda River valley was a wild place, a roadless place.

14

"Sir, will a river boat be available?"

"Yes, but not one of the navy's river boats. They are committed to supporting my men and keeping the pressure on the retreating bastards. I am not stopping until I have reached the ocean. Knight Industry will provide an old paddle wheeler and crew to transport your men. Any reason you couldn't embark this afternoon?"

"No sir," Al snapped, keen to go.

The general studied him for a moment, then added. "The last item is a rumor the Ichneumons are killing the Zircon families in the Uneeda Valley. If that is occurring, I want to know and for you to help them escape to safety."

"Just help our people escape," Al asked thinking of those murderous sons of bitches and his family, then added. "Or can I go after the bastards doing the killing?"

"I will leave that to your judgment, captain."

Al spent the rest of the day organizing his squad for the mission and meeting with Lieutenant Kurt Bär, who collaborated with the Quartermaster. Kurt would supply the explosives Al had requested. The riverboat assigned to the Uneeda mission was at the coal dock upriver taking on the boiler fuel and supplies for the trip to Westport and would return this evening to River Point. In the morning, Al and the recon squad would board while the Quartermaster troops delivered the explosives and special items.

A large swarthy man of uncertain ancestry and around Al's age waited at the gangway used to access the twin sidewheeler, Mischief, docked at the pier near the North Wharf bar. The riverboat's captain wore faded bib coveralls with rubber knee boots. He reminded Al of an impoverished Myrtle sharecropper, except for the ratty captain hat with greenish stained brass trim.

"Captain Belcher, welcome to the Mischief. My name is Bill Walker. The boss said I'm to haul your squad to Uneeda." He removed his hat and made a sweeping kowtow. "I thank you, sir, for saving us from the boredom of pushing coal barges up and down the Erie."

That the captain appeared to have a sense of humor cheered Al. The Uneeda trip would be his first experience with a civilian river boat. The navy with some justification referred to the commercial riverboat crews as river rats. His first glance about the Mischief's deck discovered minor bits of dirt and straw in the corners and under the stairs to the pilot house. A Zircon navy boat captain would never tolerate such shoddy housekeeping.

Someone, the colonel maybe, had told him the Mischief steamboat had once belonged to an Ichneumon prince. It was his private vessel, until the Wapiti soldiers captured it and the prince. It then served as the Wapiti rebels navy's only ship during the Donnelly troubles and was credited with sinking three of the Ichneumon riverboats during that conflict. The fifty-two-meter long by seventeen-meter wide two-hundred-ton steamer could carry two hundred and twenty tons of cargo, not counting the normal fuel load.

General Markel told him the boat's current captain, Bill Walker, had a background like Al's. Both were made orphans at an early age by raiders employed by Ichneumon slavers. The Mischief captain had spent his childhood working in an Ichneumon saltpeter operation as a slave. Al reckoned a man raised around that foul odorous process to convert urine into potassium nitrate did not view a bit of dirt or poorly mopped deck as cause for concern.

"My orders are to deliver your men to Uneeda," Bill said, uncomfortable with Al's silent inspection of the boat. "That swamp we will pass through is a dangerous place. You should tell your men to keep their weapons handy."

"Don't worry, they sleep with their rifles," Al said, then did a quick inspection of the engine room, which, unlike the deck, was immaculate. He decided the well-constructed older boat would serve his mission fine. He also concluded Bill was the chatty sort. The skipper had tagged along on the inspection answering questions not asked and pointing out this and that item.

On returning to the dock Bill said, "I saw you in the North Warf Bar with Larry."

The comment startled Al, and he thought back to the person he had noticed in the dump and asked, "You were at that table with that, ah, dancing lady?"

The riverboat captain nodded and said, "Sisi has had nothing but bad luck since she ran off from her family. We shouldn't have egged her on."

"Why did she do it?"

"Why, for the money," Bill said, surprised by his question.

"I meant run off," Al clarified, thinking of that large new orphanage the Clovis and Wapiti tribes were organizing in Rainelle for the war foundlings and homeless youngsters, then realized she was too old for that.

"Sisi was in one of those strict families that thought laughter and fun the devil's work. Might have been an abusive relationship, I do not know. She did talk of wanting adventure, seeing the world. Instead, a pimp hooked her on that damn sole-nut cocaine. If she does not stop, she is doomed."

Al pitied the Sisi's of the world, but that was life. Then he remembered the other night encounter and said, "I saw her that night, some pimp was beating on her, said she owed him money. Did you pay her?"

"Hell yes, we all chipped in a nice tip of twenty D-marks," Bill snapped, offended by the question. After a pause and a look at him, the skipper sighed and asked, "Did you stop the bastard?"

"She slipped off while I talked with the jerk. He was after fifty D-marks."

"That had to be Oscar. He is an ass and dangerous," Bill said, then shaking his head in disgust, added. "The bastard knew there was no sex involved, just a friendly dance."

A fine distinction on what constituted a sexual act Al thought, but Bill's earlier remark troubled him. He was not in the clear until the Blind Owl's owner possessed the otter furs. He disliked outsiders-strangers knowing about his side deals. Al asked. "Do you know Larry?"

"Yeah, he's a dealer. You act surprised. Did you expect that no one would notice Larry carrying a heavy Ichneumon army duffel bag into the back room and then later a Zircon captain leaves with the same bag? Looked like a drug deal, was it?" After a moment and a glance at him, Bill added. "Then again you're right, not any of my business."

Drugs, damn. That thought never entered Al's mind. He hoped that fur deal did not have General Markel thinking he was trading illicit drugs. Getting an understanding from the Blind Owl using a series of brief telegrams and the bag delivered to the freight office and on the train had been enough of a hassle. It nearly got him in trouble for being late to the morning assembly. The thousand D-marks added to his bank account made it worthwhile, but in future deals he needed to consider the pitfalls, not just the money, the profits.

"You need to worry about delivering us to Uneeda, not duffel bags," Al snapped, irritated over realizing he had been lucky, not smart, in the fur deal.

Bill, startled at the sudden hostility, replied. "Just trying to be friendly," and then after a moment added, "Looks like the weather is going to be nice."

By then, the troops, ammo boxes, and pallets of the dynamite arrived, saving Al from having to explain more about the bag or comment on the weather. Instead, he jumped to supervising Bill, the boat crew, and his squad on loading the cargo. Knowing a high-powered rifle bullet might detonate the dynamite, the crew's usual method of loading cargo would not be safe. Al had the explosives and ammo placed in the very bottom of the cargo holes. Unfortunately, that required first removing Bill's cargo from the hole.

The accountant, Hans Maxim, was a not-so-young agent with the Imperial Intelligence Service or IIS. Several years before the current war, the secretive agency sent him to establish an accounting service with the purpose of tracking developments in the Oztec Territory gold fields. With help from the IIS, Hans within a year had a thriving accounting and tax filing services with all the Uneeda mine owners. They were Zircon citizens with the obligation to pay the empire's taxes no matter where they earned their income. Then as Herr Bergdorf acquired various gold leases, Hans found most of his work was for Bergdorf Mining. Finally, after clearing it with the agency, he accepted an offer to become the mining company's treasurer and handle the marketing of their gold.

Then the current Ichneumon army commander, Colonel Kropp, arrived, and murdered Jesuit-educated Chief Aveo and many of his Agarwal tribe subchiefs, seized his town and garrisoned the stone fort. The invasion also scattered the Oztec people and broke Chief Aveo's Agarwal Nation into several bickering smaller tribes throughout the lands around the lake. The alien's army left the miners alone, but required they sell all their gold to Ichneumon buyers. The result was the gold started going to Delta, not the Zircon capital, Merlin.

The Ichneumon conquerors used, Hans thought consumed a better word, slaves as did his employer. The Agarwal tribe had been involved in the slave trade to a limited degree before Chief Aveo banned the practice years ago. Now in control of Uneeda and needing slaves, the Ichneumons told Chief Laredo, a wannabe warlord, who had united a few of the various remnants of the old Agarwal Nation that slavery was legal. Telling this to the Laredo clan was like telling a fox it could hunt rabbits.

Under guidance from the brutal Laredo gang, five of the western Agarwal tribes enthusiastically reverted to livestock rustling and raiding their neighbors for captives to supply the expanding demand from the gold mines and Ichneumon army for slaves. By the time the Zircon Ichneumon war started, the Uneeda Valley had become a brutish merciless place even by frontier mining camp standards. Hans believed it was only a matter of time before Chief Laredo tried to seize the mine and murdered Bergdorf men and him. And no sane human trusted those Sun God partisans like Colonel Krupp. He told the IIS he wanted out and started planning the theft of a Bergdorf gold shipment to finance his retirement.

Chapter 3

The five-hundred-kilometer section of the Erie River between River Point and Westport was peaceful now. The burned-out villages, abandoned wharfs, and farms the Mischief steamed by testified to the bitter four-year war that had raged until recently in the valley.

A light rain had driven Al inside from his preferred perch on top of the pilot house. The Mischief's captain, Bill, was at the riverboat's helm and his crew of five was down in the boat's interior. The contract with the army called for two meals per day and Al figured the cook and her helper were in the galley fixing their evening meal, hopefully something different from the pinto bean, rice, and cornbread served last night. The morning meal was eggs, bacon, flat wheat cakes. Everyone aboard liked the meal. The fresh eggs came from the twenty Brown Ridge hens Bill kept in a large wire cage when traveling. The hens were smart for Al had heard when the Mischief docked in rural areas, Bill allowed the chickens to run free on shore. A blast on the boat's steam whistle would bring the birds running for their cage.

"That abandoned fort and dock," Bill said pointing toward an old-style log post stockade on the east shore of the river. "That shit hole is where I was born and lived until Herr Knight freed me five years ago." The general had told Al about Bill's background and he asked.

"Is that the same person who owns Mischief?"

"Yes, he is my boss and a great guy. I used to compose piss and moldy hay to make saltpeter, worst damn job on the planet. Took a month, after Knight freed me to get rid of the odor and before women would allow me near them." His normal cheerfulness returning as the riverboat carried them on down the river. He changed subjects. "Are you married, captain?"

That deft topic switch gave Al pause. He was not one inclined to share his thoughts on personal matters, but knowing the chatty skipper intended no harm, answered, "No, never met the right woman. What about you?"

"No, I'm skeptical marriage works for a riverboat man," Bill answered, then with a chuckle added. "Besides, there are women at every port to be had."

"Yeah, along with every damn disease known to man," Al snapped, disgusted with the prevailing misogyny among most Zircon soldiers and rivermen or their stupidity to think that a woman's only utility was sex. Bill's startled look reminded him few of his associates shared his opinions and he changed topic again. "Think you will get your own riverboat?"

"For sure, I'm an entrepreneur and will one day have a fleet of ships," Bill said as he adjusted the boat's rudder to swing farther into the main channel. "Herr Knight has offered to sell the Mischief to me for ten thousand D-marks."

"I would have thought this boat worth at least fifty thousand," Al said surprised at the figure. The twin drive assembly with two tandem compound engines was worth three times that price. The boiler was old but of a modern design and appeared well maintained, so Bill's boss had offered him a sweetheart deal. Al hoped their mission did not result in the destruction of the sturdy riverboat as Bill explained.

"It is, he is just doing me a favor. I helped him rescue the Wapiti captives the Ichneumons held at Bone Valley and recover the hundred thousand D-mark ransom."

The second evening on the riverboat Al learned Herr Knight allowed Bill considerable latitude in entering freight hauling contracts. The Hawick farm, the largest Clovis territory hog farm, had hired the Mischief in River Point to haul sixteen fifty-kilogram barrels of their prime white lard to a market in Westport. Curious, Al had been present during the negotiations and afterward had asked what the freight charge was. Six hundred D-marks a pleased Bill told him.

"I get forty percent of the freight charges on small jobs I find. The riverboat account gets the balance, but that money also covers the costs associated with the shipment. The cut from those side deals is how I'm raising the ten thousand."

Al wanted to ask how close Bill was to having the payment saved. A hell of a lot closer than he was to his saving goal, he figured. Then again it was not any business of his, same as why that young girl, Sisi, was washing the cook's pots and pans in the boiler room.

The following morning Bill asked Al who had been honing his sword while sitting on top of the pilot house. "Where do you expect to encounter the Ichneumons after we enter the Uneeda River?"

"Their first fort is at Prenter, about a hundred kilometers upriver from Westport. I figure there, though their snipers might be encountered anywhere in the valley."

"That is my worry," Bill agreed nodding his head and then added, "The Mischief is not armored, and we will be vulnerable targets for enemy sharpshooters hiding on the riverbank."

"You're right. That is our weakness. I will assign men to watch the riverbanks for trouble, but by the very nature of a sniper attack, our defense can only be reactive. Until the enemy fires, chances are you will not know of his presence until then. That is why when we reach Westport, find some iron plates to protect the pilot house. My men will rearrange the firewood for our protection."

The Zircon Navy did not approve of false flag operations, but Al knew the general did not care. Bill was for any action that helped protect his Mischief and nodded in agreement as Al added. "Before reaching Prenter, I will switch flags to the Ichneumon golden serpent flag to help confuse our enemy."

About mid-morning on the third day and about thirty kilometers upriver from Westport, Al was resting on the pilot house roof enjoying the warm weather and sun when Bill yelled for him to look. Scrambling to his feet, he saw one of the army's new forty-meter armored warships designed for the territory's rivers bearing toward them. He had heard about them, but this was the first one he had seen. The sleek black boat used a propeller driven by a steam turbine powered by an oil burning boiler. The warship's bite came from two rotating gun turrets, each with a breech loading cannon that shot twelve-kilogram exploding shells

"Are they stopping us?" Al asked, joining him in the pilot house as several of his men gathered on the deck to learn why the Mischief was slowing.

"That is the Zircon Ray," Bill answered. "I know the captain." About then a navy officer and three armed marines exited the bridge area and walked to the forward deck as the warship matched the Mischief's drifting speed.

Al was worried the iron-clad vessel was too close and would brush against the Mischief's portside paddlewheel housing and cause damage. Bill and the warship commander, Captain Corliss were yelling insults and greetings, clearly old acquaintances and unconcerned the ships were too close, so he said nothing and just listened. By then half of Al's recon squad had collected along the portside upper deck to watch and listen. They were a group of young strong robust men. Most had been relaxing shirtless in the sun, but they all had their rifles. The commander looked concerned and asked Bill about them.

Al answered instead. "They are part of my recon group, army rangers, the Mischief is transporting them for General Markel."

Satisfied, Corliss quizzed Bill on what traffic they had passed earlier today. They told him nothing of note, only one old sternwheeler, a few local sail and fishing crafts.

"My orders are to locate and sink the enemy warship, Saukko, before it can ambush our troop carriers, and General Markel, whom we expect to arrive in two days from River Point. The warship was spotted on the Erie last night near Westport." That news had Al concerned and he asked them what the Saukko was.

The captain of the warship, Corliss, in a booming voice answered.

"The Saukko is an older sixty-meter-long armored, heavily armed sternwheeler that had been on patrol duty in Uneeda River. With us now holding Westport, we figure the Ichneumon Navy had ordered it to leave the Uneeda River to avoid entrapment and patrol the lower Erie to help the defenders at Delta."

The news cheered Al and Bill, for they both knew the Mischief did not have a chance against even one of the older armored warships like the Saukko. Bill had earlier discussed his fear of encountering an Ichneumon warship while traveling up the Uneeda

River. During their peaceful trip down the Erie River, Al had argued the Ichneumons would not want any of their warships trapped in Uneeda with their forces at Delta needing all the help they could mobilize to stop the Zircons. Captain Corliss's news confirmed that, and Bill was happy.

"Well, if the Saukko had gone up the Erie," Corliss yelled from the Zircon Ray's deck, "It would have encountered and sunk the Mischief, so I think it's safe to assume it went down the river, probably headed to Delta." With a wave, he ordered the Zircon Ray to pulled away. The sleek war ship was soon out of slight heading south on the broad river. Still an uncertainty remained in Al's mind. By rights the Saukko should have left Uneeda River before the Ichneumons lost Westport, or at least near that time, not two weeks later, if the plan were to avoid entrapment.

The rest of the beautiful sunny spring day the men checked their weapons, rested, and played cards. They reached Westport that evening with an empty coal bunker. Al had his men help Bill's crew lay in boiler fuel, wood, since coal was in short supply this far down the Erie.

Sergeant Jones, a veteran Zircon NCO, and Al went on to the fort where Jones would organize the ammo transfer from the Mischief to the fort. Al reported to the Westport commander, Colonel Haddad. The colonel knew of the IIS agent Maxim but had no current news on him. His other news worried Al.

"Something is not right," the Westport commander said. "There is no traffic out of Uneeda. The swamp fur trappers missed the annual fur and hide auction. None of them showed, nor has any anyone shipped gold for months. The rumor is that a plague killed everyone."

The Devil's Spawn

"I don't like hearing that," Al said, thinking that it sounded like the explanation for the mass Clovis graves his squad had discovered, which he now knew was from the Ichneumons effort to exterminate humans.

"Since we don't know what you'll encounter upriver, keep most of the rifle ammo you were to deliver to the garrison. You are the one that will need it." Al liked that order and sent word to Sergeant Jones.

Colonel Haddad paused to open a battered ammo box on his desk and extract a thin cigar. He offered one to Al who declined. While the colonel trimmed the end of cigar and lit it to his satisfaction, Al's thoughts, probably because of remembering those gruesome mass graves, turned to the freightened young children, orphans, his squad had helped round up after that last bloody battle across from Hickory Ridge. That Zircon attack sent those murderous bastards fleeing down the river. In the ensuing panic the Ichneumons abandoned not only items like the otter pelts, but the children they had collected while murdering their families. He learned later those monsters had planned to use the children as slaves and for living sacrifices to their Sun God. He hoped those inhuman bastards were not repeating that horror in Uneeda.

Those creatures were a mystery. The hemocyanin Ichneumons were the other species of bipedal cognitive people on the planet Erden. Other than their pupils' vertical slit, instead of the round opening of a human's eye, they looked human, even came in assorted skin tones like humans. Their empire ruled a large section of the southern continent. The locals' slang terms for Ichneumons were "blue bloods" and crabs, not because they were upper-class aristocrats, but because their blood was blue like a crustacean's.

To understand their, well inhuman behavior, he had listened to and read several opinions on the reason for the sporadic, but deadly ethnic cleaning Ichneumons unleashed on indigenous populations. The Clovis genocide in the Erie Valley was the most recent outbreak. Most of the explanations centered on the aliens wanting the targeted tribe's land and wealth for themselves. He knew humans had succumbed to similar impulses, but he also wondered if the inability of the two species to breed and produce a hybrid had any bearing on the two races' endless wars for supremacy.

Thankfully, after much striking of, and breaking of matches, the Westport commander had his cigar lit to his satisfaction and Al's thoughts returned to the here and now as the colonel spoke.

"General Paget will have a lot to answer for when our forces rout him out of Delta." The colonel was referring to the Ichneumon commander's involvement in the murdering of civilians by his soldiers. Unfortunately, Al figured that might be a while. Paget and his men were in a massive stone fort a thousand kilometers away where the Erie entered the Iapetus Ocean.

"The other rumor was those Oztec tribes attacked the gold fields. Those brown savages are no allies of ours, don't let your guard down around them," the colonel added, exhaling a dense cloud of foul smoke.

As far as Al knew, he had never met an Oztec. The scuttlebutt had them as a backward tribe of brown people that the Ichneumons had driven into the mountains from their homeland around the large western lake. After six years Al was familiar with prevalent racism in the Zircon society and army. He ignored the colonel's xenophobia. At least Oztecs are human, he thought, not more aliens.

The Westport commander after pausing to examine the ash on the end of his cigar, added, "General Markel wanted information on why no traders, gold or otherwise, were traveling the Uneeda. I told him I have no way to find out. There is no telegraph to Uneeda, the Ichneumons stripped the Westport area of steamboats, and the army won't loan me one. I was able to hire a local fisherman with a sloop to make the run to Uneeda with two of my marines, but the winds are usually unfavorable this time of the year for traveling upriver."

Al agreed, the fisherman might as well plan to row the three hundred kilometers. "If we encounter him, okay I tell him to return to Westport and take your marines with my crew?"

The colonel nodded and Al added, "My instructions are to recon the area and assist Hans Maxim. I will watch for your men, but the Saukko might have spotted and sunk your sloop."

"Yes, I thought that too. Well at least you will not have to worry about that warship. It fled the Uneeda last night. I just pray the lack of travel is not from some terrible virus killing our people." Al suspected the colonel was thinking about the smallpox virus the Ichneumons spread throughout the world a hundred and fifty years ago.

"One change, tell your men, no shooting of the wildlife for target practice, only if needed for food." That was a wasteful cruel habit Al had never tolerated in his men. The colonel, after exhaling a cloud of smoke added, "And they're not to bother the otters, they're now protected."

Curious, Al asked, "Maybe that's why the trappers didn't show, if otter fur is illegal to possess."

"Those swamp rats don't let laws interfere with business. I figured they would show to sell their muskrat and gator pelts at the open auction and the otter furs later in the black-market and bars. I am glad they changed the law. I like those otters and do not think we should murder them for their fur. People who profit off the cruel trade should be ashamed of their behavior. Well, enough preaching, just remember the general asked we not trap or shoot them."

"Okay, I'll tell everyone," Al answered, wondering if this sudden love for otters would trash his Matias Niino deal as he waited for the colonel to pen a brief note ordering his two marines to join the recon unit.

As Al waited for Colonel Haddad's note, seven hundred kilometers off to the northeast from Westport a meeting was underway in the Guderian Territory Governor's private office in New Hamburg. The official purpose of the meeting concerned candy, Beckman chocolate bars. Count Harlem Penton, owner of Highland Plantation and Myrtle Cotton Bank, had suffered considerable loss of revenue because of the emperor's abolishment of slavery. The Count had an opportunity to acquire sole distribution rights in territories west of the Erie River for the popular candy bar but had learned one of the Beckman brothers was against the deal. The other person present in the office was the governor's chief of commerce, Stan Blankenship, an ambitious and charismatic amoral man who wanted to be the next Guderian governor.

The Count said, "Stan, I need you to speak with the younger Beckman brother on my behalf. He fears my past dealing in slaves will impact the public perception of Beckman as a friendly enlightened wholesome business. God damn it, it was all legal. He acts like I'm a criminal for supplying cotton to the army."

Harlem, the overweight grandfather sort, had been responsible for much evil and misery over the years. Stan had to agree young Beckman had a point but answered, "These youngsters don't appreciate what it takes to supply the empire's cotton. I'll speak to him, clear up any misunderstandings concerning you. His older brother asked me to speak against the raw sugar tariff hearing on Thursday. I'll bring your matter up at the reception following the hearing."

"Good, liquor them up," the old slaver said, nodding in agreement with the plan.

The Devil's Spawn

"I had a question for you." Stan had hesitated for several days on whether to involve Harlem in his plans because General Markel detested the slaver over his treatment of the railroad workers. "Is your sternwheeler, the Rouser, operational?"

Harlem nodded yes and with a shrug of his shoulder, asked why.

"What about your old crew chief, Captain Reed, is he available to run it?"

"The last heard. He is not in jail and hanging out in River Point saloons drinking and gambling. He would jump at a chance to make money. What do you have planned?" he asked, helping himself to one of the small, tasty cakes on the table.

"Your old partner, Count Laumeister wants to visit Uneeda on one of his "inspection" trips and needs a riverboat. Apparently, the army is too busy fighting the Ichneumons to be able to provide transportation until Delta falls."

They both had had dealings with the emperor's distant cousin in the past. The aristocrat was untrustworthy. His method was to use an inspection to discover violations of regulations and laws. That information he then used to extort, blackmail, the managers running the agencies and programs. In return for the proper payment to him, the Count would not reveal the breeches and instead give the manager a favorable inspection report.

"Why would I want to send my only riverboat into a warzone to haul that crooked numbskull to Uneeda?"

"Bergdorf was here about six months ago on some matter, equipment for his mine, I think. He had dinner with me and bragged those placer deposits of his along the Uneeda foothills were productive. The mine was producing about a ton a month of pure gold."

"Nope, not pure gold, it averages about seven percent silver by weight," Harlem injected, adding, "It's still damn valuable. A ton,

31

you say?" They exchanged looks, before he said, "Where is it going? I know there has been no gold to come through Westport in the last few months."

"According to our friend, Bergdorf, the Ichneumon commander is storing the gold in the fort's dungeon at Uneeda." With an upturn of his hands and a shake of his head, he added, "Of course, who knows how much Bergdorf has actually mined. Hell, Harlem, you know he's a bullshitter."

"No doubt, but there could be by now several, maybe six or eight tons of gold in that fort." Harlem said and then with a smile asked, "You have a plan?"

"I do. It's a bit nebulous, especially on the amount of gold in the fort and the strength of the garrison guarding it. What I do know is Markel only plans to send a recon patrol to Uneeda, primarily to help protect the Zircon settlers from the Ichneumons if they decide to start killing our people. The army is not planning on taking Uneeda until after Delta falls."

"That might never happen," the old slaver grumbled.

"I heard Markel is sending his best recon squad. The one that prevented the snipers from blocking the spur construction." Stan knew those railroad saboteurs had been on Harlem's payroll and he was resentful the Zircon troopers had bested him. "The key point is the Ichneumon garrison can't replace their losses. And if a few of the Oztec tribes help the recon squad, the fort might very well fall."

"Anything is possible, but a squad of soldiers taking that fort, nah!"

"Think of the confusion if that surrender happens with only a captain or a lieutenant in charge with a dozen men trying to manage prisoners while protecting all that gold from that band of thieves in Uneeda. Wouldn't you want your man Reed and his crew there to help the captain protect the emperor's gold under Count Laumeister's authority?"

Shrugging, Harlem said, "I doubt the Ichneumons are that weak, but I'll concede your scenario is not impossible. That's why you want me to offer our favorite aristocrat passage to Uneeda when he asks?"

A half hour later the meeting broke up.

Chapter 4

Finished with the Westport commander, Al was eager to head up the Uneeda River and hurried back to check on his crew and Bill. The sharp foul odor that greeted him at the walkway caused him to blurt out, "What the hell is that smell?"

Bill, who was standing by the Mischief's walkway pointed toward two large iron bar cages on the rear deck area. "Mischief hauls freight, I'm doing my job. The general okayed it. Bergdorf Mine ordered them. Must have a hunger for bacon."

Al looked. The cages contained two dozen young Red Yorkshires, better known as bacon hogs. The excited animals were grunting and shitting.

"What, you've heard from someone in Uneeda?"

Al did not believe for a moment the general knew about the hogs, let alone approved the cargo. The animals' stench would permeate their clothes, equipment, and the boat. Fuming, he thought that is the damn problem with the army using private vessels, lack of control, D-marks come ahead of the mission.

"It's a standing order for bacon hogs Hawick Farm has with Bergdorf. They hired the Mischief to deliver them," a worried Bill explained while throwing up his hands in a "what else could I have done" gesture. Then, trying to convince him the animals would not be a problem, said, "You still have your space. Besides, you'll be up wind from the cages once we're moving."

Al could tell the man had more unwelcome news. "What else?"

"It's nothing. I will need your cabin for the doctor traveling with us to Uneeda." He nodded toward a lean middle-aged Zircon woman dressed in the Emperor Medical Corp's uniform of light gray pants and jacket, black knee boots, and a white blouse with a neat gray straight brim hat standing down the wharf.

"She looks the serious sort. Think she'll like your hogs for company?" Bill had no comment but did appear a bit concerned.

Dr. Karren Sebastian whose age, Al decided, was closer to fifty than forty, had kept her figure trim. The dark-haired woman had a wry expression as she waited on the pier by two large tobacco hogsheads while Al disembarked and walked toward her to introduce himself. Having just returned from reporting to Commander Haddad, he had on his officer uniform instead of his normal tattered nonregulation uniform, thankfully. She was wondering if they were competent, even if it was safe. He introduced himself. She had a firm handshake and in a pleasant voice said.

"Colonel Haddad asked me to travel with your group. He spoke highly of you, captain." She paused and looked around. Al figured she wondered at the source of the foul odor. A squeal was heard and with an embarrassed laugh, she asked, "Oh, the Mischief is a livestock hauler?"

The Devil's Spawn

"It's a commercial vessel," Al answered with a shrug, deciding on a civil comment instead of cursing inconsiderate, greedy riverboat captains.

"The colonel didn't reveal that when he asked me to tag along in case an outbreak of disease is the problem. He fears a plague has swept through the Uneeda valley."

"Let's hope that is not the case. For the record, I am not thrilled with the hogs, either, but the captain assures me that once we're underway the breeze will disperse the odor."

With a mischievous laugh, she said, "Of course, I should have known Bill had a plan."

"You know Bill Walker?"

"I'm quite familiar with Captain Walker, having patched him up several times."

Al relaxed a bit: the doctor had a congenial side. He continued, "Regardless, welcome aboard. Having a doctor available is a relief. We do have a medic, Harry." Al waved for the bashful young Wapiti man to come forward and meet her.

"General Markel loaned us Harry. He is from the Roanoke school," Al said, wondering if the young man would survive two women. Sisi already bossed the shy nurse around. Other than being awkward in the presence of females, Harry had been handy to have around.

"Show the doctor where her room is."

The blushing young intern mumbled a greeting and, with Dr. Sebastian following, lugged her two large cases to the cabin. An hour later the expedition headed upriver and west.

The lower hundred kilometer of the tea-colored river ran deep and mostly free of sandbars and mud banks, allowing Bill to operate the Mischief near her top speed of twelve kilometers an hour. The large Zircon flag with a red background and the Imperial black iron

35

cross flapped in the breeze on top of the starboard paddle-wheel housing. The Wapiti flag with a white background and a large five-pointed green star was on the port side wheel housing.

The river valley land had once been forest, but over the last century local inhabitants had timbered the forest and in recent years even cut the second growth for firewood to fuel the steamboats. Watching from the pilot house roof, Al spotted dozens of deer browsing in the scrub areas over the course of the afternoon, while always overhead there seemed to be raptors in the cloudless sky ready to pounce on careless rodents. Birds, cliff swallows, had colonized the vertical sections of riverbanks and were busy hunting bugs in elegant loops and glides over the river surface. Even a small herd of red bison drank from the river, unbothered by the Mischief passage. The sunny spring day passed uneventfully in the lush river valley, though they all kept a watch ahead, leery of what might wait around the next corner.

At around a hundred kilometers upriver from Westport, the river cut through a low rocky ridge and the swamps started. The village of Prenter and a stockade shared the location along the north shore of the river just west of the ridge. Bill had told Al the village was an important stop for firewood and coal. No refueling stops existed in the swamp. The next settlement was one hundred and forty kilometers west at Seth.

The first day was almost gone when Al and Sergeant Jones switched out their flags with the Ichneumon serpent flags below the start of a shallow canyon the river had eroded through the basalt ridge. Bill concentrated on threading the boat between several large rocks that slightly narrowed the channel.

"I hope your men are alert. This is where I would expect an attack, ambush," the concerned riverboat captain said, while slowing the boat and watching the riverbank ahead. "The stockade will be visible after we turn the coming bend."

A few minutes later, with sunset not far off, the Mischief arrived and parked out in the river across from Prenter's dilapidated wooden wharf. Every one of Al's men had their weapons ready and waited in their assigned positions. No one had emerged from the village even after several blasts from the boat's loud steam whistle. Doctor Sebastian who Al now knew was a widow, joined Bill and him in the pilot house.

"If it's not an ambush waiting for us to land, then chances are a plague has killed the people," the doctor said studying the deserted wharf area and added what they were all thinking. "No way in these remote outposts the children wouldn't have heard the whistle and come running."

Al agreed and told Bill to drop the anchor. "I'll use one of the flat bottom rowboats. Sergeant Jones and I will make a quick recon."

"Don't touch any bodies, in case it is the plague," the doctor cautioned.

There were no bodies. There were old blood trails, and something had ransacked the trading post shelves, scattering can goods and clothing items. He hollered for Bill to dock. After docking, the Mischief crew and some of the soldiers loaded the firewood stacked conveniently near the wharf while Al organized a thorough search of Prenter. Other than the fort and trading post attached to the stockade, all the rest of the shelters were one story shoddy cabins fabricated from rough cut lumber and lacking glass windows. The cabin openings used either wood shutters or pieces of leather to keep the weather at bay. All in all, dismal dwellings.

Mysteries vexed Al and he told the searchers. "It will be dark soon, so move quick, but be careful of ambushes. I want all the buildings searched. Find someone who can tell us where everyone went."

He and Jones searched the small fort and several buildings with no success, then Al noticed a well-traveled footpath going off through the weeds and brush bordering the recently planted gardens.

"We're losing daylight, Sergeant. Take the men finish the cabins and check for root-cellars. I'll check where this path goes."

Al followed the trail about a hundred meters north of the settlement to a small clearing and small wooden wharf in one of the many oxbow lakes scattered throughout the swamp area. It was a local fishing hole though several alligators basked in the clearing. On noticing Al, the reptiles slipped quietly into the dark water and disappeared. No place for a swim, he thought, while examining the area. Bits and strips of fabric littered the shore. One piece of black material had a small brass button with a tiny embossed golden serpent on it. Keeping a wary eye on the pond surface, he reached into the water and recovered the sole of a leather knee boot of the type favored by the Ichneumon army. Something had chewed most of the upper leather part off. He heard Jones holler for him.

Harry had discovered two terrorized young children hiding in one of the root cellars. One was a boy of about three and the girl a bit older. They were mute, starved, apathetic, and filthy, but alive. He had many questions for them, but Dr. Sebastian cautioned him to wait.

The doctor had the children taken to the boat where Sisi gave them a warm bath while she consulted with the cook on something suitable to feed them. They settled on a chicken rice soup. Al raided the trading post and found several articles of children's clothing among the merchandise someone had scattered on the floor.

As the medics worked with the children, Al held a meeting with his squad and Bill. They figured an unknown force had attacked the settlement and had fed the bodies to the alligators. There was no plague. There was no evidence of who had attacked the settlement or why they had gone to the trouble of removing the bodies. Based on the boot and fragment of a uniform, the Ichneumons were still there and murdered along with the dozen or so human settlers thought to have lived there. Whatever had happened appeared to have occurred recently. The evidence of Ichneumon soldiers that far east of Uneeda along with the mysterious abandonment of the village and blood trails had sobered the crew.

Bill was not happy but agreed to push on toward Uneeda in the morning. They would spend the night in the middle of the river with guards posted.

"Cheer up," Al told Bill the next morning as they departed. "Your boat now has abundant firewood. Enough fuel to see us to Uneeda even if Seth, the next fuel-stop at the west end of the swamp, has suffered a similar faith as Prenter."

"I'm more worried about living to burn the wood. If Seth is the same, you need to find horses and go overland to check Uneeda. I'll hide the boat in the swamp and wait while you complete your scouting mission," Bill said, shaking his head while focusing on keeping the Mischief in the center of the narrowing serpentine river channel.

The nature of the river channel changed above Prenter. Below the swamp, the river channel ranged from fifty to seventy meters. In the swamp the river often had side channels that reduced the main channel to under thirty meters. In some areas the riverbanks were two- or three-meter-high cliffs with patches of hardwood forest growing on a narrow shallow ridge: in other areas the thick beds of four-meter-high reeds formed the river edge. Everywhere there were birds and mosquitoes. No place for a man without a boat, Al thought.

The next day while the Mischief headed upriver from Prenter, the Ichneumon army garrison stationed in Seth, a couple of hundred kilometers upriver, was busy getting ready to welcome an important visitor, Colonel Gupta. Lieutenant Halona's orders had sent him downriver to Seth to make sure that small garrison was ready for the VIP's inspection. The garrison's main warship, Saukko, had dropped him off during its trip down the river to Westport four days ago to meet and transport Colonel Gupta of the secret police back to Uneeda.

Lieutenant Halona was excited to finally get to meet Colonel Gupta, who had a reputation for loathing humans. The colonel reported directly to the emperor. Scuttlebutt had even Erie Army's commander, General Paget, fearful of the police colonel. A man with that reputation Halona hoped would not hesitate to give him permission to start a weeding operation.

Lieutenant Halona had been waiting in Uneeda for months for permission to start a weeding operation in the valley. But Colonel Kropp had not issued the order. The Uneeda commander found the ethnic cleansing repugnant and thought it foolish. Where were workers to come from if every human was gone, was the argument against the program. Halona figured Colonel Gupta would get the program going. An hour later he heard the Saukko's distinct whistle.

"Lieutenant, I am pleased to see the Uneeda command has finally started the liquidation," the larger, scarred up, muscular Colonel Gupta said, as he returned Halona's salute. "Did many humans escape at Prenter?" The colonel knew from hard experience that humans had an amazing ability to scatter when they realized what was occurring.

Unfortunately, he learned Lieutenant Halona was not involved with the small Prenter garrison. That post was under Corporal Joshi, who had three men and answered to Colonel Kropp directly.

Colonel Gupta wanted to meet the corporal and asked. "Is the corporal with you?" A nervous Halona answered he had no idea where the Prenter garrison could be. "Then you have no idea why the trappers and their families abandoned their settlement?" The lieutenant shook his head. Well, he would find out when he reached Uneeda and turned his attention to the small river village he was currently in. There were several older town residents who had gathered near the dock to watch the Saukko and the soldiers. The colonel nodded toward the humans and said, "Well, lieutenant, any reason your men couldn't start a weeding operation now?"

Halona, with a glance toward the curious spectators, answered with an enthusiastic, "No sir, we are ready."

"Good man, put out your blocking force," Gupta said. He allowed the lieutenant's troopers a couple of minutes to corral the baffled humans before drawing his service revolver and without warning shooting three worried residents standing beside him. In moments, a massacre was underway.

Halona had not been sure if he was hard enough for the duty but was pleasantly surprised to discover screams and blood did not bother him. Colonel Gupta pushed them hard not to allow any human to escape the extermination by running or faking death. Every corpse was reshot in the head. He even ordered them to slaughter the livestock. The massacre was over in two hours but resisting Seth residents had managed to seriously wound three and killed two of Halona's men during the bloodbath.

After allowing the men to strip the bodies of valuables like rings and to quickly search the residencies for any cash and gold, the colonel ordered them to board the warship. The Saukko headed upriver, but Gupta had them stop and repeat the killing at the next two small farms encountered along the river. The farmers had not been easy prey either. Halona lost another man at the second farm. It was late in the day by the time the Saukko reached the Kerry mule farm and the colonel decided to not stop but to head on to Uneeda. The men were tired and hungry. Colonel Gupta was satisfied with the day's yield of sixty-two dead humans.

41

Bill estimated they were about fifty kilometers above Prenter when they found the Westport sloop beached in a turn. The boat's hull had a large hole chopped in the port side and a half dozen bullet holes in the cabin walls. Someone had stripped the boat of its firearms, ropes, and sails. Again, there were no bodies. The hole chopped in the wooden hull puzzled them.

"Why would they drag the boat on shore and hole it?" Al asked his group.

"It's pretty clear to me, whoever it was, wanted to be sure the boat was beyond salvage," Sergeant Jones offered. "I would have set it afire, hell of lot easier." Everyone agreed with his point.

The rest of the day was uneventful aboard the Mischief as it steamed west. Dr. Sebastian, now addressed as Karren at her request, reported no success in communicating with either child on what had occurred at Prenter. Other than being mute, the two survivors were on the mend. She wanted Al's opinion on who the killers were.

He too wanted to know but had no solid opinion or clue on what had occurred at Prenter. Based on the blood trails and ransacked store something violent and horrifying had taken place, but he answered.

"I don't know. I can say it does not fit the usual river pirate behavior. I doubt Prenter had much worth stealing and why would they waste a boat they could use or sell? Besides, I've never heard of pirates hiding the corpses." Hearing no comment from the doctor, he asked, "What will happen to these children?"

"If there are no family members in Seth or Uneeda, nothing good. I have not been able to learn their names. Sadly, I figure their parents were trappers. Prenter was the trappers' base, at least it was twenty years ago. I fear for their future. Because of the war, the Erie Valley is awash with orphans."

The Devil's Spawn

"Well, for sure I won't abandon them in Uneeda if there isn't a family," Al said. "I'll arrange with Bill to haul them to River Point where the Wapiti and Clovis tribes have a good orphanage."

They watched the land pass by for a few silent minutes and then the doctor said, "I was through here twenty years ago, back when the empires were at peace. I served a summer as an intern at the Uneeda clinic patching up gold miners. We should soon be among the hammocks."

Twenty years ago, Al thought, my parents were alive, but instead asked what a hammock was.

"They're residual knobs of weathered limestone that rise a few meters above the water. The area is beautiful. Large trees teeming with wildlife like birds, otters, deer, and even black bears covered the islands, though I imagine by now they have been timbered."

"Is that the home of those silver otters?"

"It is. I saw two of the magnificent animals one time on my return trip. I've heard trappers have wiped them out. I think they should outlaw trapping and hunting otters. There is no need to murder rare animals for a damn pelt. Anyone who deals in that bloody trade should be arrested."

The next day the riverboat took them into the hammock area of the swamp. All the little islands in sight of the river had been timbered, but a while ago, for a dense low second growth now covered them. Bill figured the Mischief would reach Seth around early afternoon tomorrow as they stopped for the night. The suspected massacre of Prenter residents by unknown parties had Bill and him worried. They decided for safety to anchor in the middle of the river at night, rightly figuring the danger of a collision from a boat traveling down the river in the dark was less risky than the unknown threats lurking in the shore brush.

43

Later Al determined the attack came a half hour after midnight. He was sleeping on top of the pilot house under a mosquito net tent when a bullet hit the lower horizontal bar of the iron handrail that enclosed the roof area. The bullet ricocheted upward, missing his chest and ripping the net along with bringing him fully awake. He knew from the report it had been a black powder cartridge, fired from an old Krupp rolling block single shot rifle or a musket. A moment later a second bullet hit the boat. It came from a small hammock on the north side of the river.

Al had seen the flash from the second shot and so had several of his men for there was a returned volley of rifle fire moments later from the boat. All the current squad members on board had survived at least one or more Ichneumon ambushes while protecting the railroad. No one panicked and his men knew to shoot back. The gunfire started the hogs squealing and thrashing about in their pens.

Then the little girl started screaming and he heard Jones tell Corporal Williams to help him with the small flat bottom rowboat and for Pete to bring a lamp, unlit. He jumped to the deck as Karren, in a robe leaning out of the cabin and in answer to his question told him the children were unhurt, but the gunfire had terrorized the girl. Helping with the boat, he thought if the ambush snapped the girl out of her muteness where she could answer questions, at least something good would result. Even better, if they could capture the shooter alive, he might learn what happened in Prenter.

The night was dark, no moon, but clear, stars everywhere across the night sky. They all had good natural night vision, not in league with an Ichneumon's cat vision, but still good enough to find a recently fired old-style Krupp rifle abandoned near where Al had seen the flash, but no bodies. Whoever it had been was gone. How was the question: no way someone would have had time to escape out of slight in a rowboat, and the alligators made swimming a dangerous choice. Using the now-lit lamp, Pete spotted a patch of blood and scratched up leaves behind a small black oak tree. The darkness and weak lamp light made determining the blood's color uncertain, but red, not the Ichneumon blue, was the consensus. The brush covered island was small, less than twenty meters in diameter. A quick search uncovered no one.

"They had to swim to that hammock," Al said, after looking around for the nearest land. He pointed to a larger knob of ground. "It's the nearest land, only about thirty meters of open water to it. Let's go check, I'd really like to learn who is behind these attacks."

The water was shallow, and they simply used the oars to quickly pole the boat across the water and lily pads. A quick search discovered no one there. However, some animal lived on the island, a large one, judging by the size of two burrow holes on the back side of the low hill. The holes were large enough for a man to crawl in. Pete, a Wapiti hunter before joining the army knew all about blood trails. He carefully checked the two entrances for blood and could not find any.

"These dens are in use," Pete said. "I'm not sure what kind of den it is, doesn't stink enough to be a bear den."

"What about otters?" Al asked, remembering Karren's comments earlier.

"Yeah, that'd make sense except I thought the trappers had wiped them out."

"Well, I'm not interested in killing otters, or letting the bushwhackers escape. Could they have crawled in one of those holes?"

No one wanted to enter the lair. Finally, Pete said, "If that is a silver otter warren, or a bear's, he's not likely to survive encountering the owner."

"Okay, we'll let the bears deal with him, lets head back to the boat." At the island's edge, Al stopped Pete from joining the others.

"Stay with me," he quietly whispered, as Jones paddled the boat back to the Mischief.

They doubled back and hid on the high point of the hammock where they could see the den entrance while the others noisily boated back to the Mischief. He was surprised how far sounds carried. He could still hear the girl crying and Bill asking about them, but soon heard only the insects. Time dragged and he was beginning to wonder if they were wasting their time when Pete nudged him.

A dark bear-sized shape had emerged from the hole and cautiously inspected the area. Apparently satisfied it was alone, the large animal moved stealthily up the slope toward their location. It detected them for it stopped a dozen meters away from the summit and stood up on its hind feet. It was not that much shorter than they were and no bear.

It sure looked like Al pictured one of those giant otters would standing on its hind legs. He stood up with his revolver, not sure of the creature's intent. The animal studied him for a couple of heart beats, then loudly snarled, exposing an impressive set of fangs while crouching down in preparation to leap and attack. Pete stood up, aimed his rifle at the animal and shouted. "Don't!"

The animal stopped. After silently scrutinizing them for several moments, it looped about and ran down the slope on its hind legs, eerily like the ways a man would. The creature dove into the swamp and vanished. In a few moments there was no sign the creature had existed.

"Pete, you saved the day. Lord, I nearly pissed myself. It would not be good to meet that thing without a gun. I would rather meet a mountain lion. How anyone could think those animals were cute, escapes my understanding."

"If the bushwhacker did crawl in that lair, he's dead. God, did you see those fangs?" Pete shook his head in amazement. "The shooter must have had a boat," Pete added, while keeping a watch on their back trail as they waited for Jones to return. Al noticed Pete also joined him in keeping a careful watch on the swamp surface while Jones paddled them back to the riverboat.

Everyone was on edge, waiting for sufficient light so Bill could get the Mischief safely underway up the river. One bullet had struck the cabin Karren and the two children shared. The bullet had passed through both filmy walls without hitting anyone, but between that and their gunfire the little girl, after a screaming and crying fit, was now responding to questions.

"Her name is Nancy, and her brother is Louis. She said large monsters attacked on a stormy night. Their mother put them in the cellar, told them not to come out until she came back. That's all she knows and wants her mother."

"I figure she's dead, but then there is no proof, nothing," Al said.

"The poor child, thankfully Sisi was willing to help and has been staying with her. She's been a real help calming the girl," the doctor said sounding sad and hugging herself. After a moment, she asked. "Could the Ichneumons as they evacuated the lower valley have seized the people for use as slaves?"

"I suppose anything is possible in these strange times. If I knew who was shooting at us and why. . ." Al paused as Jones entered with the recovered rifle.

"Whoever had this rifle didn't believe in cleaning the barrel and action. The wonder was it did not explode. Whoever they are, they're a bunch of lazy slobs, if this is an example of their equipment."

Or ignorant. Al thought of the trader's tale as he walked over to the coil of hemp rope near the bow he had been using for a seat. He remained awake, too riled up to sleep, but within a few minutes, other than two guards, everybody else had settled down to catch what sleep they could in the couple of hours before sunrise.

The Mischief had been underway about an hour the morning after the attack when Bill spotted a large Jon-boat partially submerged in the edge of a reed bed along the south shore of the river. He stopped so Al could investigate. Judging from the undisturbed sediment around and in the boat, Al decided it had been there for a couple of months. During the inspection Sergeant Jones and his men dragged the boat clear of the sand and mud with the idea of taking it. They discovered the boat's floor had a large, chopped hole that rendered it useless. Al thought of the Westport sloop they had encountered yesterday above Prenter. That boat also had a chopped hole in its hull. Weird business was afoot, though no one had an answer on why the culprit would wreck a valuable boat. Al wrote down the boat license number in his unit's operational log and they continued upriver toward Seth.

Chapter 5

On the third day the landscape changed radically as the Mischief approached the western boundary of the great swamp four kilometers east of Seth. There the topography became rolling shallow ridges covered with lush grasslands and scattered patches of hardwood trees. The river gradient had picked up, the channel narrowed more, and the Mischief required additional steam to maintain the eight km/hour speed. As a result of the narrowing channel, the Seth dock ran parallel along the north bank instead of perpendicular as was common below the swamp.

Like at Prenter, there was a dilapidated stockade near the wharf. A new Ichneumon flag flapping from the watch tower worried Al. He checked to be sure his squad was on alert. The whistle brought five rough-dressed men, laborers, he figured, out of another large structure down the street to watch the Mischief dock. They all carried rifles and waited quietly near what Al later learned was the village trading post.

A strong odor of putrefaction prevailed in the area. He figured the vultures circling in the sky above the village were after the source of the odor. Something was amiss, but at least seven humans were there, though they did not approach the dock. Such cautious behavior was unusual, as normally people flock to watch a riverboat dock.

In answer to Jones's shouted question, the older man assured him the bastard Ichneumons had left and there was no plague. Bill docked the Mischief and Al debarked and asked the man why the armed greeting. The man, Herr Odrick, after realizing they were Zircon soldiers, told him.

"I have reasons. Five days ago, the Saukko stopped here late in the day. Captain Chetan dropped off twenty Marines led by a Lieutenant Halona. The riverboat then headed down river. The soldiers kept to themselves in the stockade."

The man motioned for Al to walk with him as he explained. "Livestock has been the area's business for years along with firewood for the river boats. We raise red bison, goats, and horses and on the north range water holes are important. Two small dams that supply the water needed repairs and since everything seemed calm here, I decided to take my crew and go fix the dams. The repairs required two nights and we returned yesterday to this."

Al walked into the village with the middle-aged Zircon man, Herr Odrick. The source of the odor was dozens of decomposing bison and horse carcasses in the two large corrals. Strange land, Al thought, thinking of the two boats, the empty Prenter, and now this butchery. Who benefits from wasting livestock? The appalling sight had him asking Odrick what had happened.

"That is not the worst," the despondent man said. He walked on without speaking another block and stopped in the gravel-surfaced street to point at a partially burned two-story wood frame house. "That was my home, my wife ran the school, the soldiers herded everyone into the building and shot them. For no reason, we had lived and work with those people for years, got along fine."

"Nothing seemed off?" Al, appalled at the news, asked. The rancher shook his head no.

"I had not believed the news of Clovis exterminations, figured it was the usual empire wartime propaganda. There was no warning. The soldiers were gone when we returned to investigate the smoke."

Al knew it was not propaganda. It was the truth, but not wanting to add to Odrick's misery, did not comment. After a pause Odrick continued.

"General Markel needs to garrison the town. We will never stay and live under Ichneumon rule again." The rancher, looking at the burned structure, said. "I hope your little squad is not the valley's Zircon occupation force."

"No, I'm on a reconnaissance mission to learn why there has been no traffic from Uneeda. Do you know where that Ichneumon warship is?"

"No idea. Headed downriver the last I knew, and it hasn't gone by since we returned." Herr Odrick paused and then angrily added, "Kill them all if you get a chance, especially that lieutenant."

"I'm sorry for your loss." The possibility of encountering the Saukko had him apprehensive, but instead of rushing back to the boat, he told Odrick about Prenter and the sniper attack.

"That doesn't sound like these bastards, they didn't cleanup anything." The man crossly snapped. "It was awful, the vultures had started the cleaning up."

Al found Bill and told him what the rancher said.

The Mischief's captain had comforted himself from the start with the belief that any Ichneumon warship based in Uneeda would have vacated the Uneeda River for the safety of the lower Erie River after Westport fell. The reported sighting on the Erie convinced Bill he was right for thinking the danger of running into an enemy warship on the Uneeda River was remote. Odrick's information now confirmed that belief.

"I told you. Why would the Saukko captain chance capture? He had to know the Zircons would block the river at Westport."

Al did not agree with that thinking and responded. "Those evil spawn of the devil believe in do-or-die. What the Saukko does will depend on its captain's orders, not fear of capture."

Bill, rubbing his neck and sighing deeply, said. "Well let's hope you're wrong for we would be seriously out gunned. That warship has two breech loading guns that fire fifteen-kilogram shells along with having armor protection." After a pause and lowering his hands to a "what now" motion, asked, "What do you suggest?"

"Mount the brass cannon on the bow."

With a huff, Bill said. "Our little cannon spitting six-kilogram iron balls won't impress them. Besides, that road runs to Uneeda." Odrick had shown them the start of the valley road that ran along the north side of the river between Seth and Uneeda. Bill was pushing for Al to use it to finish the recon on horseback.

Al shared the captain's concerns about the danger of encountering an enemy warship but attempted to minimize the threat. "I agree, solid shot won't, but a load of grape will make an impression on any exposed sailors."

"I pray it doesn't come to that," Bill said, clearly alarmed by the thought. "Without armor plates, grape shot would destroy us. We should retreat to Westport."

That was not going to happen. Al would seize the boat first.

"Stop your whining captain and get the Mischief headed upriver. I will help your crew mount the cannon."

While mounting the cannon, Odrick and Bill arrived at a last-minute agreement and unloaded half the hogs. Al wished all the hogs were unloaded but said nothing. On completion of the transfer, they headed upriver.

The morning was beautiful, a blue cloudless sky. The land, open rolling ridges of tall grass with tree filled ravines and small creeks appealed to Al. He could imagine settling down in this rich land. Then they passed two recently burned-out abandoned farms about twenty kilometers upstream from Seth. Those destroyed farms had to be more handiwork of the Ichneumon marines that ravaged Seth, in Al's opinion. One shared by his men.

The discoveries were an abrupt reminder that Seth was not a onetime event. The evil was roaming the beautiful land and it reminded Al that so far, he had not accomplished their mission of protecting the valley residents. Frustrated, and having no other choice but to wait and hope the Mischief would catch up with the Ichneumon killers, Al watched the river ahead from his perch on the riverboat's pilot cab roof for any sign of the marauders. Then about thirty kilometers downriver from Uneeda, around mid-afternoon he spotted a dense cloud of white smoke bellowing up in the cloudless sky about a kilometer ahead on the south shore. At last, he thought, a chance for a confrontation with those bastards. He stomped on the pilot house roof, a signal for Bill to stop the boat.

Bill hollered up to ask why the stop order as another shout came from the deck. The forward watch had also spotted the smoke. Al, excitedly pointing toward the rapidly growing smoke ahead, shouted,

"Look at that. We caught them. That smoke is from a large fire, a barn."

Bill looked and a moment later stopped the paddlewheels as Al added, "Those Ichneumons did not leave. They are still here laying waste to our people. We are going ashore. I want to surprise whoever is at the fire. Jones, organize the squad for disembarking."

"You do know that fire is on the south side of the river." Al knew that but was not sure what Bill was meant by his remark until he explained, "The road is on the north side of the river so who ever started the fire probably came by boat since no one likes to swim across the gator-filled river. That means the Saukko is probably there at the fire or nearby." A worried Bill ran his hands through his tangled hair.

Al, on the deck organizing his squad added,

"Don't worry so much. Give us fifteen minutes to get in position, then blow the whistle, I want the bastard's attention toward the river."

"Okay, but after dropping you I'm crossing to the north side of the river." Bill had obeyed his orders to head up the river from Seth, but Al knew the captain was not happy and clearly concerned for his boat.

With a shrug, Al started to leave, but then turned back to Bill. "The general said I could count on you, right?" After a nod from the captain, Al said, "Fifteen minutes." He grabbed his rifle by the chair, adjusted its sling on his shoulder, and followed his squad to the ramp used to disembark. Bill stopped him at the ramp with a hand on his arm.

"You're a crazy bastard and will probably get us all killed, but good luck, be careful."

The land south of the river was mostly open pastureland except for a band of scrub trees and brush growing in the fifty-or-so-meter-wide floodplain bordering both sides of the river. Al pushed his men hard and arrived near the burning barn in less than fifteen minutes. Even before they were near, they heard screams of the animals trapped in the burning barn. It added to the horror of the scene and the urgency in stopping the marauders. Thankfully, there was no warship waiting at the farm dock.

He had sent Corporal Williams and two men to loop inland and find the lane used to assess the farm and fields south of the river. They would block the land escape route and the Mischief had the river route blocked down river. The rest of the squad rapidly formed a skirmish line and advanced, waiting for Al's whistle before breaking cover.

He could now see four Ichneumon marines across the open barn yard by looking through the blackberry bushes he was using for cover. The bastards' attention was on hanging a family. Two crying young children and three tied up women waited by a corral gate. They had just hanged an older man using a rope thrown over the cross member that framed the gate opening. He was still struggling. To try saving him, Al blew his whistle and shot the man pulling on the rope. His shot triggered a fusillade. Two enemy soldiers ran out of the farmhouse to investigate, and Al's men shot them.

Another enemy soldier grabbed for the hanging rope, but the squad's gunfire killed him before he could rehoist the old man. The ambush appeared a complete success to Al. He had been concerned his men might have lost their edge during their three-week break, but the sudden effective dispatch of six enemy soldiers suggested his new Uneeda squad was just as good as his old one. As he reached the hanged man, he heard the Mischief's whistle.

The hanged man was unresponsive, dead from a broken neck, but he would have the doctor check when the Mischief docked. The mother who was desolate over the death of her husband sat on the ground by the corral entrance quietly crying by his body. The two younger sons, the older of whom, looked around eight, stood mute beside their mother, looking lost as the screams from the animals died off.

The daughter, around ten years old, looked terrified of Al's men gathering around the corral. The farm family members were Zircon settlers. The daughter held the hand of an extremely attractive young woman. The wiry eye-catching female was in her early twenties, he guessed. Her light coppertone skin, black hair in a neat pixie hairstyle, and deep brown eyes suggested a strong Oztec ancestry.

The burning barn structure collapsed in a storm of sparks that ended the mules' agony. The stillness was broken only by the crackling pops of the fire and the Mischief's engine and docking sounds. As Al studied her, the young woman studied him. After placing a comforting arm across the young girl's shoulder to draw her closer and glancing toward the Mischief busy docking, she asked in a hesitant voice. "Who are you, pirates?"

"Zircon soldiers. Our army now occupies Westport. I am Captain Belcher. We are on a recon mission."

She nodded toward the Mischief that was docking and asked about the Ichneumon flag.

"It helps confuse the bastards. I had hoped they had evacuated the area. They had to know our blockade of the river at

Westport would trap any of them that remained in Uneeda. Obviously, some of them stayed."

"Those animals had plans for me and Linda, after they murdered the rest of the Kerry family." The girl's quiet sobs became loud crying. The Oztec woman's intense eyes keep returning to him as she attempted to soothe the girl and ask him questions.

"How did you know not to dock?"

"The survivors at Seth told me the Uneeda troops slaughtered their families."

She interrupted him to ask, "Odrick's family?"

Al nodded. She clamped a hand on her mouth and looked down for a moment before shaking her head and removing her hand. "I knew them, good people. She was my elementary teacher."

"I'm sorry to be the bearer of unwelcome news, but that and after passing other burned-out farms, the smoke made us cautious that the Ichneumons might still be around."

That information caused her to hug Linda tighter. "Other farms? They did this elsewhere. Why?" He could only shrug. "Well," she said in a strong voice, "I'm damn glad you stopped to investigate."

Al had seen what the bastards were up to but had hesitated a few moments to allow his men time to get in position, not realizing how fragile necks can be. A crushed larynx, according to Karren, who had rushed off the Mischief to help. Not good at condolences, nor sure what if anything to say to the mother, he asked,

"What is your name and relation to the family?"

"No relation, I'm Bari Lu and work for Bergdorf Mining in purchasing. Among other duties, I buy the bison to feed their crews along with mules and horses as needed in the mines."

Her employer's name startled Al. Coincidences made him wary. That was the outfit the agent they were there to rescue worked for. Bari, after checking on Linda, continued explaining her work.

"I was here to buy eight mules. Kerry's mules have a good reputation. . . ." She stopped and looked for a moment at the glowing bed of hot coals formed by the collapse of the burning barn, then in a sad voice added, "Those evil monsters shot my horse and mules. The jacks and breeding mares they let burn to death in the barn. Why, what do they gain?"

"The Ichneumons want to eliminate us, but they will never succeed." He then asked, "You have family nearby?"

"My grandmother has a bison ranch not far away," she said, trying for a brief smile, before adding. "Other than her, I have no family."

Considering what had just occurred, the young woman was remarkably composed. Even with his experience from four years of no quarter given fighting and ambushes, he doubted he would be that calm after just escaping rape and a hanging. Where she acquired that toughness was a subject for another time. Remembering his mission, he asked.

"Are there many Ichneumons in Uneeda?"

"There's a warship and the garrison have soldiers, but I never counted them, maybe a couple of hundred in the fort and another hundred at Silver Ridge." More than they could manage. He had not heard of Silver Ridge and asked her where it was located. A mining camp at the western end of Uneeda Lake she answered, before adding. "I--, we--owe you, Captain Belcher, so I will caution you. My employer and most folks in Uneeda are pro-slavery. They won't welcome you and Zircon anti-slavery laws."

That was unwanted news but did not change his mission. Looking about, he decided to first deal with the dead. The barn was now a thick bed of hot coals capable of thoroughly incinerating the corpses. He told his men to throw the dead Ichneumons in the fire after collecting their ID-tags.

"And you, Bari, what's your opinion on slavery?" Al asked while his troopers gathered the bodies. The mule buyer was an extremely attractive woman who he hoped had an enlightened outlook on life.

"Some of the Oztecs own slaves and plenty of the mine slaves are Oztecs. It is evil business and I hope the Zircons put an end to it. You have not seen misery until you visit the mine's slave quarters."

"Unfortunately, I have," he said, secretly delighted with her response, while wondering if she had a husband. "Come with me, you need to meet Bill, he runs the Mischief. Bring Linda, there are other children aboard that we rescued in Prenter." The girl was reluctant to move, but Bari whispered something in her ear, and she came with them to the boat.

"What happened in Prenter?" Bari asked quietly after introducing Linda to Sisi, Nancy and her small brother, Louis.

"I'm not sure, no one was there except for them. They were hiding in a root cellar." Al then climbed on to the pilot house roof and stood up to better search the area and asked, "Where are those bastards' horses?" The Ichneumon army usually had good animals and he would prefer using horses for the rest of the recon into and around the Uneeda area.

"There aren't any," Bari answered, looking up from greeting Bill, then adding, "The warship dropped them off."

The news stunned them. Bill, suddenly ashen, asked, "What warship?"

"The Saukko," she said, causing Bill to quietly swear and look upriver. Al figured he was looking for the smoke from an approaching riverboat.

A glance toward the sun told Al it was late in the afternoon, which meant the warship might arrive at any moment to retrieve the raiding party. He had an idea.

"Did the boat dock or stay out in the river and use a small boat to deliver those killers?"

Bill, wiping oil from his hands with a gray cotton rag, stopped to listen as she explained.

"It turned around and slid along the end of the dock, which allowed them to jump on to the dock. It didn't stop and after the soldiers were off, it went back toward Uneeda." Seeing their concern, she quickly added, "Oh, you're worried it will return for the soldiers?"

The possibility of the Saukko catching them tied to the wharf had Bill frantic. "I have to save the Mischief. We need to flee."

Al thought the warship's return offered an opportunity. "There are two hundred kilograms of sixty percent dynamite in the lower hole. I want to use a hundred kilograms of it for a mine off the end of the wharf." He then waved for Jones to join them while Bill shook his head in disagreement with the delay.

There were no suitable barrels on the boat to hold the explosives. Sergeant Jones suggested placing the cases of explosives in an old fishing net along with rocks to weigh it down.

"Good idea, Bill have your crew unload four boxes of the dynamite." Bill just stood there looking up the river. Al said, "You can take your boat downriver after I have the explosives." Bill rousted his worried crew.

In a few minutes, the boat crew, who shared their captain's desire to retreat downriver, unloaded all but one case of dynamite, seven wood boxes, a hundred and seventy-five kilograms. Instead of worrying about returning the extra boxes, Al and Sergeant Jones used all the dynamite to form a rough cube wrapped in a net. In a few minutes they had a tight bomb package on the dock. Then using part of an old anchor chain along with several large rocks for weight, lowered the package to the river bottom under the end of the dock. Al feared the river was not deep enough off the wharf to allow the steamboat to pass over the catch of explosives. Bari watched their activity with great interest.

The River Point ordnance officer who provided the explosives, had also provided Al with a box of the new powerful waterproof detonators. Their downside was they required the current from a special magneto and a set of insulated telegraph wires to detonate. He had other nonelectrical detonators for trip wires, blasting caps for safety fuse, and simple electric caps. The dozen detonators with timers were not very waterproof.

Al especially like the magneto-fired detonators for the control they provided him on the time of the actual explosion, a critical feature in detonating mines that requires the moving target be over or beside the explosion to be effective. But they had the downside of requiring an electrical connection between the explosive and the magneto.

His immediate problem was his squad had only brought a beat up hundred-meter-long roll of waterproof electric cable to hook the detonator leads to the current source. The open dirt yard around the dock had no hiding places with in a hundred meters, which meant the boat crew would see the man waiting to detonate the mine and that could tip them off. The boat needed to dock at the end of the wharf, beside the mine.

Suddenly, one of the Mischief's crew members shouted he saw smoke upriver. The news confirmed what Al had feared: they would not have time to properly place the charge and would only alert the devils to their presence. In that case, his mission is what would be blown-up.

"Put two men to digging a hole for me. Have others hauling or scattering the excavated soil out of sight. Bari, load the family on the Mischief so you and they are safe. Bill, you need to get the boat out of slight below that bend downstream."

"What if they do not dock, I wouldn't if I didn't see my passengers. Won't the captain be suspicious if there's no soldiers about?" Bill had a valid point. Al knew the captain wanted to flee down the river, but instead he was risking all to help him in his mission.

"I have a suggestion," Bari said to Al as she picked up and examined the small T-handle-style magneto blasting machine. "Have one of your men put on a dark outfit to look like an Ichneumon. I will act as bait. Those scumbags love gang raping women."

The woman's honest talk startled Al into blurting out, "I can't allow that!"

Bari, mouth open, looked at him for a beat, astonished by his outburst. Then in a sassy voice she answered, "Don't go all mushy on me, Belcher. I'll be fine if you do your part and blow up that damn boatload of vipers."

Bill, as startled as Al, recovered first and nodding at Bari, said, "Hell, girl, you're a real trooper," then addressing Al, asked. "So, who's going to play the soldier?"

"Corporal Williams you look like an Ichneumon in the night outfit you wear to crawl around in the woods. Get it," Al ordered, rallying from his embarrassing moment of weakness, and then adding. "Jones, will that sergeant's jacket fit you?"

Jones shrugged but yelled for his men who were busy gathering the dead not to throw that enemy sergeant's body in the fire as he jogged over to check the fit. Al told the three men waiting by him, "Why are you standing there? Start digging, I need that hole, now." They jumped to excavate a fox hole.

The only suitable protection and cover for the rest of his squad was the stone fence out past the still burning barn. The location put the skirmish line at close to two hundred meters, but still well within the lethal range of their rifles. Jones managed to get the

Ichneumon sergeant's jacket to fit him by splitting the back and then he positioned the troopers in skirmish line.

Williams was back looking remarkably like an enemy soldier. Bari and he would wait beside the hole that Al was in with the magneto. They would join him when the shooting started. The hope was the blast would disrupt any organized response from the marines they expected aboard the warship and knew to be competent riflemen.

After the Mischief was out of sight around the curve, Al, with Williams's help, re-hoisted the father's corpse to hang from the cross beam and then got in position. Jones assumed a position by the rehung body. Bari in the meantime had removed her shirt and pants and stood in her panties and a pair of laced up leather work boots. It was a sight Al would not forget, nor would his men, he expected. She could give the Wapiti nurses at Summit serious competition in the looks department. After this, he would want her at least as a friend.

The lady raised an eyebrow at his startled look and with a resolved voice told him, "It's no time for half measures. Do not let me down, captain. That boat will stop."

They all agreed on that point, but where it would stop was Al's worry as the large warship came around the last bend upriver from the mule farm.

Chapter 6

The same day the Zircons arrived at the Kerry mule farm, the fort commander, Colonel Kropp, had earlier that morning upset Lieutenant Halona's plans and ordered him to remain in the Uneeda fort and hear what Friedrich Bergdorf and Hans Maxim from the gold mine wanted. The colonel had also requested that Colonel Gupta join him on an inspection of the garrison and a tour of Uneeda.

Unknown to the Uneeda command, Gupta planned to load all the gold currently stored in the fort on the Saukko tomorrow. He made the decision after learning Colonel Kropp was not aware that the Prenter garrison had vanished. The empire's gold could not be left in the care of such incompetence. He would use the warship to haul the gold to a landing just upriver from Westport where his agents along with a company of General Paget's rangers waited. They would bypass the Zircon blockade at Westport by traveling cross country and down the Erie Valley to the Ichneumon stronghold at Fenwick.

Having a window of fewer than three days to reach the transfer location about Westport, but still wanting to complete the removal of humans at the mule farm he passed yesterday, Colonel Gupta told the captain of the Saukko to make a fast trip down river to that mule farm and drop Halona's platoon off. Since the farm was less than a three-hour boat trip down the river from Uneeda, and knowing Lieutenant Halona wanted to be involved in the killing, but not wanting to ignore the gold miners, he told the Saukko to return to Uneeda after dropping the men off for the lieutenant. The double trip wasted firewood, but the fort had plenty.

Halona thought of those crying begging humans in Seth yesterday as he started the miner meeting by expressing the colonel's concern over the recent drop in gold production. As expected by the lieutenant, Bergdorf, the owner of the mine, blamed the problem on unrest in the slave barracks.

"Unrest?" the lieutenant asked, disgusted with having to be civil with this thieving human scum. "You need to crack down on the slackers. Have you hanged the leaders?"

Bergdorf, who Halona knew had been a Zircon mercenary before arriving in Uneeda was shaking his head. "I did hang two of them, but all that accomplished was reducing our labor force. The problem is your loss of Westport has given life to their hope the Zircons will soon be in Uneeda and will outlaw slavery. Is there a chance of that?"

Halona, unhappy over missing the mule farm raid, shook his head. He was not surprised to hear that lame excuse. Just what he expected from a human: blame their failures on his people.

"Clearly you did not hang enough of the scum. As for the Zircons, the Saukko has been patrolling the river and has not encountered any sign of their activity. You must know our army stopped Markel's rag tag force below Westport. I would not be surprised to hear they have vacated Westport and fled north."

Bergdorf looked skeptical as Halona added, "The colonel wants your focus on keeping your labor force working. I hear unsettling reports the slaves are more than restless. Some are refusing to work. Is that true?"

"Those were the ones I had hanged. I told the rest of them if they don't keep the gold flowing, you'll hang all of them."

"Okay, that's the truth, and your workers won't be the only ones we hang, if the gold production doesn't pick up." The lieutenant enjoyed the startled look on Bergdorf's face on hearing that threat. How spineless humans are, Halona thought, before asking the man's accountant, "So how many kilograms of gold did the mine produce last week?"

The nervous accountant mumbled, "Hundred."

"That's less than half the normal production," Halona said, slamming the table with his hand. "Totally unacceptable. You need to get control of your men, Bergdorf. Any worker who refuses to work or is heard spreading the Zircon lies needs to be hanged."

The mine owner, a large powerfully built man, glanced toward Hans and answered, "I'll deal with it, lieutenant. However, I have another disturbing bit of information for the colonel. Chief Laredo is telling his subchiefs the Zircons will put him in charge of Uneeda and give him the gold lease."

"Not my concern who owns the mine if the Zircons manage to win."

"Of course not, you'll be dead," Bergdorf said with a spiteful smile. "However, I doubt your boss wants a man with hundreds of warriors under his command making deals with the Zircons in Westport instead of providing us with slaves to mine the remaining gold."

Gold was not Halona's concern, but as a loyal subordinate he had emphasized his commander's concern over the dwindling Bergdorf Mine gold production. His aspiration was recognition by the Sun God High Priest as one of his holy warriors in the crusade to eliminate all the free humans in the Erie Valley and prevent them from spreading into new western territories. His men had made a good start in Seth, but enough dreaming. The miner raised a good point. Letting that fool Chief Laredo make deals that might speed the arrival of the Zircon army could block completion of his sacred duty.

"I'll inform the colonel, but if he tries that, the tribe will need a new chief."

Lieutenant Halona remained in the office after the miners departed, thinking about the news on Chief Laredo and his Agarwal tribe. The chief was not much of a thinker or fighter, but his oldest son, Greg Laredo was. Fortunately, they were sort of friends, collaborators on organizing drunken orgies. He would pay the son a visit tomorrow. Today he was busy. Colonel Gupta told him the Saukko would return for him and take him to the mule farm to verify his men had done a thorough cleaning. But first he needed to report to Gupta at the commander's office.

The lunch meeting Colonel Gupta invited Halona to attend with Colonel Kropp was short. Gupta's instructions were simple. Halona was to randomly pick one of the isolated farms along the river and lake every few days and have his men kill all the humans encountered at the target. The loss of Westport had awakened Colonel Gupta to the threat of a Zircon army incursion up the Uneeda River and that had made the Zircon families living along the river potential foes, saboteurs. Colonel Kropp disagreed, arguing the loss of those farms would complicate their immediate food supply. Gupta countered that the action would also advance the emperor's goal of eradicating all free humans from the Erie Valley and that ended the meeting.

The discussion at the meeting had cheered Lieutenant Halona as he left to board the Saukko. He was confident that after the farmers, the troublesome eastern Oztec tribe would be next. They would not bother the Agarwal tribe until the gold mine was exhausted, along with its need for slave laborers. With luck, in a few years there would be no free humans in Uneeda Territory.

The sternwheeler had returned before midday to Uneeda from dropping off the soldiers at the mule farm. After the lunch meeting, the two colonels went to check the gold vault and Lieutenant Halona boarded the Saukko to return downriver to collect the soldiers. The lieutenant looked forward to seeing how his sergeant and men had performed on their own. Some of the new recruits had difficulty with the killing of children and women at Seth. He had explained the need for their task by comparing it to a garden. Think of humans as weeds that they must remove to allow the Ichneumon people to flourish.

It was late afternoon when the target farm came into sight. The smoking ruin of the barn was a loss but seeing a body hanging from the corral gate cheered Halona. His sergeant would need to understand the importance of avoiding unnecessary destruction of property, otherwise the man appeared to have performed well. Clamor from the sailors caused him to look again. One of his men was prodding a nude young female prisoner to her feet. The Sun God was smiling on them, the men would have fun tonight with that Oztec bitch. As the captain swung around the sternwheeler to point upriver and stop at the wharf, Halona wondered where his other soldiers were.

Al could see the pilot of the warship was inexperienced. He held his breath, fearing the inexperienced Ichneumon skipper who had reversed the paddle wheels several times trying to stop in front of the dock might give up and just nose the bow into shore away from the dock. After a couple of worrisome minutes, the Saukko stopped dead at the end of the dock and beside the bomb. The crew had spotted Bari and they alternated shouting demands for the captain to quit delaying the docking and promises of rape and misery to the bitch. Al was amazed at the poor discipline demonstrated by the soldiers on the Saukko.

As the warship crew hurried to place the wooden ramp to the dock, Al prayed the detonator and blasting machine worked and then shoved the handle down. Nothing. Bari threw an alarmed glance toward him as the ramp slammed on to the dock. He tried again, no explosion. The cable he had used had three wires. The white one was for the ground, maybe he had used it instead of the black wire, or more likely whoever spliced the cable sections together mixed up the wire colors. He tried the white and red wires as five soldiers hit the dock running.

The warship seemed to rise out of the water as the wharf disappeared in a cloud of muddy water, debris, sailors, and fire. A moment later Bari landed on top of him seeking shelter. As a result, the pieces of heavy wood and river mud mostly hit her, not him. The impact from one of the boat fragments had stunned her, forcing him to shove her off him with a "Sorry." He had to survey the scene and help kill any survivors before they could organize a counterattack.

The warship was on its side about ten meters out in the river smoking and hissing steam. The explosion had ripped out the center of the riverboat's starboard side. The vessel appeared unsalvageable, but six of the crew that had survived were clinging to the wreck. Seeing the survivors still had fight in them, he joined in shooting the surviving sailors. A few more of the passengers, those who had abandoned the vessel, were swimming for the north bank. The squad's arrival put an end to the returned fire and only three Ichneumons reached the far shore and vanished in the brush.

In his excitement, Al almost forgot, but at the last moment he told Williams to lower the father's body. It would never do to allow the family to see how they had treated their father's corpse. The sound of the blast would alert Bill to rush back with the Mischief and her grape shot loaded cannon. He then ran back to the pit to check on the Oztec girl.

Part of the decking had nicked her, ripping the skin on her back and making an ugly wound. They were both lucky. If that fragment of the wharf decking had hit her edge on, it would have killed her and done him great harm.

"Are you okay?" he asked, helping her stand while trying to ignore the feel and sight of her mud and blood splattered breasts and back.

The Devil's Spawn

In pain and not steady on her feet, she held Al's arm and with a shake of her head whispered. "My god that was something. Did you get all of them?" After a look about and satisfied with the sight of the destroyed warship, Bari with a slight chuckle added, "I'd always heard no one could complete you guys when it came to mayhem."

"Couldn't have done it without you," Al said. "Listen, that wound in your back looks serious and needs attention." He then told Williams who was standing there listening, "Help her to the farmhouse and get someone started on heating water. The doctor will want to clean that wound and find her clothing."

Bari's grimace on switching to the corporal's arm testified to her pain, still she managed a brief smile and whispered, "Why, captain, you're a regular mother hen."

Not hen, rooster, Al thought, watching them for a moment as Bari limped off to the farmhouse. Again, her composure impressed him. Here was the kind of woman he was seeking. Then he had a sobering thought, was he the kind of man she might want? But duty called, romance could wait, and he ran back to river where Bill was considering where best to dock.

"I need the doctor and Frau Kerry," Al shouted. "Have someone row them ashore, now, if you're planning to take all day to dock! Sergeant, try to catch those few that reached the north shore before they can alarm the Uneeda garrison."

The daughter, Linda, tagged along, so he rushed the three of them to the house while asking they help the doctor first with cleaning up Bari and then fix a meal for his men. He figured putting the grieving family to work would help their recovery. The other good news was none of his men had suffered serious wounds.

Bill and his crew had tied the Mischief off to the wreck and was stripping useful items from the still smoking hulk after making sure no survivors lurked in the wreck. Al wanted the Saukko's two cannons, but first told the crew to row Private Gunner, a sergeant until a drunken fight with MP's and two troopers crossed the river. The gruesome turbulence out in the river around a floating body of a dead sailor as it vanished, discouraged any thoughts of swimming.

"I want you to run down those escapees, especially that officer," Al instructed Private Gunner.

That evening Lieutenant Halona, seated on the only chair in his tiny bedroom-apartment and slipping a glass of that green swill sold as gin, reflected on his day. After the explosion, four of them reached the north shore, though gunfire killed one of the sailors before they could reach the safety of the brush. An alligator had grabbed another of the blast survivors swimming beside him about twenty meters from shore. Those were the most terrifying moments of his life, as he wondered if a jaw would clamp down on his leg before he cleared the water. Though the chase through the forest was not much better. Those Zircon soldiers were relentless and killed the other two men with him. Exhausted, he had finally reached the fort and those devils pursuing him finally gave up, but not before killing one of the gate guards.

That was the easy part of the eventful day. His report on the Saukko destruction and Captain Chetan's death had staggered the garrison commander, Colonel Kropp. Colonel Gupta just shook his head on hearing the news and asked,

"You're sure it was a sea-mine?"

"I did not see any warships. The Saukko just exploded. It had to be a sea-mine of some sort. Intense rifle fire from Zircon soldiers at the farm killed anyone who survived the blast and stayed by the boat."

Colonel Kropp asked. "How did you manage to survive the attack, and no one else?" Reading the message in the man's look accompanying that remark required no great insight. His commander thought he was a coward, had abandoned the ship, runaway.

The Devil's Spawn

"The blast threw me in the river. I managed to reach the north shore. With no weapon I ran."

Kropp in an angry accusing voice asked, "How could you not know there was a Zircon warship in the area? That is your job, to patrol the river and warn about the enemy's location and strength."

"Enough, the Saukko captain is responsible for the loss," Gupta said. "Not the lieutenant. Losing our steamer is bad, but if we lose this fort and gold, those damn Zircons will be the least of our concerns. The emperor is unforgiving to officers that lose warships, forts, and gold. So, who else has a steamer?"

There was no disagreement on that warning and to do his part on avoiding that fate, Halona had spent the evening looking for Juan Velasquez. The Oztec pirate owned the only other steamer near Uneeda. He claimed to be a fisherman and livestock trader, and he was, but the lieutenant knew his most profitable business was dealing slaves. His boat, Thumper, was an old thirty-meter sternwheeler with an ancient teapot boiler. The vessel was slow and unreliable, but it still beat paddling against the river current. He found the pirate in the bar attached to the Uneeda fish market, another of Juan's ventures. No surprise the loss of the Saukko was the hot bar topic.

"What happened, lieutenant? I could not believe the news. Did Zircon armored riverboats surprise Admiral Chetan?" a concerned Juan asked on seeing him.

Halona joined the pirate at his table. Of course, the location offered no privacy; every ear and eye was on him, the room's curiosity was rampant. The facts would never do. Instead, he told the story Colonel Gupta suggested if asked.

"There were no Zircon boats. I was there, the damn boiler exploded while the admiral was maneuvering the Saukko, prior to unloading my squad to capture a small Zircon recon patrol. The army, I, need your Thumper to transport my marines down the river so I can cutoff the Zircon escape. The colonel will send people to help repair

71

the boat. We need to go first thing in the morning before the bastards escape."

Juan did not want the Zircons in charge either, with their antislavery nonsense. "Have your men here, first light and the Thumper will be ready. You'll owe me." Halona nodded and hurried off to organize the men and inform the colonel.

Bari's near total nudity had shocked Frau Kerry and she was not a woman fearful to express her thoughts or allow the day's worthy deeds to influence her opinions.

"What sort of men use a young woman's body as bait? I had heard you Zircons were animals. Is my daughter in danger?" She was blocking Al from the bedroom door where Bari was recovering.

"Not from us animals," he snapped, irritated at how seeing nudity unhinged otherwise sensible people. "She volunteered and her idea worked. Their evil minds were on raping her." That brought a gasp from the mother, as he continued, "That allowed us to sink the only Ichneumon warship on the river. You need to pack your valuables, it's no longer safe here."

Alarmed, she fell back a step as he added, "Their army will be back to avenge their loss. You need to think about where you and your family might be safe until this matter is settled." He felt bad for the family. For no reason other than being human, evil had attacked them.

With the door unblocked, he entered and found Bari in a folding wood chair, wearing her work clothes, freshly laundered he noticed, and trying to lace up her boots. Based on her smile, he knew she had overheard Frau Kerry's loud reprimand. With a brief giggle, she said. "Don't you animals be harsh with her. She means well."

"I know. Here, let me," he said kneeling to take the laces and tie them. "You're a brave woman, Bari. The men and I thank you for what you did." That tribute earned him a brief smile that verified his initial impression that she was a beautiful woman.

She had shaken her head during his comments and replied with, "I am glad I could help, but your bomb was the wonder. I'm amazed that little bit of gun powder could do that." He grinned over that misunderstanding and savored a chance to impress her.

"You're thinking of black powder. That was dynamite, a far more powerful explosive and waterproof." He finished tying her other boot and stood up as she said,

"They have another river steamboat. Do you think they'll be back?" That was not good news, but it did not surprise him. He never thought the Ichneumons would not have an extra boat stashed somewhere.

"Count on it, they'll want to try salvaging the boat. Normally I would have blown up the boiler and engine to prevent that, but Bill has hope of recovering the wreck for his future fleet after we run off the Ichneumons. You need to know at least one of them escaped yesterday. Jones thinks he was one of the marine officers."

"Lieutenant Halona, I saw him, and he was getting his eye full like the others, but I doubt he recognized me."

"If you are up to it, I'd welcome your help. I am sending everyone down the river for safety, but the squad. We're going to recon Uneeda and since you know the town, you could be a real asset."

"Are you talking a quick look see, or an attack?"

"I'm after information, but I'm not one to pass up an opportunity to damage our enemy."

The powerfully built Zircon captain had a patch of scars on the left side of his face, but had a nice smile, kind brown eyes, brown hair, and great looking teeth. He seemed to like her. Bari wondered what his story was. Might he be the ally she had been looking for?

Her life's goal was ending the evil of slavery, which had destroyed Oztec society.

The young good looking mine equipment salesman, Kit Jacobs, had seemed nice too. Professed he did not approve of slavery, but he had disappeared. The other Zircon she had dealings with, Hans Maxim, was proving to be all promises, no action, for his employer kept buying Laredo's slaves.

Everyone, despite the Ichneumons' effort to suppress the information, knew the Zircon emperor had out lawed slavery in the eastern territories. She reckoned it was a reasonable hope that they would end slavery in Uneeda territory if the Ichneumons were gone. Whether the Bergdorf gang would end it was another issue.

"I'll help, but your doctor said I'll have to be careful with that back wound for a few days. While we have a boat, we should cross to the north side."

Al understood she was referring to the dirt track that connected Uneeda and Seth along the north side of the river. The mule farm was on the south side of the river. A river that teemed with critters that would eat you.

"There's a decent road over there," Bari continued. Standing up, she was pleased to discover her dizziness was gone. "And I know where we can get horses if you have any money."

"What are you talking about? We'll just take them," the captain said. He almost appeared to laugh on seeing her alarm over his threat of criminal behavior.

"That will make enemies you don't need. It's not that far, we can walk it." Were Zircons no better than Ichneumons and her people? I guess he's a scoundrel, she thought.

"Don't approve of foraging?" the scoundrel asked her, sounding amused.

"Just another word for looting, stealing," she snapped. For moment she had thought these Zircon soldiers might be a step above the sorry collection of males she seemed to attract.

The older trooper, Sergeant Jones looked in the room and asked, "Are you two set?"

"This filly wants to walk there." The captain told his man while gathering up her backpack.

"And I supposed you wanted to fly. Of course, we're walking there and need to get started."

"He wanted to steal horses." That caused the trooper to look at his captain, before addressing her.

"He's just jerking your chain, lady. You will find the captain has a peculiar sense of humor." Seeing her confused look, the sergeant added, "The general would bust him to corporal for looting. We need to get going."

The rascal, smiling, said. "The sergeant's right, time to go. You need anything?"

"Yes," she answered, and decided it was time for her to learn her status with this strange gang. "Do you guys have a revolver I can have?"

Bari, still annoyed with him, answered most of his questions with one-word, when she bothered to acknowledge them. He suspected her back wound was not helping her disposition. But the Oztec beauty was a tough trooper and did not hold the squad back. Even better, she had guided them to a rocky hillside where rock overhangs offered shelter from the sun and weather along with a distant view of Uneeda.

The lake looked like a view of an ocean. It was a far larger body of water than he had expected. Even from their elevated perch, the far shore was not visible. Al had read Uneeda Lake was an environmental marvel rich in fish and waterfowl. The most commercially valuable catches from the cold clear water were the large blue pike that ranged up to ten kilograms in size and the smaller two-kilogram yellow perch that formed huge schools of fish. Several types of squids populated the deeper sections of the lake, some exceptionally large. The lake's apex predator was the megalodon.

According to a chapter in the history book Al had read, those four-meter-long freshwater sharks depended on those schools of yellow perch and squid between the red bison and deer fall and spring migrations. The article cautioned the sharks attacked swimmers and were dangerous. The three-hundred-kilometer-long lake had a shape like an eight, two circles connected by a narrow strait located about hundred kilometers west of Uneeda. Only a half kilometer width of very deep water separated the north and south shores at that location. The late migrating red bison and deer often crossed there to avoid the long distance around the western part of the lake. Sheer chiffs around Silver Ridge and glaciers added to the animals' difficulties of reaching their winter range by traveling around at the western end of the lake. The megalodons preyed on the animals that chanced the swim, but the herd was large and the sharks few.

The other interesting lake feature that caught his interest as a lay student of mining geology was the claim a fault ran down the center of the west section of the lake for thirty kilometers. The fishermen asserted that sections of the lake there were over thousand kilometers deep. Al was dubious of that claim but he hoped to travel the length of the lake one day after this war.

Uneeda was about what he expected, a large stone fort and decrepit waterfront with a half dozen wood docks, all about thirty meters long and a matching number of warehouses, three of them decent looking brick-constructed, the rest made of wood. The antiquated wharf area had no steam-cranes for moving heavy cargo.

Behind the waterfront and surrounding the fort was a series of streets and alleys, open markets, and one-story wood buildings.

The Devil's Spawn

Judging by the laundry lines with hanging clothes a few of the buildings were residential. Other buildings appeared abandoned. The fort wall construction used cut yellow stone blocks and reminded him of the original fort at River Point.

"How many people live in Uneeda?" Al asked her.

"Not that long ago, twenty-five hundred, mostly Zircons and Oztecs. But over the last couple of years the Zircons have left or disappeared and now the other humans are leaving. Uneeda will be a ghost town in another year if the Ichneumons remain in control."

Using his small telescope, he saw eight large cannon barrels protruding from the fort wall facing the lake. Large Ichneumon flags flapped above stone towers at each corner of the lake side wall. He suspected garrison troopers had not fired those cannons in years, for they would be firing over the residents and warehouses. A misfire during practice could result in a shell landing among residents and warehouses.

To the south of the fort were two other smaller cut stone multi story buildings. They were the government buildings for the court, tax collectors, and police. Radiating out from there were a few nice-looking larger brick homes scattered on the hill side behind and above the fort. Where the VIP's and Hans Maxim made their home, he figured. He walked over to the small fire where Jones was making coffee. Bari was sitting on a rock beside the sergeant cleaning her revolver barrel and cylinders with a rod and brushes from the squad's gun cleaning supply kit.

"Which direction is the gold mine?" he asked refilling his cup with the fresh coffee.

"You can't see it from here," she said, still peeved, while carefully inserting new cartridges in her weapon. He had to grin.

"May be that's why I asked you for directions." She snapped the loaded revolver cylinder shut and stood up, pausing to holster her

David C. Brown

gun, and then returned the cleaning equipment to the kit and handed it to Jones, before pointing up the hill.

"From up there you can see the mine process plant, reject piles and slave pens," she said, then with a mischievous look, added, "And their guards might see you."

Al sensed she was warming up to him a bit. "Still, a careful look is called for. Would you go with me to explain what I'm looking at?" After a pause, she nodded while an amused Sergeant Jones shook his head.

The hike to the brush covered ridge crest was easy and provided a panorama of the area north of Uneeda to the Bergdorf mine. He had expected a hard rock mining operation but realized this was a placer gold deposit. The site's several large ponds mined out deposits.

The gold mine, several kilometers off, reminded him of a gravel pit operation without the conveyors and screening plants. Here dozens of men with wheelbarrows and ox carts supplied the effort that transfer the material through the process. Bergdorf's operation appeared archaic, not even a steam shovel to excavate the sand and gravel.

Three large warehouses constructed from corrugate iron sheets were located near the southern most pond. A large prison type of fence topped with coils of concertina barb wire and guard towers surrounding the facility added to the site's sinister ambiance. The slave quarters he reckoned. He asked Bari about the source of the slaves and received a sermon.

"That is the shame of the Oztecs, they raid each other's tribes for captives to sell to the mines and Ichneumons. There is always a new wrong requiring retribution and providing the excuse to raid. They are greedy stupid fools that the world takes advantage of. You

Zircons will do the same given a chance." He did not think her condemnation fair, thinking of the resolution to the Wapiti uprising.

"We're not angels but be fair. Our emperor is trying to rid the world of slavery and all women, Zircon, Wapiti, Clovis, Mongol, Zambian, even Ichneumon have the same rights as men, unlike in the Ichneumon and Mongol empires where women are chattel with no rights."

Crouched together behind a split boulder to spy on the mine, he could smell the soap Doctor Sebastian used to wash her, which suggested she could smell him and that would not be a soap smell.

She shrugged and after a pause spoke. "Okay, I'll agree, you guys are not the worst."

"Ah, good. Now that you are willing to admit we are not the bad guys, will you show us Hans Maxim's place?"

"Why?" she asked, suddenly quite serious and looking at him. "Are you here to assassinate or kidnap him?"

"Please, we're here to rescue him." That assertion earned a disbelieving shake of her head and brief laugh.

"I can't think of anyone less likely to want or need rescuing than Hans." She studied him for a moment. "You were serious?" He nodded and then flopped around and sat up to look behind them checking no one was creeping up on them as she spoke.

"Then allow me to explain," she said, sounding a bit like he expected a young mother would as she explained to her five-year-old son why he could not have that ten-kilogram snapping turtle in his bedroom as a pet. "The current owner of Bergdorf Mining is a former mercenary and assassin who several years ago showed up in Uneeda. In short order the Zircon thug managed to acquire all the good gold leases."

"You're dreadfully disrespectful of your boss ,calling him a thug," he said, earning a slight smile from her before he added, "How did he do that, by threatening to murder the lease owners?"

"Mostly through card games. Most miners are enthusiastic but unskilled gamblers. Though I would not be surprised to learn he shot a few. By the time the Ichneumons woke up to what was happening, he was too entrenched to easily remove. Since Bergdorf kept buying their slaves, paying their taxes and selling his gold to the Ichneumon brokers, they left him alone. With the loss of Westport, the shipment of gold has stopped. Everyone expects the Zircons to attack and rout the Ichneumon army."

"I wouldn't think Bergdorf has a problem with that, the Zircons will buy his gold."

"Oh, but he does have a problem. Involvement in an assassination attempt on Emperor Schnabel and the talk is the emperor wants revenge."

She paused, studying him for a moment, then asked, "Is that why you're here?"

That the general left out a few key facts in his briefing for this mission did not surprise Al. At least Maxim's connection to the IIS did not appear to be common knowledge and he answered, "No, in fact I don't recall ever hearing that."

"Well, that's what Maxim is telling people. So that is my point, I think the man you're supposed to rescue intends to gain control of Bergdorf's mines after you poor dogs endanger your lives kicking the aliens and current owner out."

Could all that be true? How could a female livestock buyer have obtained the information that the IIS and General Markel did not have? Especially in this society where most women were chattel. Or more likely, the IIS were being their usual treacherous secretive selves. Night was falling, but she showed no interest in moving, and since he enjoyed her company, asked,

"Bari is this true or are you spoofing me? I mean how can you know this?" A soft laugh escaped from her lips, and fearing she would think him simple he added, "I know, if you're hoaxing me why would you admit it?"

"I'm not, we're on the same side in this war. I despise those cruel Ichneumons. Most of my information comes from local gossip, bars, and the markets. Keep in mind, my job is buying livestock and supplies for the mine, the largest customer around, so I'm usually welcomed wherever I go." And Al reckoned being a good-looking affable female did not hurt.

"Hans," Bari said, with a wave of her hand, "Like most men, he talks too much when in his cups." Al figured that was not all the jerk was after. He was starting to develop a dislike for the man he was to help. Bari looked at him to learn if he cared to dispute her statement. He thought that too but said nothing. She got to her feet and changed subjects by asking, "Where are you from?"

"The York Territory," Al said and to stop any more questions added, "Slavers murdered my parents and sold me to a coal mine where I worked until I could join the army." Slightly shaking her head, she quietly asked if that meant he had been a slave. He nodded, then said, "Anyways, enough about me. Back to Hans, I would not think I'd want a man like Bergdorf knowing I planned to seize his business."

Bari shrugged, then looked briefly around the hillside before saying, "It's all talk. Hans wants me for his mistress and was trying to impress me."

Hard to fault the man's taste, Al thought. That such an intelligent woman would consider that option depressed him, but who was he to judge?

"You don't strike me as the type." It was getting dark, but he caught the frown and added, "Don't get me wrong. You're beautiful enough, but you strike me more as the queen type."

She quietly chuckled. "For a rough man, you have a beguiling turn. So, what's next, captain? Sleep? It has been a long day."

Could he trust her? He hoped so but was worried her allure was clouding his judgment. Trying to stall, he asked, "What does your father do?" He twisted around on the rock from watching the mine to where he could watch her face.

She appeared startled by the question but answered, "My father was murdered in Westport three years ago."

"I am sorry to hear that," Al said, hoping she would give details.

"My mother died from influenza the year after I was born so my father and I were close. He had one of the small placer deposits and sold out to Bergdorf a year before his death."

"Any suspicion Bergdorf was involved?"

"No, my father liked working for him. The Ichneumon police murdered him. He was in Westport to accept delivery of a shipment of winter sole nuts the mine had ordered. The police seized the shipment as illegal Wapiti contraband and, in the process, shot my father. The eight thousand D-marks payment my father had with him vanished. The police said they shot him for resisting arrest. But they shot him to steal Bergdorf's money."

Al shaking his head in sympathy with her loss, thought if all that was true, then she should be a dependable ally for his mission. He said, "I need to meet your pal, Hans Maxim. If he does not want rescue, I can complete my recon mission and head to Westport with my report."

"You would abandon us?" Bari asked. Her alarm surprised him and he hastened to explain.

"There's only twelve of us, there are hundreds of Ichneumons along with Bergdorf's thugs that are or will be after us because of the Saukko. I should leave it at that, but I will bite. What would the queen have me do?"

"Queen?" She huffed, following a moment later with, "Well, since you're here, let's go visit Hans, he's a night owl."

82

Chapter 7

Earlier that afternoon, news that someone had attacked the Saukko had Hans Maxim wondering if the Zircons were in the valley or had that incompetent crew of Admiral Chetan managed to blow its boiler as the fort was saying? Now he wished he had not told the IIS he wanted out. What he wanted was in the Hittite safe, sixteen of the foundry's lovely eleven-kilogram gold ingots rested there. A fortune of fifteen million D-marks of gold at the current war price of ninety-five D-marks per gram. He had two problems to resolve before ever having a chance of absconding with the treasure. One was moving the heavy gold to Westport without alerting Bergdorf, river pirates, and the authorities. The other was getting a fair price for the gold from brokers like that bitch, Matias Niino of New Hamburg.

The mining equipment salesman, Kit Jacobs, had been interested while he thought Hans was talking about stealing the Ichneumon gold. Then once he realized Bergdorf was not involved, he told Hans not to be a fool, the man was a killer. That was two weeks ago, and since there had been no blow back, Kit had kept his word, though yesterday he learned the equipment salesman had disappeared and now he wondered if the fool had said something to Bergdorf.

He had considered trying for a deal with Juan Velasquez. His steamboat, Thumper, could take him and the gold to Westport, but the heavy bags would scream gold. Not good, it is akin to asking a wolf to carry your pork roast home from the butcher. Same problem with the recon-IIS squad, though with the Zircons one ingot in his bag might go unnoticed. What to do, his rescuers could show up at any time. He thought of Lieutenant Halona. He knew the officer was unhappy about the colonel refusing to promote him to captain. Still the man was an Ichneumon and Hans just did not trust him.

Then he thought of Bari. She was the independent fearless sort that liked haggling and making deals. There was also no love lost between her and Bergdorf over his use of slaves, or the Ichneumons, after they murdered her father. Hans had never heard any hint she padded her accounts and as far as he knew the woman was no thief. That might present a problem. He also knew she and her grandmother were land poor and had little cash, but through her livestock dealings Bari understood the freight business and hawaladar process for transferring money and credits. She would be a useful accomplice.

Hans's thoughts turned to how he could motivate her to help him. She surely had heard during her dealings with those ranchers out of Seth that Chief Laredo was talking of seizing the Lu farm during the confusion when the Zircons kicked the Ichneumons out of Uneeda. He would remind her that Laredo planned to murder her and her grandmother first to free up the farm. His argument would be that the Lu family would be wise to leave while they could. If she agreed to make the arrangements for him and his gold to travel with her next shipment of livestock to Westport, he would give her a third of the gold. Hans decided to find Bari tomorrow and ask her to help him steal the gold. If she turned him down and threatened to tell Bergdorf, he would kill her.

An exhausted Lieutenant Halona returned to the fort to tell the colonels that Velasquez would lend the army his steamboat Thumper. He hoped after delivering his news, the colonel would dismiss him. It was near midnight, and he needed some rest before morning. From the guard outside the colonel's office, he learned Colonel Kropp had sent a messenger raven to Silver Ridge. Halona figured it was to order Captain Maqbool to return post haste with the sternwheeler, Comet. The ship was a sister to the Thumper, only in better condition thanks to the army's better maintenance, but just as old and slow.

Colonel Kropp who had been standing behind his desk when Halona entered appeared irritated. On recognizing him, he waved him in. "Did you find a boat?"

Halona explained the arrangement with the pirate and quickly learned the colonels disagreed over the best use of the steamboat. Colonel Kropp wanted to send the Thumper at first light with Lieutenant Halona's surviving platoon members and several policemen to the mule farm to attack the Zircons and secure the Saukko and its weapons. Colonel Gupta had a different plan.

"Waste of time," Gupta said, "that attack was by a Zircon recon squad that got lucky and is now halfway back to Westport. I want the Thumper to load the gold in the morning. There is still time to make the deadline for meeting General Paget's men near Westport."

Kropp was against moving the gold fearing the Zircons might ambush the Thumper and steal the gold. The lieutenant agreed with Kropp, but wisely kept his thoughts to himself.

Gupta was not a man used to having his suggestions refused. Though he was a feared secret police colonel and could have Colonel Kropp arrested, even shot, he was not Uneeda's commander. The Ichneumon emperor did not approve of removing commanders without his approval. Instead, he berated Kropp for not having installed the telegraph line between Uneeda and Silver Ridge.

"If you had done your job and installed the wire, the Comet would already be headed back. Now we have to hope some damn bird manages to survive the eagles and reach Silver Ridge."

Halona's commander, shaking his head no, snarled, "What f**king wire? Delta never sent the copper. Paget and his gang were too busy riling up the Erie Valley by murdering the farmers and workers to be concerned about needed infrastructure. Now I hear you wanted to do the same thing in Uneeda. No wonder we are losing this war."

Colonel Gupta was on his feet yelling "that is traitorous talk!" when the duty officer, a nervous corporal, entered and handed Colonel Kropp a note.

Sergeant Jones and Pete were of the opinion if the squad was going to take the risk of venturing into the heart of Uneeda, they should just grab the IIS agent and taken him to Westport. Al figured what happened would depend on agent Maxim. He did not enlighten Bari to the possible change.

Al relaxed on realizing neither the Uneeda's police, nor the garrison appeared on any special alert. He reckoned the garrison commander figured they had retreated to Westport and the Ichneumons were hunting for them down the river. The fort was dark, and no foot patrols were encountered on the way to an older brick mansion in the neighborhood on the hill behind the fort. The property had a neglected appearance, the flower beds having gone to weed. At least none of its windows appeared broken, unlike the other houses they passed that looked abandoned.

An unexpected discovery was the city had a local telegraph service based on the poles and wires they passed. Whether the system still worked, given the abandoned nature of the neighborhood he could not determine. He was not sure what to make of the wire for there was no service between Uneeda and Westport.

The trip off the ridge to Maxim's place required two hours. His watch read 23:00 hours when Bari stopped him in front of a closed driveway gate.

"Bergdorf usually has one or two off-duty policemen as guards at his home-private office," Bari cautioned. "Best I go and tell Hans you are here. We don't need the guards to start shooting."

She had invented the guards. Worried the Zircon mission had not been requested by her friend, she wanted to warn Hans and give him a chance to escape in case this was all news to him.

"Okay, just don't be too long. I want to be out of Uneeda before sun rise," Captain Belcher said while his men listened.

Bari, who also wanted to be out of town before morning, jogged up the curved driveway to the mansion. An Ichneumon soldier materialized out of a shallow by Hans's front porch and stopped her. His presence shocked her, and she realized that maybe she did not know the accountant as well as she had thought. The guard said nothing, just grabbed her by the arm and escorted her into the mansion where he called out for Hans.

"Bari, you are just who I was thinking about," Hans said, dismissing the soldier and gesturing for her to come into the office. "I have a dandy proposal for you."

Hans, in a yellow bathroom, was an older, neatly barbered, and attractive middle age aloof Zircon male. His unexpected cheerful welcoming startled Bari. She wondered if the man was drunk and thinking sex. If he was, he was in for a disappointment. "Why the soldiers?" she asked, entering the office.

"Because of these," Hans said straining to lift a heavy gold ingot out of a black case sitting on the desk. "I have sixteen of these bars. Enough so we would be rich, free. Just help me hide them and then move them to Westport with your next livestock shipment."

"You're crazy. Bergdorf would hunt you down and murder you if Colonel Kropp didn't first." She laughed. "Oh, Hans your timing is terrible."

With a confused hurt look, he asked, "You would pass up this opportunity, why?"

She had always suspected that Hans, though book smart, was at heart a fool, said. "The Zircon soldiers you requested to rescue you are at the bottom of your driveway."

After Bari disappeared up the crushed rock driveway, Al called Pete and Williams over. "I want you two to swing around back and check the area. I like Bari." His men nodded; they also were impressed with her. He added, "But I have known her for less than a day and this Maxim character strikes me as a possible double agent. Be cautious. Don't kill unless necessary to save yourself. Go."

Time dragged. After a dozen checks of his prized Longiner pocket watch, he decided fifteen minutes was enough wait and walked to the mansion after unnecessarily telling Sergeant Jones and his troopers to stay alert. He found a pleased Corporal Williams waiting at the front door. He nodded toward two bound and muzzled Ichneumon soldiers lying face down in the planter off to the right of the driveway circle.

"Judging from their shoulder patch, those two belong to the same unit that's been murdering the farmers," the corporal whispered. "Haven't heard or spotted any other activity, nor your girl."

The Devil's Spawn

The presence of Ichneumon marines worried Al. He tried the tall thick wooden front door. Unlatched, it swung open with a gentle push to reveal a comfortably furnished room. Three identical black leather cases of the size used by doctors sat in a group on the floor to the left of the office door. He heard muffled bits of conversation from a room down a long hall toward the rear of the house. He eased down the hall to hear better. An alarmed Bari was talking.

"You're making a mistake. Don't send that alert to Halona." A moment later, the unmistakable clatter of a telegraph key occurred behind the door across the hall. He heard a man laugh.

"Colonel Kropp will reward me for the capture of those Zircons. They're furious over the loss of the Saukko."

"You're a damn fool. I'm out of here." There was a sound of a flesh being punched and a moan that sounded feminine.

"Stupid bitch, you should have joined me. I cannot let you leave after you know my plans. You're a witness."

The relief Al felt on learning she was not conspiring with the agent make him realize just how much he liked the Oztec woman. He slammed open the door to reach Bari just as Pete entered the room through the rear door. The distractions caused the agent, who had a small revolver jammed in Bari's head to switch aim.

"Stop or I'll shoot." The startled man said, pointing the gun toward Al who thought Pete's arrival was fortunate. It was clear the agent was not sure who, Pete or him, was the bigger threat. Bari appeared out cold on the floor beside the man, who Al figured was Hans Maxim. Pete had a bloody leg but did not appear seriously wounded.

"You want to be rescued?" Al asked, a stickler for following his orders when that suited his purpose, while wondering about the scene he had just witnessed and what plan Bari had turned down.

"What? No, but you might if you're here when Lieutenant Halona's marines arrive." Bari stirred on the floor causing Hans to look down. Pete's thrown rock nailed the agent in the side of the head, causing him to drop the firearm. Al threw the bastard to the floor and searched him for other weapons as Williams and Jones burst into the room to tell them the fort had lit up.

"Men are saddling horses, judging from their yelling," Jones said looking at Bari on the floor, and asked. "What happened to her?"

"We need to go," Al said helping a limp Bari to her feet. "Can you walk?" She appeared dazed and did not answer for a moment, then weakly nodded and stood without help. He let go of her and told Williams to watch her.

Pete said, "There's three saddled horses in the back yard, the Ichneumon guards' ride, I figure."

"We'll take them. Help Pete wrap up the traitor so he can't talk and tie him off on one of those horses. Williams, help Bari to the other horse. Pete, you have a bad leg. You take the third one and lead the other horses to the ridge camp. We'll cover you."

Gun fire from the front gate spurred Pete with Jones' help to haul the agent and Bari to the backyard and mount up. Al heard the front window glass splinter from a bullet and went to check. Someone was shooting at the house as more guns fired near the front gate. The bullet had hit the lamp, shattering its glass oil reservoir, and spraying the oil across the table, wall, and floor. A moment later the burning wick caught the spilled lamp oil afire, and flames raced up the window drapes before Al could find anything to put out the fire with.

To buy Pete more time, Al ran to the front door and over the next couple of minutes, fired a magazine of rounds at the soldiers by the front gate, stopping their advance. By then the fire threatened to cut off his retreat through the house to the rear door, forcing him to leave.

Arriving at the east ridge rally location, Al learned all his squad had make good their escape from Uneeda. Harry Baker, the squad's medic, was busy dressing Bari's head wound while scolding him. "You need to take better care of your woman."

Al suspected Bari did not consider herself anyone's woman but said nothing to the medic or Pete, who, with a slight grin, was nodding in agreement with Harry. Their captive with his arms tied behind his back was not smiling. Hans had acquired a pair of work boots and stood in his bath robe off to the side by the three horses. His burning house had lit the night sky for a while and still burned enough to locate it from the ridge. Hans was not in a submissive mood.

"You fools are going to learn those stupid Ichneumons aren't your problem. My employer will hang, no, he'll add you to his work force, as slaves." The man was nearly sputtering with malice, acting like he controlled events, not a captive. "And that Oztec bitch, Bergdorf will take particular care of her." The unexpected behavior had Al curious and cautious.

"Why did you notify the Ichneumons? She told you we were there to help you escape if you wanted to go."

"I thought it was trick by Velasquez to grab me and that your guys were from his pirate crew. I made the call because I pay the fort commander for protection." More likely Al figured, he is an Ichneumon agent and did not want to return to Westport for an interrogation.

"So, who is this Velasquez and why would you think he wanted you?"

"One of his businesses is kidnapping. Maybe he thought my boss would pay the ransom." The prisoner's brief cackle sounded forced. "I should have trusted the whore. Too late now, that was Bergdorf's house you burned, and he will not allow that affront to go unpunished. And if for once his pack of killers are not up to the task, there are the Ichneumons."

What about the gold, Al thought as Hans sat down on a rock and added. "Captain Cortazzo cannot allow your murdering of his policemen and guards, nor can Colonel Kropp allow the loss of the Saukko go unavenged. So, we're all going to die because some Zircon bureaucrat wants to meddle in Bergdorf's business."

Their prisoner was a strange bird, forgetting who had requested their presence, but his information was interesting. How much of it was true was anyone's guess. That Velasquez character was probably a local bandit. Bari can explain when she has recovered, Al thought. He had encountered a fair number of confidence men and thought he could recognize one in his prisoner.

"You do recall that you requested the IIS rescue you?" Al said and, after a moment of no comment from the suddenly quiet prisoner, asked, "What was your job?"

In a more subdued voice Hans answered, "I advised Herr Bergdorf on his dealing with the various empires and authorities."

"Have you had much luck skimming the payoffs and bribes or swindling his gold?"

Their prisoner appeared offended, but did not answer, so Al continued. "You've already told us we're dead men. I am curious, that is all. I thought some gold might come in handy during our escape." Bari heard that and interrupted.

"Don't be wasting time with that charlatan and his stolen gold. We need to find the Mischief before Bergdorf's thugs find us." She was on her feet, though a bit wobbly, as she lurched her way to the roan horse. She refused any help, except to repeat they needed to go.

"The bitch knows what's coming," the once again hostile prisoner snapped.

"Spare us your lame threats," Al said. While the tired group got moving down the trail, Al's thoughts returned momentarily to those black bags. Might there come a chance to liberate some of those bags he had seen at the house? What would Bari's response be if he tried to recruit her to join a planned gold heist?

Sun rise was a couple of hours away as they started back down the trail Bari had used earlier from the river. Williams, another former Wapiti hunter, rode one of the horses to scout the trail ahead. Pete, who had taken a bullet in his left leg rode the other horse beside Bari's roan horse. Al walked with the rest of the squad and the sullen prisoner. They maintained a brisk pace that had Hans struggling. He sat down after about thirty minutes and refused to move. A weary Al was not in the mood for any delays and called Pete back.

"Agent Maxim, you will walk or be dragged, your choice."

"Fu**k you, the IIS will hear about this. I need that horse. The bitch can walk."

Al feared that had Bari not been there, he would have shot the troublesome ass and left his body for Bergdorf men. His men would never report him. Instead, he said, "Jones tie a rope around the prisoner's torso. Hans, walk or Pete's horse will drag your sorry ass the rest of the way." It worked.

About two hours after sunrise, Williams rushed back with news of meeting Private Gunner and his men who told of an Ichneumon blocking force ahead. They were still several kilometers west from being across the river from Frau Kerry's farm and where they hoped to find the Mischief. The garrison had responded fast and must have found a boat to get ahead of them.

"It's setup as a roadblock," a concerned Williams said. "A strong one, maybe twenty soldiers, well positioned, even has a couple of officers with it. It'll be a bloody affair to take out."

"They're the anvil, which, no surprise, means there's a force coming up behind us. Worst, they will catch up with us by noon."

Jones joined them to asked what brought Willian back. Informed, he suggested setting an ambush for the hammer. That was a favorite tactic of the squad, ambush the ambushers, but the numbers were not good.

"If we are unable to wipe out the pursuing force, then we're trapped between two hostile forces that can bring in more men from the fort or the mine. Bari," he yelled, "how dangerous is that river?"

The Oztec woman seemed to have fully recovered from the knock on her head and trotted her horse over to meet him at the river's edge. The peaceful appearing dark water was only twenty meters away and flowing smoothly with little surface turbulence as it curved to the south. The river was about thirty meters across where they stood on the north shore bank, a meter-high vertical exposed bank of gravel and sand the current was undercutting and eroding. The opposite south bank was a sandy beach typically found along the inside of a river bend. There were no signs of alligators.

"I don't see any indicators of a resident gator, but occasionally one of those lake beasts venture down this section of the river and you can't know if one is out there in the deep part of the river. I'd say except for that, this is one of the safer places to chance crossing what is an extremely dangerous river."

Al had an alarming recollection from the book he had read on the lake. When the bison did not cooperate by swimming in the lake and the large calamari that lived in the deep would not rise within three hundred meters of the surface, the megalodons would occasionally hunt prey of opportunity in the Uneeda River inlet. Was that the "lake beast" Bari was worried might be in that deep pool they were going to cross?

But several his men were listening and to avoid alarming them more, he did not ask for an explanation. Their best hope of avoiding the enemy was to cross the river, but in this section of the river there were no wide shallow rapids that offered a safe crossing.

"Pete, are you willing? You're the one with a bloody wound."
He nodded.

The Devil's Spawn

Normally Al would throw several sticks of dynamite in the river to stun any lurking gators, but he feared alerting the nearby Ichneumons. That deep pool in the river's center had him nervous, still he waved the men to the bank.

"Rake out our tracks. I want to hide where we cross the river. Follow Pete and Bari's horses across the river. Williams and I will wait for Gunner." The private and his men had been ahead of them about kilometer east on the river road when Williams encountered them. They were jogging back to join Al's group. "I will stay and rake out the last tracks after Gunner crosses and bring up the rear."

None of the men liked entering that deep dark water, but as Al knew from experience, like him, they would rather chance the crossing than appear cowardly or be caught by the Ichneumons. Hiding their tracks required a few minutes, but satisfied with their work, he told Pete to go. Hans was on his feet, yelling no. A moment later, Pete's horse dragged Hans into the chilly waters of the Uneeda River. Bari followed them as the other members of the squad waded in and started swimming across. Then Gunner arrived and crossed. Al smoothed out their tracks on the shore while Williams waited for him on the third horse in the knee-deep water. By the time he entered the water, all the men had reached the south shore where Bari and Pete waited with a very wet and indignant prisoner.

Al, a strong swimmer, followed Williams who rode on the horse with their rifles. Halfway across, the horse jerked sideways, spilling the rider. A moment later a large black shark-like creature lunged partially out of the water and seized the screaming horse by its neck. One of the terrified horse's wild kicks knocked the corporal senseless. By the time Al had them free of the boiling bloody water, the monster had ripped a massive chunk of flesh from the animal's neck and ended its life.

The horror of the moment gave Al an adrenaline boost that made hauling Williams effortless. As his feet touched the river bottom, two of the squad men were there to help drag the corporal to the beach. By then the remains of the horse and the beast had attracted a couple of smaller gators and the whole bloody feeding frenzy had drifted several meters down river. Remembering his mission, he ordered,

"Pete, set a defensive scrimmage line, in case a pursuing force arrives and discovers the crossing before we can clear out."

Sergeant Jones was already ordering everyone to get off the shore after smoothing the area and to move about eighty meters into the heavily wooded area.

"Got it covered, Captain. I'll keep four men to establish a skirmish line about thirty meters off the south riverbank."

While Harry tended to Williams's cuts, bites, and bruises, Al tried to calm down. After that terrifying experience, he wondered if he would ever again be able to enter that river. A concerned Bari came over to check on him.

"I'm sorry, I never expected that. Thank goodness those monsters prefer livestock to humans. The yearling wanted the horse, you, we all were lucky." Damn if that was the word he would use, but instead asked,

"That was a yearling?"

She nodded and then explained, "The fall bison migration must be running late."

He could not help a glancing toward the still bobbing piece of horse hide floating in the river and thinking that could be him. With a shake of his head, he asked her what that had to do with this.

She answered, "There aren't many lake megalodons."

"Thank god," Al muttered, thinking one was too many as she continued.

"They would normally be in the lake's narrows picking off stray bison as the big herd crossed the lake." She paused and studied him for a moment, "Well, I'm glad you're okay."

Shaking his head, he muttered, "So am I, woman." That such creatures existed had never entered his mind. He needed to remember this was not York and French Creek. Once again, his squad had survived a precarious maneuver without losing a man, but they were not clear yet. They would not be safe until they were on the Mischief with their prisoner and south of Seth. In the swamp, the Ichneumons could not flank them and block the river.

A few minutes later, a brief hard rain swept across the valley, further concealing the crossing location. During the downpour about a dozen mounted soldiers rode by across the river on the road they had been on. He knew when the enemy arrived at the roadblock, they would realize the Zircons had crossed the river.

Sergeant Jones said, "I'm hoping they'll waste time searching for where we crossed and not immediately cross the river to block us."

"They'll be more hesitant than we were to swim that river," Bari said, looking down the river where unseen creatures were jerking the remains of the horse about as it floated on the water surface.

"No, they won't" Al answered. "I figure that blocking force used boats to get ahead of us. They can use them to cross the river to our side and cut off our escape down river."

Earlier that evening, the arrival of Hans's telegram had stopped the bickering among the Ichneumon colonels at the fort. Colonel Kropp, who read it, blurted out, "I cannot believe our luck. The Zircons are, right now, in Uneeda at Bergdorf's mansion."

Lieutenant Halona watched, amazed, as Colonel Gupta went from being a red-faced angry man demanding the gold moment have priority to a sensible sounding officer.

"No shit, really?" The commander nodded and a smiling Gupta said, "With your permission I want to use the Thumper to haul a platoon of marines along with the lieutenant's men down the river far enough to cutoff the Zircons escape while you have Captain Cortazzo and the police pursue the bastards."

"Yes, let's nail those brazen fools." The chance for payback had roused Kropp from his despair. "I'll put my police to flushing the bastards down river to you. Kill them all. Lieutenant, organize the men and steamer boarding. Listen to the colonel. Put your roadblock before the first rapids. The danger of beasts in the river's deep water between the lake and those rapids will make them hesitate to cross the river before that. And don't arrive late, go. I'll worry about securing the Saukko wreck after we capture the Zircons."

Bergdorf had been at the mine's small foundry deciding on what portion of the week's gold production to melt and cast as ingots or leave as dust and nuggets when the guard alerted him his house was burning. The structure was a complete loss. It had been one of the better mansions in Uneeda and Bergdorf's home for three years; now it was a hot pit of coals and smoldering timbers, partially melted zinc and lead roofing, and noncombustible items like the porcelain commodes, marble sinks and the massive open Hittite safe. An empty safe. Since Captain Cortazzo, the police commander stood beside him, Friedrich Bergdorf stifled his curse and said nothing about missing gold. Ichneumon law required mines store all gold ingots in the fort vault.

The sixteen gold ingots that should have been in the open safe were missing. It was an accepted fact that no one had ever opened a Hittite without knowing the safe's combination, which made the list of suspects short. Bergdorf, being an accomplished gambler, knew one of the bandits that had raided his place might have guessed the correct six sets of double digits numbers for the safe. But since the odds of that was about one in a trillion, his accountant, Hans Maxim, remained his prime suspect. Or he supposed whoever those bandits were that burned the place might have tortured the combination out of Hans, but then where was his body?

Captain Cortazzo told him Zircon soldiers had started the fire and that the commander was organizing a vast hunt for the raiders. Lieutenant Halona and the new colonel were using the Thumper to deliver a blocking force down the river. They would have the bandits by night fall.

Bergdorf wondered why use the pirate's old boat when they had the Saukko? The police captain told him. He had a new worry, could the bandits that burned his place and the squad that sank the warship be the same gang and after him? The Zircon emperor, Wolfgang Schnabel, had a reputation of not being the vindictive sort. Still, he had been part of that plot several years ago to kill the emperor. He needed information. The problem was Halona's marines tended to kill all the humans they encountered, the mounted police were not much better, and he wanted his accountant alive to explain what happened here.

"I want those bandits caught. I'm willing to loan several of my men to help."

The Ichneumon captain liked his offer, since he knew those mine-guards always caught runaways. Cortazzo left to organize his men. Bergdorf sent for Ivan. The man was one of those large brawny men from the northern ice fields that the Zircon emperor often used for imperial guards. The army had cashiered the sergeant for murdering prisoners during the Ural insurgency. He also sent for his purchasing agent, Bari Lu. She usually was on top of what was occurring.

While awaiting his employees' arrival, the labor foreman he had brought to supervise the laborers waved him over to the part of the basement located under the office entrance. The sweaty ash coated man pointed to scorched dirty ingots, still too hot to handle that lay scattered among the charred timbers and smoking bits of leather from shipping cases. A quick count discovered twelve ingots. How the ingots got from the safe to that location and where the other four where he figured would prove an interesting story. He told the foreman to clear the rubble from around the other safe.

With that pest, Captain Cortazzo, gone it was time to check on the older Hittite safe in the far basement corner. He was the only one alive who knew the combination, so he was confident the safe was not open and empty. It was not.

"My, someone did a number on your home," Ivan said to Bergdorf, and then after dismounting asked. "They catch the bastards?"

"The police?" Bergdorf asked with a sarcastic chuckle and shake of his head, before adding, "Not yet. That is why you are here. Cortazzo told me our comrades have managed to lose their only warship."

His news startled Ivan. "They lost the warship?"

"That is right, not something one would expect from the local Oztec bandits. Halona was there, told Cortazzo the real story. A sea mine blew up the sternwheeler, though the fort is telling everyone it was the boiler. Halona just escaped with his life. He believes they were Zircon soldiers."

"Then I'm surprised a Zircon warship hasn't arrived to claim Uneeda."

"The more important question is who did this and where is Hans? I need information. I want you to make a sweep down the river road and capture him and his pals before the Ichneumons manage to find and kill them."

"Do we want to be killing Zircon soldiers?"

"No, only if there's no other way to rescue my accountant. Capture Hans, let them escape, if you can."

"What if the Ichneumons protest?"

"Damn, man, do I have to tell you everything? You know what I want. If the aliens get in the way, try to not leave any witnesses. They'll blame the Zircons."

Chapter 8

Al detected the cyclic thumps of a steamboat coming up the river. Undoubtedly the boat that delivered the blocking force and was now searching for where they had crossed the river. Bari had Jones's flask of whiskey and brought it to him as he rested beside a large shrub that offered fair concealment from soldiers on the river but allowed him to see them.

"That has to be the Thumper. Juan Velasquez owns it, and he is unwelcome news," she said squatting down beside him and handing over the flask. "The Ichneumons probably commandeered it to replace the Saukko."

That was about how Al read the situation, which meant more troopers after them. He motioned for everyone to hide and be quiet. He still did not have a good plan, other than wait for night and then hike down the south side of the river toward the mule farm. The sun would set in a few hours and heavy storm clouds had darkened the valley so hopefully the boat would notice nothing and pass on.

The archaic boat was moving slowly, about the speed of a slow walk, with a dozen soldiers standing on the main deck carefully inspecting both shorelines as they passed. Other than the pilot house, the boat had an open deck layout with several cattle pens holding ten nervous horses. The animals were saddled and ready to ride.

"Bad news, that's not the fort's commander. He's the new colonel, the one my boss told me about with the secret police," Bari whispered. Al figured she was referring to the officer in an Ichneumon army colonel's dress uniform. A foolish outfit to wear when hunting Zircon rangers, he thought, as Bari softly added, "Bergdorf told me he is here to organize the roundup and killing of free humans."

The temptation to end that crab's days of murdering innocent people was great, but avoiding discovery and reporting back to Westport had to be his priority.

"Help, help!" Hans suddenly started screaming as he jumped from the hedge Pete had used to hide behind. The sergeant grabbed and muzzled the bastard, but the damage was done.

Several excited Ichneumon soldiers on the river boat were shouting and pointing to where Hans had been and started firing shots. Al had grabbed his rifle with a scope and had the crosshairs on the colonel in moments. The enemy officer stood beside the boat pilot studying the woods along the south riverbank with a spyglass while shouting orders.

That son of a bitch Hans, Al thought, now a lot of people are going to die as he watched the pilot reverse the Thumper's paddle to slow the boat. After a moment, he heard the Ichneumon officer shouting some command and saw the pilot switch the paddle forward, neatly turning the boat towards the south shore. They were landing.

It was an audacious move, but foolish against an entrenched veteran foe of unknown size. To dither was to die, so Al shot the officer as he stood on the stairs to the pilot house yelling for his men to disembark and kill the human scum. Within moments the Zircon squad poured a murderous fusillade into the boat. The horses, going wild, broke out of the pen and leaped in the river. They were swimming toward both shores when that monster grabbed another horse. How many horses could that thing eat, Al wondered, or were there more than one in the river? He reloaded his rifle.

The horse's fate convinced the Ichneumons aboard the Thumper that escape by swimming was not an option and they fought back, refusing to surrender. After the last soldier hiding behind the boiler fell, Al checked the time out of habit to know it for the unit operational log. That only three minutes had elapsed astonished him.

Pete was dead, a bullet in the neck, everyone else escaped serious injury. Al thought about feeding that despicable Hans Maxim to the gators for causing Pete's death but decided to let the IIS deal with the traitor. Al was at a loss for why the fool thought he would be better off with the Ichneumons, unless he was a double agent and feared both Bergdorf and the IIS.

Besides Pete, thirteen of the enemy were dead. Two of his men had wounds, none of them life threatening. The colonel Al had shot was not among the dead on the boat and must have been one of

David C. Brown

several enemy soldiers the gators were now tearing to pieces in the river. By some fluke, the pilot had survived with a minor leg wound. Al knew steam engines and boilers and a quick check determined that mechanically the boat was usable, though the hull was taking on some water from bullet holes.

"The gunfire will bring those mounted police to investigate," a worried Bari said joining him in the pilot house. Somewhere during the fight, she had gotten hold of a rifle.

"Jones, tell Otto I need him and then reload the five horses that survived." God had smiled on them and now he had a workable plan. "We'll use the boat to escape and find the Mischief."

The squad needed several minutes to load. He used that time to convince the pilot that the only way he would see another sunrise was to cooperate with their pilot, Otto. Unfortunately, the mounted police returned before they could leave. The leader rode to the edge of the riverbank and instead of opening fire, yelled, "Who is in charge?"

What to do? Now the Zircon squad was in an exposed position that was worsening by the moment as the police dismounted and found shelter behind trees.

"Don't stand there with your mouths open, move, find cover, use the damn bodies," Jones shouted.

The men jumped to arrange the bodies of two dead horses still in the pen, which provided a decent shelter for five Zircon troopers. Hurriedly stacked bodies of the dead enemy soldiers formed other shelters. Three of Al's squad stayed on the south shore and found cover. In moments, his men were behind shelter and ready to extract a heavy toll from the police if they fired. Their leader, still on a horse, had to realized he was in a precarious spot. Al wondered if he did that on purpose to ensure there was a chance for a negotiation before the shooting started. Apparently so, for the man shouted,

"Don't shoot. I only want Herr Maxim. Hand him over and you can leave."

104

The Devil's Spawn

"We don't have anyone by that name," Al bellowed. Bari was beside him and, after studying the policeman, whispered.

"That is Bergdorf's man, Ivan. He's a Zircon and will know we have Hans."

Bergdorf's man added, "You do appreciate all those crab soldiers that were waiting for you down the river will be here any time now. I can make the trade, Maxim for letting you escape, until my comrades arrive, then we will have to kill each other. Only the Ichneumons benefit then. I don't know who you are, but I figure you're smart enough to know you have a poor hand."

There was more to this than the accountant, but Ivan was correct. Al had to decide now or have a lot of dead humans.

"Okay, you can have him." Al figured he would catch hell for that decision, but he valued his men's lives and asked, "How do you want to do that? I wouldn't suggest swimming."

"No, no, you can't," Hans screamed. "Please, don't." Al was not sure if it was the threat of swimming or returning to Bergdorf that had the weasel sobbing in a heap on the deck. He did not care.

"I'll trust you," Ivan said. "Fire up the boat and back over here and toss him on the bank. Then get the hell out of here. The soldiers coming will want the Thumper."

"Ivan, take me too."

"I'll be damned, the boss was looking for you. Sure, girl, come with Maxim. Okay Zircon?"

Al did not answer. Instead, he looked to Bari for an explanation for the sudden change in plans.

"I can't leave my grandmother." She might be a grandmother, but Al wondered if she did not want Hans out of her sight and feared what lies he might tell Bergdorf. Or he wondered if those heavy black leather cases had anything to do with her change of plans. Gold made people do crazy things.

105

Al wanted her to stay and tell him what Hans planned. He said, "Listen to the guy, he's terrified of returning to Bergdorf. He'll rat you out in a second."

"About what," Bari snapped. "How you Zircons kidnapped me and set fire to his house. I had no choice but to go along until Ivan got the drop on you." There was no time to waste trying to convince her returning to Ichneumon authority was a bad idea.

"It's your life, good luck then. Otto, back to the shore. Jones, toss Hans off and let her have one of the horses, then, Otto, downstream as fast as this sorry excuse of a riverboat will manage." As she maneuvered the horse to leap to the riverbank, he asked. "What's your grandmother's name?"

"Helen Lu," she shouted, making a clean leap to the riverbank. After that display of horsemanship, or should it be "horse-woman-ship," he wondered, Jones asked about the wounded pirate pilot.

"He's the only survivor, an Oztec, goes by Abdel. Should I shoot him, or toss him overboard?"

"He might be useful. Have Harry look at his wound and then secure him until I can question him."

Three of the new propeller-driven armored riverboats built at the River Point boatyard and a mix of older stern and sidewheelers steamboats cluttered the river around Westport's waterfront. One of those new armored riverboats, Zircon Ray, was the one that had stopped the Mischief a week ago. It had suffered extensive damage from cannon fire. The navy had parked it next to the No. 2 repair dock that Al had the Thumper tied off to. The Mischief was at the livestock dock where Bill was trying to sell his remaining hogs.

On shore the Zircon army had erected a small city of tents. There had been none there when Al had left for Uneeda. The thousand or so troops were of Al's old unit, the 88th Mountaineer

106

battalion. He also encountered many bandaged wounded soldiers on his way to Colonel Haddad, commander of Westport. In response to Al's comments on the number of troops in town the colonel told him the Ichneumon army had stopped the Zircon advance at the Fenwick Plantation, a fortified stronghold on a high ridge inside a loop in the Erie River about a hundred kilometers south.

Another contentious development: the navy had delayed the assault on Delta for a month. To wait for his military partner to become organized General Markel had pulled the bulk of his forces back to Westport. The general's detractors were saying he had gotten his ass kicked. Regardless, the general was using the river town as a staging area for a renewed assault against Fenwick, which according to Haddad would occur when the navy attacked Delta.

After listening to Al's report Colonel Haddad thought he had shown good sense. The information that there was no plague in the Uneeda Valley was a great relief to the army and Westport community. Colonel Caprivi, on the other hand who had also listened, thought surrendering the very man General Markel had asked Al to rescue to avoid a fight suggested a meekness not wanted in a Zircon officer.

"The general is due this evening, be available, captain," the stern colonel added, nodding toward the office door.

Dismissed, Al went down to the wharf area to check on the repairs to the Thumper while wondering if his army career was about to end. The old pirate's boat showed the effects of lousy maintenance. The Mischief mechanic was replacing the bearing at the port pitman rod connection to the Thumper's paddle wheel crankshaft. A crew was busy descaling its tea pot boiler. General Markel would decide the question of whether Velasquez's vessel was a spoil of war.

Three hours later, the summons for the meeting came and Al headed back to the fort. The colonel had earlier warned him to expect an angry general. Not sure what to expect, Al learned at the fort the general was using the old tobacco warehouse by the river for his command post. The general had a reputation for tolerating spartan amenities, but on arriving at the man's office, Al thought this was a bit much. Two thirds of the structure had burned, but one end of the large building still had a section of roof. The army had enclosed that area's open sides with tarps. The set-up kept the weather out, but the pigeons managed to get in the roof trusses. Al figured protection from the bird droppings accounted for the large open-sided tent erected within to cover the office area. Two oil-fired heaters warmed the area used by the general and his staff. Another tarp separated the general's corner of the space used by a dozen other officers, clerks, and telegraph machines. Scattered around the rest of the area outside the inner tent were large stacks of rations, ammo, and weapons.

A sergeant major sat at a deck in front of the far corner that the general was using for an office. Al told him General Markle was expecting him. The man told Al to part the curtain and entered to report. The general wore the same type of gray camouflage fatigues all the soldiers used in the Erie campaign.

"I've been looking through your unit operation logs." General Markel said, returning Al's salute and gesturing for him to have a seat. The weary man did not appear angry. "Taking out the Ichneumon warship with a mine amazed our navy comrades. I compliment you and your men on destroying that warship. It speaks well of your ability to improvise."

He thought of Bari and gave her credit for the success of the ambush. Markel was amazed to learn about her idea to pose naked as bait. After a laugh and shake of his head, he said,

The Devil's Spawn

"I've heard everything now. I hope to meet Frau Lu one day. Captain, that kind of thinking will help you to accomplish this mission. And I am thankful you had enough sense to save your squad by giving up that Maxim character, but disappointed you allowed the enemy to put you in that position. Learn from it. Now how strong is the enemy in Uneeda?"

"Bari Lu is Bergdorf's livestock buyer." Her name caused the general to smile, but not to comment, as Al continued. "She and the pirate pilot we captured, both believed the garrison was around two hundred and fifty soldiers before their losses associated with the Saukko and the Thumper engagements. I would estimate thirty dead in those two fights. The soldiers also serve as the town's police, so there is no other armed group in Uneeda except the gold mine, which has armed mounted guards, maybe a dozen. I doubt the garrison counts on them."

"You lost a good man in Corporal Pete. Did you write his family?"

"I did, he was one of the Wapiti warriors that helped us track down those saboteurs trying to blow the bridges on the spur railway."

"The remains of Burney's squad are available, eight good men," the general informed him. Al had heard Lieutenant Barnard, Burney to friends, had lost his right leg in the Fenwick Plantation attack. "I want you to incorporate them into your squad. That will bump your squad to twenty-four men. Could you take the Uneeda fort with them?"

With a lot of luck, Al thought. He answered, "That fort is a larger version of the one at River Point. The cut stone walls are in good repair and high enough to make any attempt to storm them a bloody business. My preference would be to nibble away at the enemy's strength in a series of small sudden attacks and withdrawals

109

while avoiding major engagements. The strategy ought to succeed against an Ichneumon garrison that had no hope of receiving reinforcements to replace loses while we block the Uneeda River at Westport."

"I agree that is a workable plan, but what if the Laredo tribe decides to aid the garrison? Or they manage to ambush you," the general said, studying Al.

"Let me have Sergeant Gunther's mortar squad. A couple of dozens of those thirty-kilogram shells would wreck the fort. The garrison would have to leave the fort and attack. My crew with our new repeating rifles could deal with that."

"I will think on that and get back to you. You think some of those ranchers might join you in the fight?"

"I believe the ranchers I met at Seth will help."

"If you get in trouble, do not expect help or a rescue, I have no men to spare now. Do what you can to harass that garrison of murderers. That will help to halt their ethnic cleansing that has been occurring. That is your mission, ending the Ichneumon slaughter of our people in Uneeda Valley. That reminds me, what did you do with those two orphans? A boy and a girl I recall, what are their ages?"

Al knew Markel was referring to the two children rescued from Prenter. "Nancy is five and Louis is three. I'm delivering them to the church's orphanage today." The general nodded in approval.

"What happened to those children is why I want you to focus on stopping the Ichneumons' murderous behavior. Now tell me about the boat's owner, Juan Velasquez."

The Devil's Spawn

Al explained he had never met the man, but Bari Lu had referred to him as a pirate and slaver hiding under a front of being a fisherman.

"I believe she's correct about Velasquez for the pilot of his boat is a branded slave. The other point, the man was allowing the Ichneumons to use the boat."

"I don't figure Velasquez had much choice but to accommodate them after the loss of the Saukko. As to his boat, I will leave that to your judgment. Returning the boat would deliver the message we are after Ichneumons, not the lake people property. Still, what kind of person brands his help? If he is really a slaver, the hell with him." Then the general offered some advice, "Establish a strong hold along the river below Uneeda from which to operate."

Al explained about using the Kerry farm. The general liked that and added, "Good, as I can, I'll have the navy run extra men and supplies up the river to the farm. Last point, the IIS said some of the Agarwal tribes are making threats to move on Uneeda. Don't let that happen, or we'll have another war to fight."

"I've been told there are thousands of Oztec warriors in the Agarwal tribes," Al said, apprehensive his commander was confusing his squad with a battalion. Markel waved that point off.

"The tribes are disorganized and feud among themselves, have been for years. I will be able to move on Uneeda in force before some chief can unite the tribes. The IIS told me a couple of Agarwal chiefs are talking about moving on the gold mines, but Bergdorf is capable of blocking that move. Remember, stopping the Ichneumon murder of humans is your goal."

The general's aide-de-camp, Colonel Caprivi, entered the office and handed Markel a telegram and left. After reading the message, the general shook his head and, in a disgusted voice, said, "The IIS is sending Count Laumeister to the Uneeda front on an inspection tour. They want a report on the Oztec tribes' attitude toward slavery and Zircon governing of Uneeda after the Ichneumons leave. Do you remember the Count?"

"Yes sir." Al had seen the aristocrat only once, from a distance, and never met the man but heard stories from other officers. Laumeister was a second or third cousin of the Zircon Emperor. The Count was one of the poorer peers of the realm. He had a reputation for requesting favors from the person he was investigating in return for not looking too hard.

"He's a treacherous bastard," the general snapped, then after a moment, in a normal voice, said, "You know what I want, focus on that. Let the Count do his thing. One final caution, the remote danger exists that the enemy forces at Fenwick and Delta might mount a joint push on Westport and break the Uneeda River blockade. Just be aware, you could be attacked from down river."

On his return to the Mischief, Al found two MP's and a frantic Dr. Karren Sebastian, the two Prenter children, and Bill discussing an abduction. Two men had grabbed Sisi on the way to the orphanage. Fortunately, the thugs had ignored the kids with her. Nancy, showing good sense, had grabbed her brother and run. She later found the two MP's and told them.

"Captain, we looked, but that area is a maze of dives and apartments controlled by criminals," the MP corporal said to justify their lack of success. "I fear your friend is gone, but at least the children are safe."

The corporal then suggested they go to the Westport police and Al agreed that was the path they would take. After the two MP's

The Devil's Spawn

walked off and Karren had taken the children aboard the Mischief for a hot chocolate, Al, disgusted, said. "The town's police are worthless." Then seeing two young prostitutes near the entrance to the wharf the Mischief was berthed at caused him to ask Bill. "Oscar in town?"

"Good chance, he likes to follow the soldiers. You are his best customer."

"I need to head upriver and don't have the time to patrol the streets looking at prostitutes," Al said, not caring for Bill's remarks about soldiers. Besides, he was still making up his mind about Sisi's character and could not help wondering just how much resistance she had put up. Then again, there was no proof her former pimp, Oscar, was in town or was involved. Not sure why, he still felt a certain obligation for her safety and asked, "What hole does your pal operate out of when in town?"

"If he is in town, he will be at the Grand Hotel. I am going to check, your help would be much appreciated," Bill said with a hopeful look.

Bill was critical to Al's mission, so having little choice, he asked Sergeant Jones to come along and the three of them went to the misnamed Grand Hotel. It was late afternoon so Al figured many of the pimps and prostitutes should be there organizing for the night.

The Grand Hotel being more a large saloon and bordello than a hotel, he assumed most guests rented rooms by the hour, not the day. Since Bill knew the saloon owner, he went in while Jones watched the front entrance and Al went around back. There he found a loading dock and saw several cat-sized brown rats vanish in holes under the dock and in the three metal bins used to store the garbage. Judging by the smell, the trash collectors did not empty the bins often. The propped open door on the dock allowed easy entrance for him and the flies.

The room opened into the saloon's scullery. To Al's left through another closed door with a window was a kitchen where two heavy middle-aged women of Zircon ancestry worked. One was stirring several pots on a large cast iron stove, the other one was busy chopping greens. The room's aroma reminded Al of the mine's mess hall's bison stew, a pleasant smell in sharp contrast to the alley.

The larger lady with the knife spotted him as he stepped into the room and said, "Captain, please, close that door. This is not the customer entrance. You need to go in the front door."

"I am here for a health inspection," the imp in Al made him answer.

The lady stared at him for a moment, then laughed, and, after a second look at him and shake of her head of curly gray hair said, "That's nonsense; in this lawless town? You need to leave."

Her partner, the pot stirrer, chuckled and said, "Honey, our boss, Herr Lindy, doesn't have a sense of humor. If you are trying to avoid paying to visit your sweetheart, save the girl a lot of heart-aches and go in the front."

"Actually, ladies, I am looking for Oscar. Know which room he might be in?"

The request sobered the cooks, and after they traded glances, the knife lady said, "We can be fired for talking."

"Or dead," her partner said in a worried voice. The women traded looks again, nodding their heads over some silent agreement between themselves. The knife lady explained as the other woman suddenly started stirring one of the pots that appeared to be boiling over, "Oscar is a mean one. Are you going to arrest him?"

114

"That depends on him, but he will not know where I obtained the information."

"He and his sluts are in rooms 112 and 114." She pointed at another door off the scullery and added, "Those stairs will take you to the rear of the second floor. His door is just down the hall." After another worried pause, she said, "To save our necks, I have to shout a warning to the front desk that a stranger ran up the stairs." Then apparently seeing his concern, she grinned and added, "I'll give you a minute, then I'll yell."

He nodded and ran for the door and up the stairwell. The tracked-in dried mud and leaves on the stair's treads testified to the lack of cleaning. The hallway had a grimy carpet runner with an area of the carpet worn to the burlap backing. Light came from a window at the end of the hallway. The darkness made reading the room numbers difficult, but he found room 112 and tried to open the door, but it was locked.

Al knocked and said loudly, "Telegram."

The door to the next room down the hallway opened, and the pimp with the goatee he had encountered in that River Point alley leaned out. Later Al learned that was the entrance to room 114. Oscar reacted fast, but not fast enough. The door was no match for Al's kick and parts of the wooden door and Oscar tumbled into the room to sprawl on the floor in front of a ratty couch that two young naked girls sat on. The pimp attempted to retrieve the revolver he had dropped, but Al stepped on the gun. Then he heard the cook's yelled warning followed by shouts from men below. That motivated Al to move fast.

He yanked the pimp to his feet and threw him against the door that connected the two rooms. "Where is Sisi?" He noticed one of the girls starting to get up and snapped, "Don't move."

"I haven't seen the bitch," Oscar cried spitting blood.

Al opened the interior door that connected the two rooms and saw a gagged and struggling naked Sisi tied spreadeagled on the bed, her clothes scattered about the room on the filthy floor. Then he heard men in the hall and pulled Oscar into the room bolting the door.

"Free her," Al ordered, and shoved the pimp toward the bed while he checked the window. A quick glance showed the drop was too great to chance a jump to the alley. Then there was pounding on the hallway door and the shouting, "Police, open the door!"

Al ignored them and helped Oscar free Sisi, using her ties to secure her abductor. Men were pounding on both doors. He was wondering what could be delaying Bill and Jones. A gun shot in the hallway stopped the pounding followed a moment later by Jones yelling, "You okay, captain?"

That remained to be determined, Al thought as he opened the door. One of Westport's notoriously corrupt police officers lay sprawled on the hallway floor with another policeman, his partner, Al guessed, trying to rouse the down officer. Two of the hotel's thugs-bouncers were in the dark hallway with their hands up. Bill and Jones, with their revolvers drawn, had them covered.

"Is he shot?" Al asked Jones who shook his head and answered, "No, the fool's gun went off by accident when I hit him."

The young thug asked Al, "Did you find what you were after?"

He nodded. "I did and if you don't mind, we will leave and avoid any more unpleasantries."

116

The Devil's Spawn

The young thug, reluctant to wait, crowed by Al to enter the room and address Sisi, who was hastily covered her nudity by pulling on a large green sweatshirt, "Are you one of Oscar's whores?"

Oscar started arguing, "yes and she owes me money." Saying no, and crying, Sisi rushed into the hallway into Bill's arms.

While Bill assured his friend of her safety, the police officer who had been down got totteringly to his feet. Looking around, he recognized Sergeant Jones whom he demanded his partner cuff and arrest. Jones just laughed and told the angry officer to be quiet.

Al learned later the young thug was Herr Lindy, the manager-owner of the establishment. He was a young brute of a Clovis man missing his front teeth and his left ear. Whether the man lacked humor, as claimed by the cook, Al never learned, but he was a sensible fellow who knew both Bill and Oscar and which one to believe.

"Forget that arrest nonsense," Lindy told the police officer. "None of us wants trouble with an army that has a thousand soldiers in town. Captain, take the bitch and your men and leave."

Oscar, shaking a fist, shouted, "You'll pay for this."

Al just waved off the pimp's threat. As he walked away, he heard Lindy asking Oscar how he intended to pay for the damage to the rooms. On their walk back to the Mischief, Bill and Sisi held hands, Jones keep over his shoulder. His sergeant was having a tough time believing the Grand Hotel gang had dropped the matter. Besides watching for the patches of horse manure and double-checking alley openings they passed in the grimy waterfront neighborhood, Al thought about what needed done to head back upriver. He decided to say nothing to Bill about the general's warning he might abandon Westport.

117

The ladies in the kitchen seemed normal, but they worked in a brothel whose business resulted in the abuse and devastation of young women and their future. The brothel's procurer-owner was more concerned about damaged doors than the devastation Oscar and his business caused to the lives of the prostitutes. Then again that was life on the frontier, and Al's thoughts went to Bari Lu and the coming mission.

Chapter 9

The slight of Velasquez's riverboat running down the river shocked Lieutenant Halona and his stunned gawking had nearly cost him his life. The Zircon rangers aboard the Thumper had swept the roadblock camp with rifle fire as the boat rushed by. He lost one soldier. Whether his men hit anyone on the riverboat, he did not know; for sure the boat never paused.

He realized the roadblock no longer served any purpose, broke camp, and marched his platoon back upriver to search for Colonel Gupta and the men that had been with him. About two kilometers back toward Uneeda they found on the shore the half-eaten body of one of the soldiers from the Thumper, and nearby, chewed pieces of horse. Another dozen meters up the shore in one of those tall reed beds that grew along the edge of the river, they heard a scream. A small gator was struggling to drag a body into the river. A quick inspection revealed it was the colonel. His men shot the gator.

The unconscious mutilated colonel was more dead than alive. The gator had grabbed his left foot, which was now a mangled bloody mess of boot, flesh, and exposed bone. Doctors would need to amputate the colonel's ankle for him to have any hope of recovery. Halona organized a litter to carry Gupta back to the fort and sent a man ahead to alert the commander.

After leaving the Zircons and the riverboat Thumper, Bari Lu rode back to Uneeda with Ivan and his men where they parted company under a clear starry sky. Ivan, with his prisoner Hans

David C. Brown

Maxim, went around the town and west to Bergdorf Mine. Bari went north to her grandmother's ranch. She arrived an hour before sunrise, in time for the ranch's breakfast. By then she had made the decision to spread the news about the Ichneumons' murderous behavior at the Kerry mule farm.

She spent the morning reassuring her grandmother that what happened at the mule farm might have been rogue soldiers on a rape and plunder expedition, not the first act of an organized ethnic cleansing operation. However, if the Ichneumons were on one of their rampages to exterminate free humans, they could flee to the Eastern Oztec nation and ask for Chief Mantas's protection. Meantime their best hope was for the Zircon army to attack Uneeda and kill the monsters. The next day Bari sent a rider to alert Mantas while she left on a two-day journey to warn all the farms in the area along the river between Uneeda and Seth.

While Bari was warning the farmers, Al learned the Mischief owner had sent the boat's old armor plates left from the Donnelly troubles to Westport. Bill was delighted to acquire them. His crew quickly reinstalled the iron plates that would provide some protection from shore rifle fire. While that was occurring, Al had the Westport dock crew install several mismatched iron plates on the Thumper to protect the pilot house. The old pirate pilot, Abdel, and Otto thought that a wonderful improvement. Al had assigned them to captain the Thumper together.

The other addition to their small fleet was a stout oak coal barge loaded with firewood, which would help feed the boilers. The thick side wooden barge and its cargo would also serve as protection to the seven riflemen assigned to the barge when the time to fight came. Another amazing turn, headquarter had assigned Al's former first sergeant from the railroad campaign, Sergeant Gunther, to his

120

unit. The man had two experimental 40mm guns that the navy and army did not want. The guns had sliding block breeches and fired cartridges that looked like giant rifle ammo.

"Think of these guns as large rifles. I have an extra two hundred and forty shells, but only forty fully loaded 40mm cartridges. After firing a shot, save the brass casing. Gunther knows how to reload them." Lieutenant Bär, Al's go to ordnance-explosive expert, explained as he inspected the open wood crate that held twenty of the loaded cartridges.

There had been rumors of new cannon developments. Al could see this design would be a huge improvement over the little muzzle-loading brass cannons, especially if the shell exploded when it hit the target. He asked about that, and Gunther removed the lid from another wooden crate that contained rows of black shells about the size of a salami link and handed one to Al. It was heavy.

"There are two types of shells," the lieutenant explained. "The black ones contain trinitrotoluene and detonates on contact. The green shells are incendiary rounds. The blue shells are inert and intended for training. The black and green shells are expensive. Do not waste them on practice shots and be aware these are all the 40mm rounds in the Erie Valley. That's the reason the navy and army didn't want to bother with them now."

Al's men spent the next day mounting the two new guns, one on the barge and one to replace the Mischief's brass cannon, which they removed and mounted on the Thumper's rear top deck. Lieutenant Bär told them to keep the guns covered until they were out of Westport and well up the Uneeda River. While Bill and Gunther's crews were busy, Al visited the fort's armory and obtained several flair guns and the ammo for signaling.

Colonel Gupta would recover according to the Uneeda fort's medic despite his still festering shoulder wound and missing left foot.

Lieutenant Halona did not share the doctor's certainty that the difficult patient would avoid blood poisoning. Regardless, standing in the dim hallway by the entrance to the commander's office, he knew because of a series of unwanted events, he was now in effect Gupta's assistant and gofer. Having no choice, he entered the office.

"Colonel Gupta has asked I have him moved from the infirmary into your office," Halona told Colonel Kropp. The commander looked at him like he had asked for permission to shit in the corner.

The colonel's office had an unusual history that shed light on why the Ichneumon forces were in trouble in the Erie Valley war along with why Gupta wanted to recuperate there. Several years ago, stonemasons had removed the rock wall between two of the narrow old fashioned rifle firing slot openings cut through the thick stone wall of the tower. The enlarged opening was to create a port for one of the new rifled breech loading cannons.

The cannon never arrived, and Kropp had a two-meter-wide window made from nine square glass panes installed in the opening. Opening the bottom panes allowed in fresh air. The colonel like the air, and the unobstructed view of the lake and dock area the window provided. That the missing cannon and glass window weakened the tower and the fort's defenses did not concern the commander. Only the Zircon army could threaten the fort. None of the local bandits would dare fire at the window. Until the promised cannon arrived, Colonel Kropp planned to use the room for his office and to enjoy the view. Now that smelly pest, Colonel Gupta wanted his office to loiter in.

"Lieutenant, I'll manage your patient, our honored guest," Kropp sarcastically said and, after another shake of his head, added, "I need to speak to him about his prosthesis to replace the amputated ankle and why my office is not suitable as a hospital room. I want you

122

to find Captain Maqbool and answer his questions about the Zircon force you encountered."

Finally, Al's little fleet was ready to embark on its mission. Bill had sold his remaining hogs to Herr Lindy at a small profit after having to haul about half of them back to Westport since they never reached Uneeda. Al had the cages and the Mischief cleaned. Four cavalry horses replaced the hogs. Al and Sisi had delivered the two Prenter survivors to the orphanage with a promise to check on them on the next trip. With all the supplies, chickens, horses, and passengers aboard, he told the boats to head up the Uneeda River.

At Prenter, still empty of people, Al stopped and tested the new guns on the abandoned stockade. The inert blue rounds punched fist-sized holes completely through the heavy upright logs that formed the stockade walls. The consensus among them was the practice rounds could breech most riverboats hulls. The two black-explosive-rounds that Al allowed them to fire, on impact, blew substantial openings in the fort's log walls. The one green-incendiary-round fired made an impressive fiery display on hitting the fort's wall but did not penetrate through the wall. However, the shell did set the log afire and started small fires in the weeds and leaves at the base of the wall. The gun crew saved the fired 40mm brass casings. Later, as the riverboats traveled up the Uneeda River, they cleaned and reloaded the casings with smokeless gunpowder and the black shells

About fifty kilometers past Prenter, on the second night, a curious incident occurred. One of those giant otters climbed aboard the Thumper in the area where on the original trip they had discovered the Westport sloop beached. The boat was moving at the reduced night speed of four kph. The animal attacked the watch. The soldier suffered a serious bite in the shoulder and a mean clawing of his right arm and face, but thankfully his eyes were not damaged.

The animal's aggressive behavior did not surprise Al, thinking back to his experience on that hammock after the gun fire incident. What did surprise him was the guard's claim the otter wanted his rifle. The crew figured that in the turmoil of the attack the rifle fell in the river. Al was not so sure, remembering that old Krupp single shot rifle they had found on that other hammock, but offered no comment. He transferred the soldier to the Mischief, where Dr. Sebastian who had agreed to accompanied them on the return Uneeda mission, treated the man's injuries. She had no rabies vaccine. They could only hope the animal was not infected.

Al felt safe from an Ichneumon ambush when in the swamp. The gators and maybe now the silver otters were dangerous, but they did not worry him. The enemy response did. They now knew a Zircon raiding party had been in Uneeda and had killed many of their men before fleeing down the river in the stolen Thumper. The Ichneumons were competent soldiers. They had to expect a return visit. If it were him, he would set an ambush along the river at some point since there were no roads connecting Uneeda and Westport. Well, of course, one could march around the swamps, but that would require a couple of weeks or more and passing through the unmapped territory of several waring Oztec tribes.

The first spot for an ambush was the old stockade at Seth where the swamp ended. After there, any number of locations would work, though he figured north shore was best because that was the side the trail-road between Seth and Uneeda was located on. No sane person would want to row a boat or swim in that river when hungry lake monsters were hunting for gators and livestock to eat.

The river had cut a narrow short canyon through the low escarpment that formed the west border of the swamp and the start of the grasslands. The fast current and submerged rocks required the pilot to exercise care when traversing the gorge. The Mischief had to give the Thumper a pull to reach the calm upper pool above the entrance to the canyon where the two boats stopped.

The crew used the stop to replace the Zircon and Wapiti flags with the Ichneumons' golden serpent flags. They switched the barge from the powerful Mischief to the Thumper to push ahead. If an ambush cost him a boat, Al would prefer the older boat be the sacrifice. Bill never commented, but Al figured the skipper agreed with his thinking.

The snipers assigned to the barge rearranged the remaining firewood to provide protection in the event of an ambush. Bill loaded the little brass cannon on the Thumper with a double grape shot charge and installed one of the new snap igniters in place of the troublesome match-lite primer. Both 40mm rifles traveled with black rounds chambered, ready at a moment's notice for action.

Williams and Gunner, volunteering to do the first recon for ambushes, off loaded their horses. Al figured they would need a couple of hours to ride to Seth and determine if the Ichneumons had returned, or if an ambush waited there. To pass the time, Al inspected the exposed rock strata in the canyon.

The dark outcropping was primarily gray granite like rock with bands of black rock. He wondered if the black rock could be hematite, a rich iron ore, or even better, one of the manganese ores. Knight Industries might be interested in the deposit if it were manganese, since they were developing a large red hematite deposit in the upper reaches of the Erie River. There was even talk of Knight building hot-air blast furnaces and a rolling mill, though Al figured iron masters back in Zircon's capital, Merlin, would not welcome new competition from the territories.

Using his boot to scratch away the vegetation at the base of the rock layer, he uncovered a fist-sized piece of the dense heavy black rock. He decided to have it sent to New Hamburg for analyzsis. Never know, he thought, he might have stumbled on a valuable mineral deposit. Hard rock mining appealed to Al more than an army career. On hearing Williams return, he pocketed the heavy nugget and hurried back to the boat.

"No one was in Seth," Corporal Williams said on dismounting. "We looked for that rancher, Herr Odrick, but no sign of him or his men. There was one thing, our flag was replaced with a new serpent flag."

"A patrol must have paid a visit and alarmed the rancher."

"Or they arrested him."

"Well, let's hope not," Al said and, after a look toward the Mischief, added, "Load up men, we're heading upriver to Seth."

Halona wanted Captain Maqbool, a tall handsome man with family connections to the emperor and the most talented officer he knew, to think well of him. The special force captain had already heard about Colonel Gupta's disastrous encounter with the Zircons. The captain, shirtless, was helping his men bolt iron doors on the Comet's pilot house when Halona arrived. The four doors were scrap left from when the colonel had replaced several cell doors in the dungeon with new doors. The doors were the only suitable iron plates the fort's maintenance crew could locate. The iron would help protect the sternwheeler's pilot house. Another crew was constructing two small redoubts with sandbags on the forward deck to help protect them from enemy rifle fire.

"You need to be cautious and not overload the Comet," Halona said observing the closeness of the lake's surface level to the hull's load lines. The captain's startled look made him smile, but carefully. He did not want to offend the aristocrat by laughing. It was not often he had a chance to correct his connected friend who quickly checked with the Comet's captain.

The Devil's Spawn

"Tell me about the Zircons," Maqbool asked after stopping the sandbag crew and telling them to help with the cannon. "How many and who is their commander?"

Halona realized he knew little about the enemy, nor their number, though he estimated twenty, nor the rank of their commander, nor what explosive they had used to wreck the Saukko. Or even how Colonel Gupta had managed to lose the Thumper.

"Do you know anything useful about the raiders?" his irritated friend asked.

"Well, I did send a platoon to secure Seth and block the river."

Ivan showed up at the Lu ranch several days after Bari had left the Thumper. He asked her to return to the mine with him. Bergdorf had questions for her concerning the night of the fire. She had only been back a day from alerting other families about the Ichneumons' attack on the mule farm and was behind on her reports and accounts on purchases. She doubted the meeting was about late reports, but instead Hans and the gold, subjects that made her uneasy.

Her boss was a former Zircon mercenary with an unpredictable temperament. He was older and not as large as Ivan or Captain Belcher, but like them, Bergdorf was a solid built muscular man who Bari figured was capable of great violence against those he believed had wronged him, like Hans Maxim. She had known the accountant planned to steal the gold and had said nothing to Ivan. Having no real choice in the matter, she went along with Ivan to meet Bergdorf.

When they arrived, one of gold mine's security men escorted her to the holding cell at the warehouse, where she met Bergdorf and a bloody bruised Hans, who was lying on the cell's concrete floor in urine, blood, and obvious pain. Bari figured Ivan or her boss had beaten a confession out of him. The lack of concern or pity she felt for Hans alarmed her. The misery and cruelty she seemed to encounter daily was making her callous, even corroding her affability.

"Thanks for coming," Bergdorf said to her while gently prodding the man with his boot toe. "Hans, say hello." The prisoner moaned. "Well, I guess he's not feeling sociable. He did admit he was planning to steal my gold. To your good fortune, he said you refused to help him steal the sixteen ingots."

He paused to inspect her and then in a threatening voice shouted, "176 kilograms of my gold, a fortune. That is bad enough, but now the commander wants an explanation of why the gold wasn't delivered to the fort."

Bari, relieved, but still concerned by her boss's wrathful look and hostile tone decided there was no question asked and said nothing, same as Hans who remained curled up on the floor.

"Why were you there and with Zircons?" Bergdorf suddenly asked in a sharp voice and with a hard intent look.

"The Zircons asked me to show them where Hans lived," she answered in a slightly wobbly voice that embarrassed her. She did not want to appear frightened by the questions and managed to collect herself. Then in a clear steady voice she added, "Captain Belcher was concerned about the guards, so I went in first to tell Hans about the captain wanting to visit." She considered telling her boss about Hans's request for rescue but figured the poor man did not need more trouble.

"No, that is not my question, why were you with the Zircons? Did they pay you?"

Hans's moans and her boss's intimidating tone were not helping her nervousness, but she managed to answer calmly. "No. I was with them because they saved me from the Ichneumons, who attacked the Kerry mule farm. I went with them for safety." Bari paused, her explanation appearing to satisfy her boss, and added, "After I turned down his request, Hans attacked me and then alerted the fort command that Zircons were in the neighborhood, which resulted in a gun battle. The Zircons grabbed him and me and you know the rest."

"Not all of it, did they have any interest in me?"

"Yes, Captain Belcher had questions about the mine and you as that related to Hans," she said realizing too late she should not have mentioned Hans as Bergdorf interrupted her.

"Why would a Zircon recon unit give a damn about some local thieving accountant?" After a glance at her, in a suspicious voice he asked, "Were they in cahoots with you two and after the gold?" Hans moaned loudly as Bari comprehended, she had better worry about herself, instead of a man who had tried to kill her.

"The captain told me Hans had asked to be rescued. He asked I show him where Hans lived. That is why we went to your house."

Bergdorf went quiet for a long pause, rubbing his bristly chin and studying her, then asked, "Was the IIS mentioned?" Bari nodded. "Well shit, you're an IIS agent," he said to Hans followed by a hard kick to the prisoner's body that made her cringe. He then turned and asked her, "There are four ingots, forty-four kilograms of gold missing. Who stole them?"

"Not me."

Captain Reed arrived in Westport two days after Al Belcher and his crew had departed on their return trip to Uneeda. Reed had no knowledge of or reason to ask about Al's crew, though later he would wish he had known about the Zircons.

Reed was captain of the riverboat Rouser, Penton's old sternwheeler. Past its prime, it was still a dependable machine. Reed's only order had been to take the riverboat and crew to Westport and then await orders. He was familiar with Harlem Penton's clandestine way of operating. Since Penton would continue to pay, he was content to wait. The Rouser crew retired to the Grand Hotel to do their waiting.

The recon squad and Al reached Seth around noon, only a few minutes after a mounted unit of a dozen Ichneumon cavalry soldiers had arrived. Afterwards, Al figured the false flag act delayed the enemy's response enough to allow the riflemen in the barge to deliver the first volley. Only three of the mounted enemy escaped up the river trail. One of the men in the barge suffered a serious wound and would be out of action. Once again, they had beaten the enemy, but it cost them the chance to surprise the Uneeda garrison.

"We now have six horses," a pleased Williams said as he finished inspecting the fine, but still agitated animals. "We could recon in force up the river road, maybe catch the Ichneumon soldiers before they can sound the alarm."

They were standing by the wharf's entrance looking upriver. Al sympathized with the corporal. He too would prefer hunting the enemy from a horse to waiting on a boat for the enemy to attack.

"Best not, you could blunder into an ambush charging after them. Do not forget the soldiers who were at the earlier roadblock. What if they remain camped out above the Kerry farm and those riders warned them? What I want is for you, Gunner, and a third person, your choice, to carefully recon for ambushes along the river. If you encounter any activity, one of you ride to the river and warn us. I will bring the boats slowly up the river and one of you will ride to the river every few kilometers, so I know you are okay. I will be on the Thumper. The Mischief will trail us."

With surprise lost, Al's original plan of picking a hot sunny afternoon when Ichneumons liked to nap and blowing a hole through the wall to storm the garrison no longer appealed to him. Bergdorf's response was unknown, would he stay out of the fight? What would the lake pirates do? Hell, what would the garrison commander do, now that he knew a Zircon force was in the valley? Hide inside the fort or come looking for them. He then thought of Bari. She would know the latest news and rumors in Uneeda.

"Abdel, do you know Bari Lu?"

"The pretty bison buyer?" Al nodded, she was well known, no surprise.

"Do you know where her farm is located?" The ex-slave assured him he did. Then once the men had the stronghold and the Zircon defenses established to his satisfaction, he would call on Bari. For her knowledge of the local environs and people.

The sun was low on the horizon when they reached the abandoned Kerry farm. On arrival, Al had half his men land on the north shore to help Williams who had arrived before them construct a temporary log redoubt and corral for several of the horses. They unloaded the rest of their horses on the south shore and placed them in Kerry's remaining intact corral, including the five Ichneumon horses they had captured at Seth.

131

The striped Saukko hulk, partly submerged, made a decent anchoring spot. The Thumper and its barge tied off on the riverside and the smaller Mischief tied off between the hulk and the riverbank where the farm dock had been. The crew positioned both 40mm rifles to cover up the river and the north shore. Lieutenant Bär, whom the general had ordered to accompany Belcher's recon unit, had divided the trained 40mm gunners into two twelve-hour shifts. Each gun would always have a two-man crew manning it for the next two days until Al had a better understanding of the Ichneumon army's reaction to the Seth confrontation.

Chapter 10

The return of the surviving members of the platoon sent to Seth by Lieutenant Halona galvanized the garrison. Colonel Kropp fearing the immediate arrival of General Markel's Zircon army, wanted the gold loaded aboard the Comet. Then, if the Zircon army arrived, the Comet crew would have time to steam out to the deep part of the lake and dump the gold. That move, Colonel Kropp argued, would ensure the enemy did not acquire the treasure. Colonel Gupta, still bed ridden, ranted about missed opportunities to ship the gold down the river on the Comet to General Paget's men.

The worried, even defeatist mood Captain Maqbool and Lieutenant Xavier encountered among Halona's men and the police, even the colonels, surprised the young ambitious officers. The change in the garrison's mood from when they left to inspect the small garrison at Silver Ridge and a possible alternate route for the gold through the high mountain passes was alarming.

At that point the Uneeda command was eagerly awaiting an expected Zircon recon up the river. Admiral Chetan, captain of the Saukko and Lieutenant Halona and his marines had orders to bloody the Zircons so bad, they would hesitate to bother Uneeda again before General Paget returned to hurtle the Zircon force out of Westport. Instead, the Zircons had destroyed the Saukko and killed the admiral.

While the colonels quarreled in the fort commander's office, Captain Maqbool assembled Halona's surviving men in the cafeteria to question and feed them. He decided there was no invading army, only something like the earlier Zircon recon force had returned, to finish whatever their original mission had been. He went to inform the commander.

"The Zircon recon force has returned to Seth with two riverboats, one of them the repaired Thumper." He noticed his news caused Colonel Gupta to sit up and pay attention. "The other riverboat they're using is Prince Cherukuru's private riverboat, the one Wapiti appropriated several years ago. I want permission to use the Comet and Lieutenant Xavier's cavalry to ambush the Zircons down the river."

Colonel Gupta asked, "Why jeopardize the Comet? Could not concentrated rifle fire from shore accomplish the same results?"

"Yes, if field cannons were available to rip up the iron plates and expose the enemy crew. The men reported the boats have armor and the Zircons have a small cavalry unit with them. I fear if we don't hit them with a powerful blow, they will get entrenched and block access to the river valley and our possible reinforcements."

"How does using the Comet change that outcome?" Gupta asked, hobbling over to sit in the empty chair by Kropp's desk.

"I have mounted on the Comet the extra wall cannon the fort had. It fires a thirty-kilogram shell. One shell could destroy a riverboat."

"If you hit it," a skeptical Colonel Gupta said, and looked at Kropp for his comment.

"The colonel has a point. If your first shot misses, reloading a cannon is a slow process. Do the Zircon boats have cannons?"

"Just a small brass cannon," he said, waiting to learn if they would grant him permission.

Colonel Kropp focused on a farfetched outcome as the reason to approve the mission. "If your men recovered the prince's riverboat, the Uneeda Garrison would be rewarded. You would be a hero. Do it."

What passed as sound strategic reasoning in the fort commander's mind appalled Maqbool. Still, the colonel's approval to attack the Zircons pleased him and he rushed off to organize the attack.

Friedrich Bergdorf had conducted many interrogations over the years and believed he could sort the lies from the truth. Hans had willingly answered all his questions and Bergdorf believed him. He also now understood why the recovered ingots were where they found them. There had been four identical bags by the office door. Hans had been certain Bari would help him. She condemned Hans when she turned his scheme down, especially with the Zircons waiting on the driveway. Whether she might have joined Hans if the Zircons had not been on the property no one would ever know. To salvage something, Hans had alerted the fort with the hope of making a whistleblower deal with Lieutenant Halona by ratting out the Zircons and the mine's diversion of half the gold production.

It was a foolish move. Thankfully, the Zircons had grabbed Hans before the Ichneumons arrived. He did not need Colonel Kropp wondering if he was conspiring with the Zircons. Knowing Ichneumon thinking, Bergdorf feared Kropp might decide why chance it and have him arrested and hanged. Hell, the monsters are already openly murdering harmless farmers, for no reason other than they are human. He was safe with Ivan's squad to protect him and figured Kropp was not interested in another shootout with the mine men while an unknown number of Zircon soldiers were prowling about the valley.

There was still the missing gold. Someone had carried off one of the bags prior to the fire. Suspects were Captain Belcher and his raiders, Lieutenant Halona or his men, the firemen, and one of the neighbors, or in other words everyone who was in Uneeda that evening. Bari Lu never had an opportunity. The guards would have seen her in the time before the Zircons arrived, and then after Hans knocked her out, she could not have carried off the bag. Hans said the Zircons were traveling light, no heavy bags or backpacks in which to conceal ingots.

If Halona was the thief, did he hide the ingots or tell Colonel Kropp? If the lieutenant told his colonel and the mine did not report the theft, that would expose their skimming of gold from the reported mine-production. After blaming the reduced gold deliveries on a restless work force, he would have no credibility with the Ichneumons. Worse, the Ichneumons might already be on the way to arrest him. Best to keep Hans alive and if the issue arose, blame him.

By the time he finished Hans's interrogation, one important fact he had learned was that he did not know his people as well as he had thought. Hans was an IIS agent, Bari was in league with Belcher, and Jacobs' equipment salesman knew of the planned theft and instead of telling him, had run. He told Ivan to have Hans patched up and locked in a cell.

Back at his office, Bergdorf poured a double shot of Simpson whiskey and sat down to organize his thoughts. The most pressing unknown was whether and when the Zircons would get serious and take Uneeda from the Ichneumons. One reason for the delay, besides, General Markel having all his forces committed to capturing Delta, was that for at least a century the Zircon Empire had considered the Erie River the western boundary of their territorial interest. That was one of his reasons for fleeing to Uneeda after the failed coup. Now Bergdorf believed it was only a matter of time until railroads and iron bridges breeched that barrier. Already, the Wapiti and Clovis people were clamoring for a high railroad bridge across the Erie River at River Point. After that occurred, the rails and empire would expand to the far western ocean.

In the process, the empire would replace the power of local warlords, like himself and the tribal chiefs like Chief Laredo with laws, regulations, and territory governments. Fortunately for him, that change would require years. In the meantime, he needed to talk with Captain Belcher and learn if there was a Zircon arrest warrant out on him. He told Ivan to ask around about the missing gold and find the missing salesman, Kit Jacobs.

The next day Al had the men build another redoubt beside the gravel-surfaced road-trail that ran along the river valley between Uneeda and Seth. Information on the Comet came from Abdel, who had seen the Ichneumon steamer when it docked near the Thumper. He said it was a sister to their Thumper. Al figured after their disastrous loss of the Thumper, the Ichneumon attack would come from land, from the north side. They would save their only steamer for hunting down stragglers afterward. Their superior night vision almost guaranteed a night attack, and soon.

Al was at the road redoubt with Williams and six men when that very evening thirty-some cavalry soldiers burst out of the dark and charged the redoubt by the road. The gun fire was intense as the cavalry soldiers wildly emptied their multiple shot revolvers at the redoubt. One of the bullets hit Al's right hip, knocking him down. He recovered his footing and managed to shoot the rider trying to force his horse to climb over the redoubt wall. The rider had been determined to slash at the defenders with his sword after having emptied his revolvers.

Within a minute or so, Al could see his men's carefully aimed rifle shots that rarely missed had cut the attacking cavalry to shreds. The result convinced him the general had the right understanding. Direct assaults on a fortified position defended by men armed with repeating rifles were foolish. Maneuvering to force the enemy to withdraw to avoid encirclement and attacking him during the move was best. Feverishly inserting a fresh magazine, Al heard a large cannon fire out on the river followed by several rapid 40mm shots. He had guessed wrong.

The Ichneumon cavalry, still mounted, found themselves between two redoubts and suffered appalling casualties of men and horses both. Only a handful of the several dozen cavalry riders retreated up the road toward Uneeda, whether to regroup or flee, Al did not know. His leg was bloody but working. Using a handheld torch, Williams checked the enemy dead scattered around in front of the redoubt while Al checked on his men. Two of the men with him in the redoubt were dead, another wounded but still alert and holding his rifle. Al then limped over to meet Private Gunner in the field between the redoubts. He was checking the enemy dead and wounded.

"Send Williams three of your men and no shooting the enemy wounded. Put a guard on them while I check with Lieutenant Bär," Al told Gunner as they stood by a silent and fearful wounded Ichneumon soldier pinned down by a dead horse. They dragged the enemy soldier clear of the horse.

"And what am I to do with him?" the ex-sergeant asked, nodding toward the young Ichneumon now curled up beside the dead horse.

"You heard me, soldier," Al answered, as Lieutenant Bär arrived. The lieutenant had been assigned to the Thumper and the wooden barge. After they were a dozen meters away from the wounded soldier, Bär spoke.

"The Thumper got hit by a large cannon ball that scrambled its boiler and engine," the lieutenant said, "but those 40mm guns are a wonder. The real surprise was how effective the incendiary rounds were. That's what saved the Thumper's crew. The fires started by our shells stopped the reloading of Comet's killer cannon."

After Al verified none of the 40mm gun crews had serious injuries, he asked Bär about the Comet.

"I think the faint glow you can just detect up the valley is the Comet burning, but whether it's out of action I don't know. It was hit many times before it reversed back out of slight toward Uneeda."

The Zircon force was still intact. The Thumper still afloat, but crippled. Six soldiers were dead with several wounded including himself. The doctor, Karren, treated his leg wound and afterward, he had ordered a hesitant Bill to attach the barge to the Mischief. He wanted to try and catch the Comet before it escaped. While Lieutenant Bär rearranged the 40mm rifles, Al had Williams organized a mounted patrol to scout the road into Uneeda. He told his sergeant his main interest was to learn where the enemy cavalry had retreated to and use his judgment on whether to engage or not.

Three hours later, the Mischief entered Uneeda Lake and Al could see the Comet had reached the protection of the fort's cannons. Al had the gun crew lob several incendiary shells into the fort to alarm the garrison. Unfortunately, the action also alerted the garrison to their presence and resulted in return cannon fire. One of the fort's iron balls had slammed into the wake behind the Mischief, startling Al. The fort's cannon crews were better and more of a threat than he had expected.

Bill wasted no time in seeking the protection of the river and headed to the mule farm where Williams informed him the cavalry survivors had entered the fort. That the Zircon small force had made the larger enemy force race back to the fort gave Al and his men some satisfaction. Al also thought their success in repulsing the Ichneumon attack would make the crabs leery of venturing down the river valley to murder more farm families. Another development that boded well for his mission was the arrival of three men from the nearby ranches that offered their help. He learned Bari had been warning the farm families about the Ichneumon attack on Kerry Mule farm and telling them to be alert.

The day after the skirmish the owner of Bergdorf Mining sent a rider with a letter requesting the Zircon commander visit him to discuss how they might work together for a peaceful resolution of various matters.

The Zircon captain was one of the few men Bergdorf had met who was bigger than he was. Judging by the facial scar, Al Belcher had had a narrow escape from an enemy cavalry saber sometime in the past. The blood-stained leg bandage indicated he had not emerged unscathed from that bloody engagement east of Uneeda with the Ichneumon garrison. The young captain was a monster of a man, built like Ivan. His guards were two equally large tough Zircon NCOs armed with rifles and revolvers. That his man, Ivan, waited by the office door with Belcher's men helped Bergdorf relax a bit. His temporary office, since the loss of his home, was now the rear of a large wooden barn that functioned as a warehouse for mining supplies.

"I heard things got hot the other night down the valley. My messenger said your men nearly shot him. Is your limp from that?"

The Devil's Spawn

"Just another scuffle with the crabs. Your message said you wanted to talk," the Zircon captain said in a strong businesslike voice while looking around the office and adding, "Not quite as cozy as the one in your home."

"Yeah, well some assholes burned it," the miner answered crossly. "We're both busy, so I'll get to the reason I wanted this meeting," Bergdorf said in a brisk voice with an undertone of irritability. "Did you or your men steal four of my ingots the night of the fire?"

So, Al had guessed right on what that ungodly heavy leather case contained. How to answer? He had not precisely stolen the gold, nevertheless he knew where one of those bags might be if none of the other visitors, police, firemen, and neighbors had not found it. The only reasons he had not taken it were the bag's heavy weight and his need to flee on foot up the mountain to avoid the Ichneumon police.

"Nope, my men did not carry off any gold that evening. Besides, why do you call it stealing? I thought the gold belonged to the Ichneumons and could be considered spoils, war booty." That remark brought the miner to his feet. Before Bergdorf could respond, an alarmed Bari burst through the office's rear door.

"Hans has started bleeding again and needs medical attention, a doctor," She said in an excited voice.

Bari had a frazzled look, though she was still the beautiful woman he had dreams about. Was Bergdorf pestering her over that missing gold?

"Don't worry about that thief," the mine owner snapped. "If he dies, it'll save me the need to hang him."

141

Bari did not like that and shouted. "He served you well for years. He made a mistake, and he deserves better." She then turned to Al, for his support, but he remembered Pete who was dead because of that bastard and spoke before she did.

"He deserves nothing. He would sell you, all of us, out to the Ichneumons." Bergdorf nodded in agreement, but on seeing her stricken look, Al relented a bit. "If he can reach the stronghold, I'll have Karren look at him. I'm not risking our doctor for that treacherous double agent."

"Take the son of a bitch. Ivan, help her get him ready to travel with the captain." Bergdorf ordered while shaking his head.

Bari studied the mine owner and him for a moment, decided they were serious and exited the office by the rear door without comment. Ivan went with her. Al reckoned they went to organize Hans for traveling to the Zircon camp. After they had left, Bergdorf sat back down, muttering, "Big mistake, big mistake not shooting him." Then with another head shake and his normal strong voice, he returned to the gold question.

"That gold belongs to the mine until the Ichneumons pay for it, so no nonsense about booty. You want General Markel to know you're more interested in my gold than your mission?"

"You are the one who requested the meeting and brought up gold. Well, we didn't carry your gold off. However, if my men find gold lying around, don't expect them to walk by it. Now, what's the deal with your accountant?" Bergdorf told Al about Hans's confession.

"Kind of an ass backward way to organize a heist," Al said after learning how ad-hoc Hans' robbery had been. He also thought, if Hans was an example of an IIS agent, no wonder their intelligence was often mediocre and even flat wrong. He said, "You're supposed to arrange your accomplices first and have a plan."

Bergdorf shook his head in disgust and said, "You would think, but then I thought the Lu woman had more sense than to feel sorry for that man who is a serious threat to her and my wellbeing, if the Ichneumons grab him." Seeing Al's questioning look the man explained. "The army requires the mines to sell all their gold to them in exchange for rupees. Colonel Kropp would not take well to learning I was planning to divert half the gold to independent buyers for D-marks, not more rupees."

Well, that was an interesting confession, but why tell me, Al thought. Thanks to his little side deals, Al knew a good bit about the various currencies and their exchange rates. The rupee was the name of the Ichneumon currency and used thorough the western territories. Before the war, ten rupees equaled one D-mark. Business and people the length of the Erie Valley used both currencies. A person could in theory convert both paper currencies to gold. A Zircon paper D-mark was convertible to one fiftieth of a gram of gold or flipped around one gram of gold was worth fifty D-marks, one kilogram worth fifty thousand. The rupee had a similar comparative value. No one ever bothered with redeeming the paper for gold since that required a trip to Merlin's royal treasury or the Ichneumon remote capital deep in the south continent.

"My problem," Bergdorf explained. "Due to the war and its inflation the D-mark is worth only about a hundredth of a gram gold. The rupee even less. Currently twenty rupees are equal to a D-mark everywhere, but Uneeda. The colonel still insists on using the old valuation to pay the mine."

"That's why you started skimming the goal?" Al asked, his curiosity overcoming his worry about Bergdorf motivation for telling him these details.

"Yes. I was receiving only half the real value of gold at the fort, compared to what other buyers outside of Uneeda were paying. And they pay in D-marks, not devalued rupees. It's a recipe for going bankrupt with inflation doubling operating cost."

"And Hans was going to tell Colonel Kropp about the skimming," Al said. Bergdorf nodded. "Why would he do that?" The miner shrugged with his hands and appeared truly perplexed.

"I need to go. Where is Hans?" Al wanted to leave before the miner remembered that the question of who had taken the missing ingots remained open.

"Wait a minute, I have a question for you," Bergdorf said as Al thought, damn, too slow, but still got to his feet to leave. "Is there an arrest warrant out for me?"

The question cheered Al. The miner with more serious concerns to worry about would quit pestering him about the missing gold.

"I've heard the rumors you participated in some coup attempt, but no, no one has mentioned any arrest warrant for you. The IIS's only interest was in your accountant, Hans." Al paused at the door to learn if his answer satisfied Bergdorf while suddenly realizing he might be able to use the man's concern to obtain some useful information.

"I heard an old sewer once ran under the fort. Do you have information on it? Help me and I'll write the general and give you a glowing commendation." The mine owner studied him for a bit, trying to decide if what he said was true.

"Kropp knows about you," the miner said. "He now has patrols watching the streets, day and night. You can't just ride up to some building behind the fort and kick in the door like you did to my house." Al made a motion with his hands to explain. "You'll need a diversion, have one of your men fire several shots down by the wharfs. That will draw any foot patrol out there away from the neighborhood you're interested in."

Gunner, Williams, and Bari were waiting with the captain's horse outside the mine's office. She arrived with Hans on a horse whose reins she handed to Al as he walked up. "I need to return to the ranch," she said, "promise you won't just shot him as soon as you're out of sight."

Hans, though savagely beaten earlier by Ivan, had recovered enough of his belligerence to sneer, "That's right, boy, listen to the lady."

Al ignored the jerk and said, "Gunner give her the rifle." The trooper handed her a new Mauser bolt-action magazine-fed rifle chambered for the 7.62x65mm smokeless powder cartridge with a scope. He added, addressing Bari, "General Markel asked I give you the rifle as a token of his appreciation for your help in sinking the Saukko. I had Gunner put one hundred rounds of the new rifle ammo in your left saddle bag."

"Oh god you didn't tell the general what I did." Bari asked, shaking her head, looked flustered. Damn, she should have known the soldiers would talk. Hopefully, her grandmother would never hear about it.

"Of course not, I wouldn't do that." The suddenly embarrassed brute claimed. She nearly laughed at Al's pathetic denial. The captain realized he needed a new topic. "You and your grandmother need to be on guard. Word will find its way back to the fort commander about you warning the farmers. By the way, that was a good move, Bari, thanks for doing it. But the Ichneumons might think you'd be a fine hostage for dealing with the Zircons and who knows what's in Bergdorf's mind."

Bari nodded. They shared the same worries.

The last two days had been stressful, even terrorizing as she witnessed the treatment of Hans. Thank God she had nothing to do with the missing gold. Until just now she had not been sure Bergdorf would let her leave. The timely arrival of Captain Belcher helped to remind that psychopath she had a powerful friend who would ask questions if she disappeared. And now the man was giving her a gift of an expensive scope rifle, why? Judging by Gunner's amused look, he wondered the same thing, figured she had traded sexual favors. If Captain Belcher wanted her, he did not need gifts, he had had her interest from their first encounter.

Al and his men were anxious to leave for down river and their stronghold as Bari rode off. Before they could go, Ivan, the mine's security chief, yelled from the office to wait. He jogged over and handed Al a rolled up dusty blueprint.

"Herr Bergdorf told me to give you this."

Not sure what the roll was, he asked Williams to hold one edge of the large print and carefully unrolled the brittle blueish paper enough to determine what the print showed. It was drawing of the foundation plan for a building across the alley from the north wall of the Uneeda fort.

"Tell your boss, Ivan, that I appreciate this. Men, time to ride."

By then, it had been a long day for Al and his men, and they were anxious to finish the trip. Sunset was less than an hour away. As he rode, his thoughts returned to Bari's reaction. It had never entered his mind she would be sensitive to the general's learning about her willingness to expose herself to help them accomplish the heroic result of destroying an enemy warship. He obviously had much to learn about women.

The mine office was five kilometers north of Uneeda and the Zircon stronghold was ten kilometers east of the town. As a result, the last kilometer of the road Al's party used to reach the river road from the mine camp went through east Uneeda, a mostly abandoned suburb area near the fort. He was not overly concerned about those patrols Bergdorf had cautioned him about. The darkness would help hide their passage.

Luck was not with them that evening, however. A three-man mounted Ichneumon patrol waited at the livestock water trough off the intersection where the river road left the Uneeda streets to head east. The dismounted soldiers were talking with two of the residents. Prostitutes Al judged by their state of undress. One of the watch soldiers, more curious, than alarmed, asked who they were.

"Miners, we're taking an injured worker to the doctor," Al said not stopping.

"Dangerous work, that mining," the soldier said. "Move along the curfew starts in twenty minutes." He turned back to the woman just as Hans yelled.

"They're Zircons, stop them."

Al shot the soldier who had halted them. His men shot the other two soldiers before they could react as Hans kept screaming, "They're Zircons, kill them."

147

Al, who was leading the traitor's horse, started to shoot Hans but, remembered his promise to Bari and instead pulled on the reins to bring him close enough to reach over and club him with his revolver barrel. The hard blow stopped his yelling, though now the prostitutes had started screaming, "Help, Zircons are here!"

"Gunner, stop that, don't shoot them, just ride," Al ordered and they galloped away toward the redoubt.

A century before the Ichneumons forced the Agarwal and other Oztec tribes from their ancestral homeland in the land bridge between the north and south continents, the Lu family had been part of a much earlier exodus north. The Lus were among the first Oztec families to settle in the uninhabited north Uneeda range where they established a ranch. Over the following decades Bari's ancestors acquired four of those 500-hectares fee simple deeds issued by Jesuits to homesteaders who volunteered to live on and farm the uninhabited western land. Bari was the fifth generation of the Lu family that had lived on that 2000-hectares spread.

The Zircon Empire had recently decided to recognize those deeds that backed the Lu family's claim of ownership. Despite knowing that and having no legal claim to the land, Chief Laredo wanted that ranch with its springs. A complication was the Zircon captain. Jose, the Lu ranch's range boss, had told his sons that the Zircon captain with the recon squad knew Frau Lu's granddaughter, Bari. The current small Zircon force was no great concern to the chief. Even if the captain did not approve his seizure of the Lus' place, he could not stop him. Besides, Colonel Kropp would help him with any interference from the Zircons, especially if the Laredo warriors were to help the colonel defeat Captain Belcher's recon squad. They had given the Ichneumons heartburn. Frau Lu's anti

The Devil's Spawn

slave stance had alienated the colonel and the chief figured he would be happy to see her gone.

However, time was not on his side regarding whether to make the move and seize the ranch. Once the Zircon army arrived, captured the fort, and controlled Uneeda, they would protect the Lu family. His opportunity would be gone. The time to strike was now. Claim the land belonged to the tribe. The Zircon Empire would not care about the change in ownership of a remote ranch, especially if the Lu family were not around to complain. He sent for his sons and subchiefs. Greg arrived first.

"I'm going to seize the Lu property," the chief said, watching his son's reaction. If he were in favor of the action, most of the subchiefs would be. "And I don't want those women escaping to Westport and pleading for Zircon help."

"It's about time father, that bitch is getting too chummy with those Zircons and if those bastards take Uneeda, she'd be untouchable," Greg said, looking satisfied with the idea. Chief Laredo knew his oldest son was the smart one, though his thuggish appearance caused most strangers to assume Greg was a thoughtless brute.

His son added, "However, we shouldn't underestimate that captain either."

"I'm pleased to learn you're thinking that way, son. Best not to underestimate your enemy. Just so I am clear, some of our subchiefs are soft on the Lu women. I want you to eliminate the Lu women. I know the young one is a looker, but I do not want one of our subchiefs making her his plaything. I want them dead, disappeared, vanished without a trace. Can I count on that?"

149

Chapter11

Bari had a lot to consider during the ride out to the Lu ranch after leaving the mine and Zircons. Was there actual missing gold? Hans had claimed to have sixteen ingots. Bergdorf claimed to have recovered only twelve ingots. Both men were liars. She was certain the Zircons and Hans did not have any ingots with them the night of the fire. If gold was missing, in her mind, the thief was Lieutenant Halona, or one of the police, or firemen who had the run of the burning house after they escaped. But that was not her problem. Her other worry was the Laredo gang doing something rash. If only General Markel would take Uneeda, then the chief would be afraid to bother them.

Taking her prized new rifle after turning her horse over to the stable hand, she hurried into the house, finding Grammy and Jose, the range boss, in the office on the main floor. That she was there and unhurt had Grammy happy and hugging her. No one asked her about the rifle.

"We may have a problem," Jose said. "Chief Laredo is raising a group of warriors. They are meeting tonight. He's planning a raid and my usual chatty sources on tribal news claim not to know the raid's target." That silenced the room.

"Reckon that means it's us?" Bari asked after a moment, releasing her grandmother. Jose nodded and Grammy looked alarmed. "I think now would be an appropriate time for the three of us to check out the high range, maybe do some fishing, disappear until we know what is going down."

Grammy, bless her frontier spirit, nodded in agreement. When her husband was alive, they would often spend a week in the high ranges camping out. Then with a worried voice, Grammy asked, "Could we go to the Zircons for protection? They owe you."

"Our problem is the greedy bastard, Laredo. I doubt the captain with his small Zircon force would appreciate us dragging him into an open conflict with the tribes. He has enough trouble with the Ichneumon army." Bari needed coffee and she moved to the kitchen with Grammy following her saying,

"I heard the stable hands talking the day after Ivan came for you. They said the chief told the Agarwal subchiefs they needed to act before the main Zircon army arrived. I did not think it concerned us, but after what Jose said, I am worried. What do you suppose that meant?"

"Nothing good for us," Bari said, knowing she needed to decide to stay or flee. "We don't want to be hostages and I don't want to be beholden to the Zircons." She cared what the captain thought of her and did not want him thinking she was one of those women who could not look after themselves. So, she said. "Jose, help us pack our camping goods. Tell everyone who ask we are going to Seth to buy a milk goat."

"A goat, we have several now?" Grammy said.

"Well, our plan is to hide, and Jose has to tell our people something." She then told him, "Then tell them we are going to Seth to buy two horses. Regardless, we are going to slip into Clear Fork's high ridges for a few days while we wait to see if Laredo is a problem. It's important none of our men know where we went."

Grammy and she left an hour before sunrise the next day with two pack mules for their camp on Goat Ridge in Clear Creek valley. The camp was a stone hut Grammy's father built for fall hunts and winter skiing. The three-room structure was on a sheltered ledge just below the crest of the front range separating Uneeda from the western prairies and the high southwest range and glaciers. A remote cold place, the trip required two long days to reach the hut.

The Devil's Spawn

On his return to their camp at the Kerry mule farm, Al learned General Markel had kept his promise to send supplies as he could. Anchored beside the Saukko sunken hulk was one of the new style propeller driven riverboats that the River Point boatyard built for the commercial river traders. He learned the riverboat had just arrived after making a quick trip up the river from Westport. The boat was dropping off twenty more soldiers, First Sergeant Duncan, and Lieutenant James Duffield, a cavalry officer, along with a large quantity of rifle ammo, five-hundred kilograms of dynamite, several cases of various 40mm shells, the men's pay and ten thousand D-marks. And he assumed, the cash for expenses and bribes. A new experience for Al, having money. Either General Markel had faith in his honesty, or the quartermaster screwed up. He decided to ask Dr. Sebastian to hold the cash and run a simple ledger for him on where the funds went.

There was no Count Laumeister aboard to Al's relief. Sergeant Duncan he knew from their brief campaign in Myrtle Territory two years ago to rescue Herr Leslie, inventor of the telegraph, from kidnappers. The sergeant could be depended on when the bullets started flying. The other new officer, Lieutenant Duffield, was a recent graduate from the Zircon Military Academy. With two squads, each with a capable leader, Al now had a force capable of confronting the Uneeda garrison. Even better the riverboat captain agreed to take Hans Maxim back to Westport and deliver him to the general.

If the old blueprint was accurate, which Al had not yet verified with a recon of the building, at one time there had existed a stone culvert where the fort now stood. The culvert was part of an older storm sewer system to gather storm runoff from the residential neighborhood on the north ridge behind the fort. For sure no sane

153

engineer would build a fort over a drain way that the enemy could use to mine the fort's walls. But stormwater off the ridge was going somewhere, and engineers have been known to make mistakes.

Al spent the next several days strengthening the Zircon defenses in the Uneeda valley. The first order of business was to stop the Ichneumon soldiers from venturing down the river valley and preying on the remaining Zircon farm families. Al organized under Lieutenant Duffield and Sergeant Duncan twelve mounted soldiers and under Sergeant Jones ten snipers. The snipers would go with the Mischief and the Thumper's firewood barge up the river while Duncan's cavalry went up the road to make a coordinated sweep of the north side of the river valley and drive off the Ichneumons. Over an eight-day period, three hot firefights erupted as Ichneumon patrols tried to travel down the river road or slip by in small boats. Al's forces lost three men and the enemy eight, but now the Ichneumon soldiers and pirates would consider the river valley a dangerous place.

The Zircon soldiers also constructed two entrenchments with log parapets to replace the redoubts. One on the south side of Lake Uneeda outlet to block lake traffic from the use of the river and one on the North River Road to block enemy cavalry raids down the valley toward Seth and the ranches. He had Bill install the two cannons salvaged from the Saukko wreck, one to each strong point. When word the Zircons were establishing those simple fortifications had spread through the valley, local men started asking if they could join up. Al sent word asking the Seth rancher, Herr Odrick, to join him and help him form an irregular militia from the volunteers.

From the start of that skirmishing in the river valley Chief Laredo's scouts kept him informed about the Zircon captain's activities and the pathetic Ichneumon army's response. In the opinion of the chief's oldest son, now the time to seize the ranch while the fighting had the Zircon captain and fort command distracted. The chief finally agreed, and that evening the Agarwal warriors struck. They discovered the women were gone but their foreman, Jose had stayed behind to keep an eye on the Lu ranch. Unfortunately, the man successfully escaped along with Frau Lu's wolf, which had warned him in time to avoid being surprised in the ranch kitchen. The foreman had grabbed one of their saddled horses and galloped away toward the mine. The old wolf had slipped off before Greg could shoot it.

The chief was angry over his son's failure to capture the foreman and made his displeasure known, bellowing, "That bastard knew where those bitches went. Now how are we going to find them?"

"The same damn way I always find what I am after, organize a hunt." Greg snarled in return. "I will split up the men. One group will search the river valley and road going to Seth and another group to search Clear Creek to the source spring at the toe of the glacier above the tree line."

After two days, neither group found a sign of the women, but the chief decided they had found their way to the Zircons' camps on the river. Chief Laredo then settled into the ranch house, but a day later he had second thoughts. Zircons appeared to be winning and his scouts reported the women were not in the camps. He needed the Lu women dead and asked Greg to thoroughly search the Clear Creek high ridges. Another team of five under Zack would search the mine, check with the garrison commander, and patrol the wharf and Uneeda areas for the Lu women. The team that captured them, or bought their heads, would receive a five-thousand D-mark reward. Dead women could not contest his ownership.

While Al's crew was busy securing the upper river valley, trouble was arriving in Westport. Harlem Penton and Count Laumeister had used the plantation owner's newer riverboat, Cotton Belle, to travel from the rail terminus at River Point to Westport where Captain Reed and his crew of pirates waited.

"You tend to forget how large the Zircon army is," Count Laumeister commented appearing pleased with the camps and equipment parks they passed on the approach to the dock area. "I believe the general will be successful this time in capturing Fenwick."

"Ah, you think our fine navy might this time allow those battleships to actually fire their cannons at Delta?" Penton asked sarcastically.

The plantation owner hated the Count's uncle, Emperor Schnabel, over his decree that prohibited slavery. He tolerated his passenger's pro Zircon opinions, but the intense activity and number of soldiers in Westport made Penton wary in voicing his anti-emperor opinions. He knew General Markel despised him and the army would arrest him if he gave them any excuse. At least the general and the Zircon army appeared close to being ready to embark from Westport and head down river. With the general gone, Westport would be back under the control of Colonel Haddad's control who was the Guderian Chief of Commerce Stan Blankenship's brother-in-law. Stan was Harlem's partner in this Uneeda project.

The IIS had helpfully advised the Count their rescued Uneeda agent was recovering from various injuries in the Westport hospital. The agent was under arrest for aiding the enemy and attempting to rob his employee, Bergdorf Mining. The IIS had suggested the Count might wish to speak with their local IIS station chief who had conducted the Hans Maxim interrogation for the latest news from the gold fields.

The IIS chief meet their riverboat at the north dock where Penton's man, Captain Reed, had Rouser docked. The Count went with the IIS chief to meet General Markel and for his private IIS briefing. Penton and the captain went by coach to visit the arrested agent.

The station chief had arranged a pass earlier that allowed Penton to enter the ward where Hans Maxim lay with his left arm in a sling. The man looked rough. Most of his skin that was not bandaged had dark bruises and scabs. His front teeth were missing. His left eye crusted shut, evidence of a severe beating.

"I gather Bergdorf didn't take kindly to you trying to carry off his gold." Penton said while making a quick check of the water closet as the captain closed the room door.

"F**k you Penton. I was setup by that bastard Belcher and his Oztec bitch. Hell, you're the real criminal here," Hans answered in a weak but defiant voice while trying to sit up in bed.

"You're right." He looked toward the door where Reed gave him a thumbs up, which meant the hallway was clear. "Answer my questions and I'll help you escape with a stake to start over. So, let's start with your estimate on the amount of gold held in the Uneeda fort."

Over the next hour Penton questioned the IIS agent and because of the man's answers decided an Ichneumon gold hoard of a ton or more in ingots sat in the fort. He also learned the miner, Bergdorf, had a private safe that contained a large amount of gold dust and nuggets in small canvas bags. After Reed suffocated Hans with a pillow, they retired to the Cotton Belle to finalize their plans.

"This is a bit of a long shot, but the potential payout is enormous," Penton said as he tasted the rum drink the attractive young Clovis female had served him before continuing. "Since the Ichneumons never installed the telegraph line to Uneeda, I will buy four of the Westport homing messenger ravens for you to take along to Uneeda so we can communicate."

"That will work. I have a cage and a man who is used to working with the birds," the captain said as he finished rolling a skinny joint using some of the good Wapiti red marijuana and a strip of old newsprint.

"Your job is to use Rouser to take the Count upriver to the Zircon army base. Be useful and friendly to Captain Belcher, he's no fool" the plantation owner cautioned Reed. "Same applies to our friend Count Laumeister while you await developments. What I want to know is the moment the fort falls. Sent two birds so one is sure to arrive in Westport."

Reed, after a toke, returned to digging a broken cork out of a new bottle of corn whiskey while listening to his boss. "None of that should be a problem if our army wins the fort. So, what's the plan for getting the gold?"

"I'll get to that. When the fort falls, produce some reason the Rouser needs to return to Westport." Seeing his collaborator's confusion, Penton added. "Offer to take the wounded to the army hospital in Westport. I'll have an experienced crew ready for you to take back to Uneeda and at that time explain my plan. Remember, send the birds when our men have the fort and get Rouser back to Westport without the Count," Penton held his glass out for a refill with the corn whiskey.

The Devil's Spawn

"What if he wants to come?" Reed asked, emitting a cloud of smoke, and standing to walk over to pour some whiskey in his boss's glass.

"The man's whole purpose in going to the war-zone was the gold. He will not want to let that gold out of his sight. He'll stay, hoping he can convince the emperor that he's entitled to a share of the finder's fee. Remember the Count is not involved in our matter, let him do his own thing."

"What about Bergdorf, might he be interested in using us to ship his gold?" Reed asked, standing beside his boss waiting to learn if he wanted the glass topped off.

"That's a good point. Check with him. If he used the Rouser to transport his private gold, the Count would have fewer qualms about recommending the army use us to move at least part of the fort's gold."

Reed was pleased his boss like his idea and explained, "I'll offer Bergdorf a price he can't pass up. I'll tell him the truth, if he ships his gold with us, I can use his favorable decision to convince the Count and army to use my riverboat to ship the fort's gold. Then I can cover most of my cost in their freight charge while cutting him a good deal."

"I like your plan, run it by Bergdorf and let me know his decision." Penton laughed and added, "What sweet haul that could be, the miner and army's gold together. And we know hijacking the Rouser would be a hell of a lot easier than a navy warship."

While the Rouser gang was scheming in Westport, Al was at the south entrenchment, where he could see the Uneeda fort, about

159

four kilometers across the lake. How Colonel Kropp would respond was the question they pondered by the fire pit at the south stronghold. Duncan and Jones figured the colonel would sit tight in the fort and force them to attack. Al did not share their certainty, but the hesitation of the Ichneumon steamboat Comet to leave the protection of the fort lent support to the idea. But to attack the fort, he needed to establish if mining, placing a large explosive charge under the fort's wall, was feasible.

That evening he left Duffield with most of the mounted soldiers and took Duncan with two cavalry troopers as guards to pay an unannounced evening visit to Bergdorf at the mine office. The man had been drinking but he was in and received Al while Duncan and Ivan remained in the hallway and traded greetings. Later Al learned those two knew each other.

"I'd heard you had blocked the river. Is the main army with you to take Uneeda?" the mine owner asked. Al could not tell if that possibility cheered the miner or depressed him, as he added. "Or are you just harassing Colonel Kropp with a squad of men?"

"I intend to do more than harass that bastard and wanted to ask you about the blueprint," Al answered, "and the latest news from the fort." Al looked about for a place to unroll the blueprint. The desk had a small beam scale on it along with two teacup-size clean glass dishes that contained tiny amounts of gold dust.

"Not much happening at the fort, but Chief Laredo seized the Lu ranch about a week ago. No one has heard from Bari and her grandmother. I asked Baron Gilmore if he knew the fate of the Lu women. He didn't."

The news shocked Al. Bari was a woman he could imagine partnering with and had intended to court the wildcat after dealing with the Uneeda Ichneumons. If Chief Laredo and his thugs had hurt her and the grandmother, the savage would pay dearly.

"I don't understand why. There is plenty of land. What is so special about the Lu land that Laredo would start a fight with an established family?" Al thought of the native copper deposit he had heard about on the Lu's family's land and added, "Is the copper deposit the attraction?"

"There was a time when people thought there was gold with the copper. Bari's father asked me to have the metal analyzed right before the police in Westport murdered him." That was news to Al, and he asked the miner to explain.

"Like his daughter he was good at haggling with the Wapiti and Clovis traders that traveled the Erie. I used him to oversee those purchases. He was killed in Westport about three years ago while there to buy tasty winter sole nuts for the mine's laborers."

Well, that was close to what Bari had told him, but he asked. "Was there any gold?"

Bergdorf shook his head, "In the copper? Not a trace of gold, though there was a trace of silver. Just little bit of metal in a lot of hard black rock, not enough copper to pay mining the Lu property. I doubt the chief is even aware of the copper. The metal was too pure and soft to be of use to the Oztecs for arrowheads and knives. He probably just wanted the house and water."

"How is that even legal?"

Bergdorf after a sarcastic laugh, said, "What law is he violating? The only law in Agarwal tribal land is the chief's and he only recognizes Jesuit deeds and private property when convenient. I would not be surprised to learn the chief considers women owning property an abomination. I hope Laredo did not kill them, but instead made them slaves. I might be able to buy them in that case."

"Buy them?" Al exclaimed. What a miserable country, he thought, but asked, "Any thoughts on what Colonel Kropp thinks about the chief's move?"

"I doubt he cares one way or the other. Killing you and getting the stored gold to Delta are his concerns."

"If the chief didn't kill the Lu women, where would he keep them?"

"Laredo knows about you and the Zircon threat. If he thought the Zircon army was about to land in Uneeda, if he has not already, he would kill them to break any claim on the ranch. One bit of luck is that the chief wasn't impressed with you as a threat, so he might keep Bari alive for entertainment, but the grandmother, not likely."

"Think the chief has moved into the Lus' house?" Al asked, thinking the chief was not the only one unimpressed by his opponent.

"I figure he has, along with hundreds of warriors. You need to focus on taking the fort, not rescuing maidens in trouble."

Ture enough Al thought, but that Oztec maiden had his interest and if he could help her, he would. As he walked to Bergdorf's desk, Al said, "Move the gold out of the way," finally getting to the reason for his visit and unrolling the print. He pointed at a dashed line. "Could that old culvert still be under the fort?"

"The story I have heard is Laredo's grandfather built that fort using Ichneumon plans and a Zircon army engineer to supervise," Bergdorf said, getting up from his chair to remove the dishes with the gold to the top of the file cabinet and then walking around the desk to better see the faint print on the drawing. "So would a Zircon fortification expert leave the old culvert?"

"I wouldn't think so, but there's still the stormwater that needs a way to reach the lake. I would have built a moat and diverted the water into it to bypass the fort. Get some value out of the water."

"There's no moat, it still rains, and the water goes somewhere," Bergdorf said. "You'll have to go look."

Chapter 12

The incendiary rounds fired by the Zircon sailors the night the Comet attacked the Thumper shattered Maqbool's experienced crew manning the large cannon. The crew's first shot had been perfect, right into the Thumper's engine room. They never had a chance for a second shot, which would have finished the enemy's boat. Instead, the Zircon defenders unleashed a storm of exploding shells that along with enemy shore rifle fire battered the Comet and threatened to destroy the riverboat. The enemy had a new weapon, a rapid firing small cannon that shot a mix of incendiary and explosive 40mm rounds

The explosion of the two black powder charges that the crew had ready for reloading the cannon caused considerable damage. Several small pellets of white phosphorus and debris from the explosion wounded Captain Maqbool. The cannon crew was not so lucky. They died. Despite the considerable damage sustained by the Comet, the tough boat managed a desperate escape backward up the river far enough to put a river bend between them and the Zircon guns.

Maqbool organized the surviving crew to extinguish the fires and save the warship. He later docked the Comet by the fort for protection. Maqbool had little faith in that protection. He knew the fort's cannon crews had not practice fired the weapons for years, until recently. The gunners needed practice. The other lesson was that

164

against rapid firing cannons, the poorly armored Comet did not have a chance. His conclusion was a land battle would decide the winner in the river valley war.

The captain went to see Colonel Kropp to report on the action and try to convince him the Ichneumons needed allies like the Laredo warriors to provide replacements for the soldiers lost over the last month. The murdering of humans needed to stop; all Colonel Gupta and Lieutenant Halona were accomplishing was creating enemies.

The morning after the Ichneumon captain told his commander he needed to stop killing humans, Bari was worrying that Greg Laredo and his warriors had returned to Clear Creek for a more thorough search. She knew the chief's oldest son was a competent hunter. She also knew hiding all the tracks of several pack mules and horses across the hillsides and bogs was impossible. The recent dry weather did not help. It preserved the few tracks Bari missed by not raining and washing away the disturbed ground.

Seven days after setting up camp, Bari was out hunting marmots for Grammy's camp stew. She used her grandfather's crossbow to shoot the fat rodents as they popped up among the rocks to avoid gun shots that could alert any warriors still hunting them. They had a scare last week when several of Laredo's men had searched the Clear Creek valley, but after two days they left. Jose's failure to arrive worried her and she hoped he had escaped. Yesterday she had seen a Laredo warrior on the ridge across the valley. Today the wild goats that hung out on the ledge below had again disappeared.

Probably nothing, but she unshouldered her rifle to use the powerful attached 6x40 scope to study the hillside near their camp. Just more rocks with a few small bushes, nothing threatening. The entrance to the ledge was about a half kilometer distance. She watched the mountain slope below the entrance another fifteen minutes, nothing, but her sense of danger remained strong. She needed a different vantage point for a better view of the camp and left the two marmots she had shot on a rock to retrieve later.

Grammy and her grandfather had brought Bari to the camp all through her childhood and, as a result, she knew all the best views and hiding spots around the camp. The boulder field on the ridge across from the camp ledge was a good spot to watch the front of the hut. Hanging the crossbow sling across her back and holding the rifle, she climbed up the slope to the boulders. By crawling into the space between two large boulders she could look past another large rock and see the hut's entrance, but for anyone at the hut looking toward the ridge, the shadow behind the rocks would hide her. She saw a man with blue zigzag bolts painted on his face standing by the hut porch, about two hundred meters away, and looking down the slope. Bari had not seen him before. Unwelcome news, Laredo's men had found their camp. Had they caught Grammy?

The loud cry of an eagle made her look down where she had left the marmots. Two eagles were fighting over the rodent bodies. The noise of bird scuffle brought another warrior out of the hut with a rifle. After a moment, both men slipped around the ledge. Bari realized they were planning on shooting and wanted a better shot at the birds now on the ground. Having realized there were two prime rodents, each large bird had claimed a marmot to rip apart and eat. She knew the Agarwal warriors prized eagle feathers and wondered if she could use that to her advantage. The two warriors standing by the camp were easy targets now. What to do? Was there a third warrior in the hut with Grammy? Was her grandmother hurt?

The warrior's rifle was an old rolling block Krupp single shot with iron sights. She waited and alternated watching the rifleman and the hut entrance. The man fired. Only one eagle flew away, the other, wounded, flopped down the slope. The two warriors yelled something and ran to catch the wounded eagle. Their yell brought a third man, a large brute she recognized, out of the hut. He had Grammy in front of him. Greg Laredo, the meanest of the gang. He shoved Grammy to her knees and yelled,

"You stupid asses, now that bitch knows we're here." Based on the evil bastard's next order, Greg was also an eagle feather fan. "Only one of you go get the bird."

With her grandmother caught by the Laredo, sneaking off was no longer an option, she realized. She watched the two warriors stop and argue. After a moment, the younger one turned toward the camp with the rifle while the other warrior ran after the bird, which was rapidly getting away toward the lush bog where the goats normally foraged.

"I don't know why you worry, they're just an old woman and a young girl," Bari heard the warrior with the rifle say when a favorable pause in the wind allowed his voice to carry.

Bari had the crosshairs on the center of Greg's upper body. She still hesitated to fire because she knew the Agarwal were fanatics about avenging slights, real or imagined. Killing one of Chief Laredo's sons was as real as it got. If the chief learned she had killed his favorite son, she and her family would have to watch their backs forever. Grammy must have said something, for the brute whipped out a wicked looking knife and pulled her grandmother's head back by her hair, exposing her throat. Greg shouted some threat, but the wind was unfavorable and whatever he said was inaudible. After glaring about, Greg put his hunting knife against her throat.

Bari had always thought Greg the smart one in the Laredo family, despite his history of abusing women. Did he think she would

167

not have a rifle with her, or would be too fearful to shoot him? The misogyny rampant in the Agarwal tribe explained the foolish behavior, she figured. Regardless, there was no other option for her. Those Agarwal warriors were out to kill Grammy and her so their chief could claim the Lu property. Neighbors had warned her. The blood appearing on Grammy neck pulled Bari's trigger. The brute dropped his knife and released the woman as he staggered back into the hut. The shot report stopped the other warrior with the rifle who was looking wildly about to locate the shooter.

No stopping now. If one of them escapes, she is dead. When she shot him, he flopped about, dropping the rifle, before crawling behind a rock. The eagle man had stopped, but on hearing her second shot, he bolted down the hill. Bari was good but hitting a running target at six hundred meters was beyond her marksmanship. Still, she chanced a shot. The man went down. Whether her shot hit him, or he had misjudged a step and stumbled she could not tell. Whatever the reason, he had enough sense to stay down, and she had no clear follow up shot. A quick check on the other warrior showed no change in his position. Grammy, thankfully, was on her feet, blood dribbling down her neck as she stumbled toward the boulder field. The wounded eagle had disappeared.

Still not sure as to the number of warriors about, Bari decided to hell with caution and raced across the boulder field to meet her grandmother. Whatever Greg had managed to slice on Grammy's neck bled a lot, but the wound was not fatal, and a large cotton wrap around her neck stopped the bleeding. Bari knew she needed to go to the hut and make sure Greg was dead.

Grammy sensing her hesitation spoke. "Don't chance an ambush by entering the hut. He may be still alive and waiting for you. Your shot wounded him bad. Let the wolves and bears deal with them. We can reach the horses without going near the hut and make our escape."

Not good advice, Bari knew, but she would also be endangering her grandmother. Grammy needed a doctor. She was weak and without Bari's help, the elderly woman would never survive the trip out of Clear Fork walking. Just the hike across the ridge crest to the horses started her wound seeping again.

While Grammy rested, Bari saddled their horses. The Laredo horses were there. She knew a wounded Greg and his thugs, assuming they were still alive, would have a tough time reaching help without horses. Bari stripped the Laredo horses of their tack, saddle, and halter before chasing them off the ridge.

The Lu women then considered their next move. They were lucky this time, but Laredo had more warriors, and someone would come to investigate Greg's disappearance. Joining forces with the Zircons now seemed their only good move, so they headed down the mountain to Uneeda and east.

While Bari and her grandmother cautiously made their way off the high range Sergeant Duncan and two of his men went with Al to search for the sewer shown on the old blueprint. Jose who had showed up two days ago with news of Chief Laredo's treachery, had tagged along and joined them to wait with the Zircon horses a block down the street from the abandoned school. The Lu foreman had verified Bergdorf's news that Laredo had about a dozen Agarwal warriors hunting for him and the Lu women. That news had Al seriously concerned. Bari knew the country as well as Laredo's men and would know to come to their stronghold if she felt endangered. He was in no position to go hunting for her, but after he settled matters with the Uneeda garrison, he planned to offer his help.

Bergdorf's response to the chief's lawlessness toward Bari confirmed Al's suspicion that he should not count on the miner in a pinch. His more immediate concern was whether Bergdorf might tell the Ichneumons of the Zircons' interest in the abandoned school directly behind the fort and the old sewer. His hope was the culvert shown on the old blueprint Bergdorf provided still existed under the Uneeda fort's present location. To verify the culvert's existence, he needed to gain entrance into the school's basement. He figured the school plumbing had used the old culvert as a sewer and there should be a manhole.

Private Gunner, who would be a master sergeant, except for his inability to control his urge to always have the last word, had volunteered earlier to slip into the alley behind the fish market and raise a bit of hell by firing several shots. Al, waiting at the intersection where the river road joined the Uneeda streets, heard a couple of gun shots near the wharf. Whether that gun fire was from Gunner or just the usual waterfront fights, he did not know, but the shots served their purpose. The foot patrol they had spied in the neighborhood north of the fort where Al wanted to go jogged off toward the waterfront on hearing the shots.

After the night watch left, Duncan and Al entered the school by prying open a side door. The rough stone building had at some time in the past been partially demolished, but for reasons unknown, the job was never finished. Most of the roof beams and roofing slate tiles cluttered the ground floor, except the area toward the fort where the floor had collapsed into the cellar. Sentries on the north fort wall could look into the building where the roof was missing. Al hoped Gunner had also attracted the sentries' interest toward the waterfront. Only by keeping the rear school wall between them and the fort and staying low against the inside of the wall, could they avoid a watchman on the fort's wall spotting them. It required crawling across the roof debris to reach where the first floor had fallen into the basement. The hole allowed them access to the cellar.

Old trash and cobwebs littered the basement. The ground floor supports had failed in spots, dumping bits of the roofing tiles and pieces of the first-floor slab concrete into the basement. The whole structure looked poised to collapse without warning into the basement. Under a tipped-over wooden student desk Al spotted a cast iron manhole cover. With Duncan's help he cleared the desk and pried the rusty cover free. The foul sulfurous odor that greeted their nose told them it was a sanitary sewer manhole, a rank one.

They had come prepared. Duncan had a small lantern on a thin hemp rope to lower down the manhole. The feeble light showed the stone manhole was four meters deep, just wide enough that a small laborer could fit through. The manhole structure sat on top of the older cut rock arch tunnel that served as the sewer. Whoever had constructed the manhole had cut a hole through the sewer's roof to allow liquids flowing into the manhole to enter the sewer. The difficulty was the hole's size; the lantern could just fit through the jagged opening. The overall drop from the manhole top to the water was seven meters.

The lantern's light reflecting off the water surface ripples allowed Al to estimate the sewer had a flow of a couple of liters per second, which at this time of night meant creek water along with sewage. Even better the lamp kept burning, so there was oxygen and little methane.

"Is this what you hoped to find?" Duncan quietly asked as they replaced the lid and dragged the desk back to cover the spot.

"I now know there's a culvert," Al whispered, thinking what a difficult dangerous task this would be. First, they would have to remove and excavate the stone manhole to reach the culvert. Then

171

enlarge the hole so a man could drop into the sewer and accomplish all that while not alarming the nearby fort guards. And he still didn't know if the culvert went under the fort or around it.

"Whether I can use it depends on where it goes and if there's a better access into it," Al said, looking up through the hole in the old school's ground floor slab to check for a sentry on the fort wall.

"It's clear," he said. They hurried out of the cellar to the shelter of the wall and then around to where their horses waited.

As they approached Jose waiting with the horses, the ranch foreman held a finger to his lips and whispered, "There are several of Laredo's warriors down the street by the water trough."

At some time in the past there had been a police-guard post there by the road intersection. The Ichneumon army had ended the practice and the small two-story cut stone building had been abandoned after a fire destroyed the building's roof last year. However, as Al knew from the earlier trip, the spring-fed watering trough still worked. Its presence accounted for why the painted warriors had waited there with their horses. It was the same location where that asshole Maxim had nearly gotten them killed.

Al studied the men by the water trough. The darkness interfered with determining if the men had the blue zigzag lines painted on their faces which would identify them as Laredo's warriors. After a moment said, "Yeah, I think that's who they are. What are they waiting for, the night watch?"

Whatever their purpose, it was a complication. The warriors blocked the entrance to the river road they had planned to take out of Uneeda. He knew with the fort only two blocks away this would be a damn poor location to start a firefight. Then another warrior galloped up to the group by the water trough and spoke in an excited voice loud enough for Al and his men to hear.

"I checked with the whores. They saw two hooded riders with pack mules pass their place, headed out of town." In response to a question, the rider added, "About an hour ago." After some inaudible conversation, the Laredo group mounted up and noisily clopped away on their horses in apparent pursuit of the strangers.

Looking at Duncan and Jose, Al asked, "Any chance those two hooded riders are Bari and her grandmother?"

Jose, after a moment checking the wolf, said, "They had two mules, but Grammy's wolf is not reacting, though that might be because the wind is away from us, or they passed by too long ago." He shrugged, adding, "Only way to know is follow and see if the wolf picks up their scent."

His men waited for his decision and for Gunner who had not returned from creating the ruckus at the waterfront. After a pause Al said, "Let's follow those warriors, maybe learn who they're trailing." At Duncan's questioning look, he added, "Gunner said not to worry about him, he'd find his way back."

Because of the way the lake shore curved around a small bay, the land route to the Zircon's north stronghold was a trip of nine kilometers from Uneeda, though by boat across the lake the distance was four kilometers. East Street ended at Uneeda's city limits and became the North River Road that went to Seth about sixty kilometers east.

Al and his men followed the five warriors, maintaining a separation of a couple of hundred meters. Sunrise was a couple of hours away; still, the warriors had to know someone was behind them. They seemed unconcerned.

"They're not expecting Zircons, figure we're the night watch," Al told Duncan and Jose in a soft voice. He still did not know who the warriors followed for sure, but every step brought them closer to Jones's men in the stronghold. Then the wolf bolted ahead down the dark road. The animal's action cheered Al. The mystery riders must be the Lu women. Though how Laredo's warriors would react when a wolf dashed through their ranks was a concern. A minute later, several powerful shots spaced apart at about the time required by a proficient rifleman to work a bolt action rifle ripped the night. Over the next minute or so after those shots, many revolver shots, yells, and flashes happened.

"Duncan, you and your two men cover our rear while I go ahead." Still not sure what was occurring, Al eased his mount cautiously down the dark road toward the dead horses he could see. He heard more shouted curses and two additional shots but could not see who was fighting. Then a bullet hit his horse and the animal collapsed, pinning him for a moment with its body. As he struggled to free his leg, he realized there was a good chance Bari had shot his horse while trying to kill the rider. The incongruity of the woman he was trying to rescue killing him made him laugh.

Free of the horse, and on his knees in a muddy ditch, he looked about the area in which he had landed. The land around the river road in this area was used by farmers to grow crops like wheat, oats, and barley. The fields were flatland, offering little cover to hide behind. There was a larger drainage ditch the road crossed over and that seemed to be where the other party fending off the warriors had holed up. The darkness made it difficult to determine who was who and where.

A dead mule with baggage lay in the road with two horses. A dead warrior lay in the road near the mule and another warrior used the mule body for protection. Al could not locate the three other warriors from his location in the roadside ditch beside the still twitching horse. Three riderless Laredo horses milled about in the field toward the river. Nor could he see who hid in the irrigation ditch and culvert about a hundred meters east of his spot, though he now had an idea who it was.

"Is that you, Bari?" Al shouted, figuring no need for caution though his shout did alert the man hiding behind the dead mule. The warrior had not noticed his presence but, on recognizing the Zircon uniform, turned to shoot him. Al beat him to the shot.

"Watch your right, there's two in the field," he thought he heard a woman yell. The gun blast had his ears ringing as Jose landed in the ditch.

"We have trouble. Duncan told me the gunfire has drawn the night watch," Jose said, then asked, "Are the Lu women by the culvert?"

"It sounded like a woman. For sure whoever they are, they are not friends of the warriors. Grammy's wolf ran that way. We need to locate the missing warriors," Al said, worried the foreman might rush to join the women and make an easy target for those warriors in the bean field. He then asked, "Where's Duncan?"

"He said he'd slow down the watch and join you later," Jose answered, while nervously glancing about. After studying the roadside ditch, he added, "This is not a safe location you picked if the watch gets by Duncan."

Al figured explaining the bullet that killed his horse picked the location was pointless and

spoke. "Don't stand up, I figure those missing warriors are lying in the field waiting for a shot. They cannot see us, same as we cannot

175

see them. Our best bet is to crawl along the ditch to the culvert and hope they're the Lu women."

The crawl along the wet ditch bottom, dragging the saddle bag and his rifle, was not a pleasant trip. The feel of a creature squirming in the muck under his hand caused thoughts of giant leaches until he realized it was a small frog, one of those raucous peepers that lived in the muddy ditch.

Then he heard Jose, who was in front, say "It's me." And a moment later they were in the irrigation ditch beside the road culvert with the Lu women. Bari uttered a soft thank God as she recognized Jose. A quick glance told Al that her grandmother was in trouble. The elderly woman was quiet, trembling, and curled up on the ground under the road crossing with a bloody bandage around her neck.

"I don't know where you guys came from, but I'm thankful you're here," Bari said, while alternating between watching down the southern irrigation channel and the road toward Uneeda. "I fear Laredo's boys are going to reach this ditch and have a direct shot up the channel at us. Grammy's hurt and exhausted."

A bullet plowed across the soil ditch berm and slammed into the culvert stone headwall. The sprayed dirt caused Al to yank his head down from looking where Bari had pointed. The shot came from nearby in the southern field. Running along the south edge of the bean field and the river was a hedgerow. The drainage ditch they were sheltering in cut through the hedgerow to the river. When the enemy realized he could move around behind the hedgerow and go to where the ditch discharged, he would have a straight shot up the ditch to the culvert.

"We have to move," Al whispered. He vaguely remembered crossing this irrigation ditch they huddled in on his last trip to Uneeda from the north road stronghold and estimated they were about three or four kilometers from the stronghold. There were no high ridges between their location and the stronghold; it was mostly flat land though there were some large patches of timber among the farmlands. The moonless night was clear with a vast display of stars.

"I don't think my grandmother can walk," Bari said, and adding in a resigned voice, "I am not leaving her."

"Lieutenant Duffield and his squad are about three kilometers away. I figure they've heard the gunfire along with the fort," Al said, while opening his muddy saddle bag. "I have a flare gun in the bag. If I fire a red flare followed thirty seconds later by a yellow flare, and Jones sees them, he will know I need help. Unfortunately, so will the fort and the night watch, which are after us."

"Well, it's not like the bastards don't know where we are now," Bari said. "So, fire them, maybe your men can arrive in time."

"We're not waiting on them," Al said, opening the flare gun breech and checking that the barrel was clear. He then pawed in the bag for the proper color flare shells and handed her the gun with the proper color flares. "Cheer up, you're the one who's going to fire them."

While she examined the single shot gun, Al added, "It's simple. Loads like a single barrel shotgun. Remember, fire the red, then the yellow. I'm taking your grandmother and running down the ditch to that bend." He pointed to where the fields on both sides of the ditch ended, about hundred meters away at a thick hedgerow, and the ditch bent out of sight. "Jose, you stay here and cover her until she reaches the hedgerow, and then you run. I will cover you. One of you bring my bag."

The lightness of Bari's grandmother surprised and worried him. The woman did not weigh forty kilograms and was no burden as

177

he jogged down the muddy ditch toward the hedgerow. Halfway there a warrior sprang up from the bean field to shoot them. A shot from behind him knocked the warrior down before Al could bring his revolver up to fire. A few moments later he reached the hedgerow. A quick check discovered no enemy behind it. The red flare reached its zenith of several hundred meters as he finished making Grammy comfortable among the hedgerow bushes.

Chapter 13

While Al was deciding to follow the Laredo warriors on the East Road, Zack Laredo had stopped at the fort to ask Colonel Kropp if his brother Greg had been around. The guard directed him to the storeroom across from the commander's office where the colonel had moved his office. "No one has heard from Greg and I'm growing concerned. Have you heard from him?"

"No, your brother has not been by. I wouldn't worry," the colonel said thinking if any human could take care of himself, Greg Laredo could. He thought about asking how Laredo's rash move to seize the Lu property had played out. So far, he had not heard a thing and he wondered if the Lu women were dead but did not ask. "Have you checked the bars and bordellos around the waterfront?"

"We don't like to bother you and I checked his usual haunts before coming here. Nothing, no one has seen him in several days. Could the Zircons have captured him?"

The Devil's Spawn

"I haven't heard a thing. There was some gunfire in the wharf area earlier, but it was some drunk the watch reported." The officer of the day entered the office.

"Sir, there's reports of heavy gunfire out the north river road. The watch had gone earlier to investigate reports of Agarwal warriors on the East Road. Should I alert Captain Cortazzo?"

"Yes, tell him to form up a dozen mounted men and report to me on the east castle wall. Satisfied the officer understood, he asked Zack, "Are those your men on the east road?"

Zack with a wry expression answered, "Yes, they're looking for my brother. The watch knows about them. They shouldn't be firing guns unless someone attacked them."

"You need to check on your men. I'll advise Captain Cortazzo your men are in the area." The colonel showed Zack out and then went to the castle wall to meet his police captain. Colonel Gupta had commandeered his office and window. The tower roof offered a better vantage point of the east. He arrived as a red flare was streaking skyward. The police captain arrived as a yellow flare sailed into sky.

"Those flares sure look like Zircon army ones," the very worried police captain said. "Could their army have arrived?"

"There would be a dozen armored steamboats in the lake unloading a thousand soldiers if Markel was here." What a numbskull, he thought, and wondered if he was any better after agreeing to relieve Captain Maqbool of his command for speaking the truth. "It's that damn recon force that has been pestering us. I hope the watch has them cornered and you can finish them off. Do your duty."

179

The hedgerow was a good defensive position against attacks from the road, but not so good if the enemy got behind the hedgerow. Sunrise was less than an hour away when Al saw a half dozen of Laredo's warriors cautiously moving down the road toward the road crossing. Judging by their action, the enemy thought they were still in the irrigation ditch culvert. Then a dozen mounted soldiers thundered into sight and charged to the road culvert, where several dismounted and searched the ditch.

Al hoped Duncan was safe. The sergeant had to have seen those flares and known Al was still alive and where he was located. Now the question was if Lieutenant Duffield and his men at the stronghold had seen the flares and would send reinforcements. Then Jose, who was beside Bari and him, and had been watching in the Uneeda direction the area between the hedgerow and the river, spotted Duncan and alerted them.

"You've kicked the hornet nest," the sergeant cheerfully said, dropping beside Al. "There's more of those blue-faced warriors waiting up the road behind those police searching the culvert and ditch. Only a matter of time before those geniuses realize whoever had been shooting at them escaped. We're seriously out gunned if Duffield doesn't show."

"Then let's hope they decide we bolted east for the stronghold," Al answered, not sharing his sergeant's jaunty mood. His question, "Any sign of Gunner?" merited only a head shake from the sergeant.

Bari had checked on her grandmother, and satisfied the old lady was no worse, she crawled back through the hedgerow to join them with her rifle. "What's your plan?" she asked in a soft voice as the group watched the mounted police milling about the culvert. With a sigh Al answered her.

"Wait here quietly. I have faith, between Sergeant Jones and the lieutenant, the men will come. Once they have them engaged, we'll hit their rear."

"They're a tempting target now," Duncan said. Al had to agree. The police were standing on the road smoking and talking, unconcerned about the hedgerow a hundred meters off to the south by the river. After a moment, Al replied,

"My concern is not knowing how many Laredo warriors and soldiers from the fort are hanging back toward Uneeda." The two Zircons understood the danger of two armed groups encircling and trapping them.

"If there are more than a few of them and that oldest son of the chief is leading those warriors," Al worriedly explained thinking of the grandmother, "he won't hesitate to attack us if we're discovered."

Bari thought about telling them what happened up Clear Fork, but she still harbored a hope the three warriors had died from their wounds. If they were all dead and she did not tell anyone, the surviving Agarwal tribe members would not have reason for revenge against the Lu family. She was a firm believer that when two people knew a secret, it was no longer a secret.

Then there was sudden activity by the culvert, the police captain deciding to pursue east on the river road. The police mounted and galloped east, followed a moment later by eight mounted Laredo warriors. She did not have a pocket watch, but later reckoned only a few minutes had elapsed before an intense firefight erupted in the direction the police had gone.

"Bari, you and Jose need to stay with your grandmother and cover us. The rest of you follow me. We're going to jog along behind the hedgerow toward the gunfire and surprise those bastards."

The eastern horizon was lightening. Al and his three men, after five minutes of a fast jog, reached the site where the two forces had collided. His leg wound was painful but not bleeding, so he put it out of his mind and studied the couple dozen riderless horses milling about the fields on both sides of the road. Patchy gun fire meant both sides had dismounted and scattered. Who was winning was anyone's guess. The light allowed Al to identify three Laredo men across the road trying to collect the horses. Duncan and his troopers, following his hand signal, brought their rifles up and fired, and in moments the three warriors were down.

Their action instantly attracted return fire, but they escaped injury. Al could not locate other targets, though irregular gunshots continued for another several minutes as the night became day. Then suddenly the surviving enemy troopers made a break for the woods bordering the north field. Al knocked one more warrior down. Several other running men dropped as Jones's troopers laid down an intense fire. Then quiet.

A quick check of his men showed Duncan down. Concerned, Al jogged to his location. The sergeant had a high left shoulder wound, not good, but not likely to prove fatal. Duncan told him not to worry and Al went to find Sergeant Jones.

"An expensive mix-up," Jones said, on meeting Al in the road by two dead Ichneumon police officers. "I thought they had you pinned down, didn't expect to run into them charging down the road. Do not say it. Expect the unexpected, I know. I lost two men with two wounded." Al asked who. "Harry, our medic, and one of the new men. The wounded will be okay, nothing serious."

"Duncan got clipped, but again not too serious. So how did the enemy do?" Al asked as they walked over the battlefield and Zircon troopers secured the uninjured horses. The Uneeda police had borne the brunt of the fight and that showed in their dead, six patrolmen and a lieutenant.

Sergeant Jones' squad, Al's old squad had done well, and Al added, "Your men sure shot that bunch up."

"Yeah, they were more surprised than we were. I counted four of those painted warriors. Why were they involved?"

"I am not sure. They were hunting the Lu women and just joined forces with the police. The chief seized Lu's farm." Jones indicated he was aware of that with a shake of his head as Al continued, "I need to collect the women. Have the men gather all the abandoned weapons and bring me the ID disks from the dead Ichneumon soldiers." After a moment he added, "Pass on the firearms of no use to us to the farm families. I'll meet you back at the stronghold."

Captain Cortazzo and Zack stopped in the fort hallway by Colonel Kropp's office. Zack was thankful and amazed to be alive. They had charged after a couple of women and two men fleeing down the river road and ran head-on into a Zircon cavalry. The worried Ichneumon captain muttered, "I dread this. Give me that flask."

Zack did not mind sharing but being ordered to irritated him. Handing Cortazzo the flask, he had the thought, the wish, the colonel ought to have the inept asshole shot. The man took a double shot of gin from the flask, then carelessly tossed it back uncapped, and entered the commander's office. Closing and pocketing the silver flask, Zack knew to wait until summoned.

Cortazzo, after entering the commander's office, saluted and spoke. "Six men and my lieutenant dead, along with their horses dead or missing." The colonel blinked, appearing to have difficulty processing the information for a moment.

"What about the enemy? What about the Laredo warriors, did they not help?" the ominously calm commander asked.

"Yes, Laredo lost men helping. They were after the Lu women but joined us to go after the Zircon recon force. They lost several men. I saw several dead Zircons."

"Several. . .? What about those women?"

The captain answered, "I saw no sign of any women. Zack's men were chasing two hooded riders they thought might be the Lus." The colonel looked a bit lost. After a long pause, asked him to tell Zack Laredo to enter.

"Tell your father if he wants to keep the Lu farm to send me one hundred warriors and Greg. With his men and my troopers, I will kick those Zircons out of the valley, and he can have the women."

After the Oztec savage left, the commander said, "That recon force is bleeding us dry. I've lost around thirty men now. I have only about hundred and fifty left and half of them are garrison type, more of use for guard duty and the watch patrol. You need to hire a dozen Uneeda residents to bolster the watch patrols." He studied his police captain for a moment. The man appeared flustered, one of those bureaucratic officers who had never been in a firefight with an armed enemy. "Don't disappoint me again, dismissed."

Colonel Kropp next went to his office to consult with Colonel Gupta, who he feared might recover. Lieutenant Halona was there. The ass wipe was telling about Cortazzo's failure to subdue the Zircon patrol. He motioned with his hand for the lieutenant to leave as he greeted the disheveled religious police officer.

Lying through his teeth he said, "Glad to see you're looking better." That earned a weak curse from Gupta. "I want to advise you

The Devil's Spawn

I'm putting Captain Maqbool in charge of Cortazzo's men and will ask him to organize an attack force. I can't allow the Zircons to nibble away at our patrols."

"I agree Cortazzo is worthless, but I don't care for the captain's attitude. Use Halona, he thinks right."

"The Oztecs have no respect for the lieutenant. Since I want the chief to provide us with a hundred warriors and Maqbool and the chief's oldest son are friends, I figure the chief is more likely to agree if the captain commands the unit."

By then with some groaning Gupta had sat up with his legs over the edge looking ill. He made a shooing away motion with his hand when Kropp reached to help him. "Belcher needs to be beaten. Do what you think best. Just remember the Lord High Priest considers officers like Maqbool heretics."

Al, the Lu women, and the wounded went straight from the battle site to the Mischief, which was anchored near the north stronghold. He first informed Dr. Sebastian of the death of her friend and colleague, Harry Baker. Afterward, he had a hot shower taking advantage of the Mischief's boiler and changed into a clean fatigue outfit. A clean Bari found him, and they went to see her grandmother. One of the two new army medics delivered by last week's supply run out of Westport had cleaned and rebandaged Grammy's cut after adding a few surgical sutures.

"The medic said your grandmother was lucky to have survived that wound. How did it happen?" Al asked Bari after exiting the tent.

"A couple of those warriors surprised us earlier. During our escape one of them sliced her before I killed him." A clean but worried Bari said, "Now I fear infection or lung congestion. She's 78 years old and that night in the ditch couldn't have helped."

185

David C. Brown

Al figured that was not the full story, but not wanting to disturb Frau Lu, dropped the subject. Instead, after they were clear of the tent, he said. "Could you ask her if she went to the Uneeda school as a child? I'm trying to learn about that culvert that runs under the town and fort."

"Why?" she asked, diverted by action in the horse corral. Then like a switch thrown, an energized Bari turned and directly addressed him. "You're planning a mine! A repeat of the Saukko take down, right?" Her dark eyes sparkled in anticipation of his acknowledgement.

"Maybe, if I can place the explosives under the wall. I need a way into the culvert, the abandoned school is too close to the fort. The guards would see us excavating the sewer there. I was hoping your grandmother might remember where the sewer started, and if it was far enough away from the fort the guards couldn't see us entering it."

Another local predator that Al had not yet encountered was Juan Velasquez, former owner of the steamboat, Thumper. His home was Uneeda Lake and its environs, where he operated a small fleet of sail=powered fishing boats and owned the Uneeda fish market. The market was a sprawling collection of small shops around and in a large open-sided warehouse by the main wharf. The middle aged Oztec man also owned the Port Hotel, an old gray three-story wood frame building with a dark slate roofing. The hotel served as a saloon, a bordello, and Juan's office, and even occasionally rented rooms to travelers.

Juan showed the wear and tear of clawing his way up from an escaped slave to head of the lake pirates. He was missing his front teeth, left ear, and two fingers from his right hand, and had a large scar on the left side of his skull from an old cutlass sword wound. Juan had never attended a classroom but could read and understand

186

basic math. The lawless man had a strong entrepreneurial spirit and was open to innovative ideas.

Until recently, Juan had thrived doing nasty work for the Ichneumon commander, Colonel Kropp. Need a couple of raped and murdered females or prisoners disposed of? Call Juan. The lake monsters were always hungry. Need a couple of nameless humans for their evil religion? Juan always could part with a couple of old, ill, or lazy slaves. In return the Ichneumons did not interfere in his business. He was king of the Uneeda docks and the lake fishing industry. Then that son of a bitch, Lieutenant Halona, had demanded the use of his steam-powered boat, Thumper, to chase down a few Zircons. The fool lost Juan's boat.

The scuttlebutt of Uneeda waterfront denizens was that the days of the Ichneumon rule were ending along with slavery. He believed that might happen, after hearing about the exploits of that Zircon recon squad. Any group that could burn down Bergdorf's home, snatch his accountant, carry off the mine's gold ingots, destroy the Ichneumon warship, steal his Thumper, and in the process kill many soldiers, he did not need as an enemy. If he had known that a month ago, he would not have abducted that machinery salesman Kit Jacobs. Now he wondered if the salesman had any value for the Zircon commander.

Captain Maqbool, in Juan's opinion, the most sensible Ichneumon officer in the Uneeda garrison, had consumed a bottle of the better local gin with him a while back while trading lies and news. He learned that in the captain's homeland people raised minks and foxes for their pelts. That gave him an idea for a new business.

Wild silver otter furs commanded decent prices, but the animal was scarce and the swamp where it lived was a hazardous place. Otters eat fish and Juan had ample fish, water, and land. He had bought the abandoned Agarwal prison seven kilometers west of Uneeda on the north shore of the lake several years ago for a place to hold his slaves. The building had previously served as a slave holding pen for the Agarwal tribe and a jail for tribal lawbreakers. Converting part of the facility to hold giant weasels was not difficult.

The difficulty was obtaining breeding stock and settling on the proper diet and care for the animals. The otters' pens required periodical cleaning to keep their fur healthy. The slaves waiting at the facility performed most of that work, including the animal's feeding. One of the orphans his men had collected on a raid several months back, a young Oztec girl, had a way with the creatures. She could safely enter the pens and clean the floors and bedding. He had kept her, not sold her to the fort garrison for that reason.

The trappers that operated out of Prenter had supplied him with two young male otters, a large dangerous older male and four females, two of which were pregnant and two nursing young puppies. Until the reckless Ichneumons managed to lose his steamboat, he had planned to visit Prenter and order six more breeding pairs. The older male otter had killed a careless guard and needed to be put down. Even the girl feared it. The pelt from the animal would have financed his trip to Westport. The sale would have also helped spread word throughout the Erie valley that Velasquez had silver otter pelts for sale. But now, without his boat, his plans were in limbo.

About the same time the pirate was wondering how to proceed, Chief Laredo, if asked, might have answered that his plans were also in an ambiguous state. Greg's large palomino stallion had shown up at the Agarwal stable with several deep wounds from bites and claw scratches. Zack's opinion was a bear or mountain lion could have gotten his brother.

"No way a cougar or bear killed all three of our men, especially Greg," Chief Laredo snapped as he paced by the corral holding his morning cup of coffee and watching the groom clean and calm the nervous animal. The abrupt disregard of his speculation irritated Zack. Then again, he ought to be used to it. His father, even that Ichneumon colonel, thought his older brother was the only Laredo son of any account.

"Maybe they encountered one on a narrow trail and their horses panicked and lost their footing. Some of those trails edge along hundred-meter drops. Wouldn't hurt to check those spots out in Clear Creek."

His father looked at him. "If he is dead, someone, Zircons or Bergdorf's men, ambushed him. But you are right, it needs to be checked. I want to resolve what happened to your brother before sending men to Uneeda." The loss of seven warriors and the escape of the Lu women had him frustrated. Rubbing the back of his neck, he eyed his son. "Just how many Zircons were there?"

Stepping away from leaning on the corral rail, Zack said, "Your surviving bounty hunter told me afterward, two or three Zircons jumped them after they had cornered the women in a ditch. I was with Colonel Kropp when the gunfire started, and he sent a dozen mounted men to deal with the Zircons. My six men followed to assist the police and help the bounty hunters grab the women. Next thing I knew there was Zircon cavalry in front and behind us. I do not know how many, but twenty or thirty guns were firing. It wasn't any rinky-dink squad."

The chief flung his cold coffee on the ground and yelled out an obscenity. Zack thought he was about to receive one of his father's screaming fits; instead after kicking the stall wall and muttering several curses along with shaking his head, his father said,

"We need to get on top of this. I will pay the colonel a visit while you check those Clear Fork ledges once more. Find your brother. We'll meet back here in two days."

Bari woke her grandmother and asked her if she remembered where that old culvert that drained the school's neighborhood started.

189

She did. The inlet was located three streets north of the old school in the former residential area for the Uneeda professional class that left when the Ichneumons arrived.

That evening after the river road dust up, Al visited the neighborhood that was now a near-slum of huts and shacks among the few still standing, large two- and three-story homes. Chickens roamed the neighborhood and in several of the backyards a goat or two wandered about. All the remaining large homes had been converted into low rent apartments by their owners. As a result, plenty of witnesses living in the neighborhood around the culvert inlet to observe Al and his men activity at the culvert. Any one of the residents might report Al's activity to the Ichneumon garrison.

No watch patrol was encountered, but several residents saw them inspecting the site. Unfortunately for Al's plans sometime in the past the city had extended the culvert with two smaller diameter pipes to serve as sanitary sewers for side streets. A concrete junction box now enclosed the old storm culvert inlet. Entry to reach the large stone arch culvert was through a narrow drop inlet used to capture the water from the small creek. The narrow inlet manhole would complicate installing a mine. They would have to open the dynamite boxes and drop the individual sticks of explosives into the culvert through the manhole. A time-consuming operation when they would not have much time before the locals alerted the fort and the Ichneumons investigated.

The other difficulty presented by the presence of witnesses was having enough time for him to even enter the sewer and determine if it went under the fort. Knowing he needed to rethink the fort attack, he returned to the stronghold.

Bari was in the back tent near the river on a low stool feeding her bedridden grandmother some of the evening's corn and bean chowder. Concerned he asked, "How are you Frau Lu?"

"I'll be fine if my granddaughter would quit treating me like an invalid. Did you find the inlet?" Grammy, asked pushing the spoon away. She appeared very frail to Al as he helped her sit up. She asked about the inlet.

"The inlet won't work without removing a concrete junction box, which would require a construction crew. No way the fort would not learn and mount an attack on the crew. Where is the sewer outlet?" Al asked the two of them after explaining the problem with the inlet location.

"It's just east of the fish market wharf. The outlet is about fifty meters out in the lake," Bari answered. A submerged outlet, he realized and inaccessible. Mining the fort wall was not panning out. Lieutenant Kurt Bär interrupted them with a message that Herr Bergdorf was at the river road stronghold requesting a meeting.

The mine owner was talking with a shirtless Sergeant Duncan who had his left shoulder bandaged. Bari had tagged along with Al, and the sergeant, on seeing her, volunteered to get his shirt. Bari told him not to bother as Al greeted Bergdorf.

"I'll get right to the purpose of the visit," Bergdorf said. "Chief Laredo asked me to ask you if the Zircons had his oldest son, Greg, or knew where he was."

"No, none of my men have had any contact. Is the sociopath missing?" Al asked.

"He's been missing five days. What about you Bari, he was supposed to be looking for you."

"Can't help you," she said, adding, "Why are you Laredo's message boy?"

"I don't have a riverboat to jump on and flee to the Zircon army. The chief is gathering 100 to 120 warriors and I want to stay on his good side." Turning his attention to Al, he said, "Kropp's special force squad is being reorganized under Captain Maqbool who knows his business, right Bari?"

191

"Yeah, he does. I hate to hear he's back from Silver Ridge," Bari answered, fueling Al's curiosity about the new officer.

"The colonel is a dithering old man trying to hang on," Bergdorf added, which Al agreed with. After a glance toward a young Oztec boy leading a red bison toward the stronghold, the miner added, "Maqbool will come after you, won't rest until he's driven the Zircons from the river. The sensible move for you would be to pull back below the swamp and wait for the general at Prenter."

Al liked Bergdorf but did not trust him. Still, he agreed that the miner's suggestion was sensible because they were outnumbered. But those spawn of the devil had not bested his men so far, and it was not his nature to run. Glancing toward the red bison, Al fleetingly wondered if that animal meant the cook planned on roasted bison steak this evening. He answered the miner,

"That's not a bad suggestion. I will think on it. Have any idea how many soldiers the garrison has?"

"A lot more than you have. Maybe 100-130 Ichneumon effectives and add Laredo's and you are outnumbered ten to one."

Al had enough of this talk. "I've been meaning to ask you, what happened to that equipment salesman?" He noticed that this question had Bari's interest.

"I wish I knew. He had my order for a new boiler and engine, but Velasquez was not departing to Westport for another week. Kit told me he wanted to try his luck in finding the source of the west placer gold deposit for a few days. He never returned, you arrived, and Velasquez lost his boat. I have word out to the various Oztec tribes that I will pay a reward for information and Kit's safe return. Nothing in two weeks, kind of reminds me of Greg. According to his brother, he has vanished."

Al was not in the mood to gossip but decided to use the miner to deliver a message to the chief. "The chief shouldn't squander his remaining men over Ichneumon foolishness. He'll need them when the Lu family comes to reclaim their stolen property."

Wanting their visitor to remain unaware that the Uneeda valley farm and ranch families were joining Al's command to help in the fight, he said, "You need to leave. Sergeant Jones, escort Herr Bergdorf to his horse."

Herr Odrick, the bison dealer from Seth, had arrived yesterday with six fellow ranchers and their men. Many of them had suffered loss of property and loved ones from the earlier Ichneumon raids. They wanted to help. Bari and Jose had convinced several of their ranch hands to join the fight, but the other Oztec families would not buck Chief Laredo and stayed away.

Al was not sure what to make of that timid response. He hoped it was just fear of Laredo thugs and Ichneumon reprisal and not a harbinger of the tribes uniting against the Zircons. Still, he was pleased that some had joined his force. With his twenty special force troopers, he now had another thirty tough men and women who were familiar with firearms and hunting. He asked Jones and Lieutenant Duffield to organize and familiarize the volunteers with the Zircon army basic command and control procedures for small units. The irregular local militia marksmanship was good and required little additional training, other than to become accustomed to the new bolt action rifles.

Next Al went to the barge attached to the Thumper. He had enclosed the center section of the wooden barge to make a secured place, separate from the Mischief's magazine, to store part of their arsenal and ammo. He had seen Bari head that way and wanted to ask her about the new Ichneumon officer.

"Lieutenant Halona was like a kitten compared to that tiger Maqbool," she said, while filling small ammo pouches carried by the soldiers with 7.62 x 65mm cartridges from the bulk container. "He was also in cahoots with Juan Velasquez in the slave trade and furs, pelts. Maqbool seizes the people and animals, and Juan brokers the sales and oversees shipping to dealers along the Erie River." Bari's information reinforced Al's opinion that the slave trade underpinned much of the misery he had encountered in life. He thought, God bless the emperor for wanting to end the business.

"I figure they might make a grab for the Thumper, but it's out of commission. Still, you need to be on guard," Bari said, stopping her ammo transfer to better observe him. "We can't afford to lose this," she said with a hand motion indicating the weapons and crates of ammo and dynamite stacked around her.

"I agree, that's a concern," he said, pausing to considered whether to explain his plans to Bari. The beauty was a competent woman he trusted, and with that knowledge, he explained, "I thought their desire to strike back could be an opportunity to deal a telling blow to the devils. I might use the riverboat as bait for an ambush. Chances are the Ichneumons don't know how damaged it is," Al offered while checking her response. Seeing her concern, he clarified, "Not with the barge and magazine."

After telling Captain Maqbool his new mission, Colonel Kropp took him to the rear cell in the Uneeda fort dungeon basement for an appreciation of their dilemma. Stacked on the concrete floor of the cell were a hundred and forty-seven dust- and cobweb-covered eleven-kilogram gold ingots.

"General Paget and the Delta command needs that gold," the colonel told him while holding up a lamp to better illuminate the area.

"Is Bergdorf's mine that productive?" Maqbool asked, knowing it was not, but not wanting to ask his commander why he allowed such a valuable inventory to accumulate in a vulnerable location.

The colonel shaking his head, in a weary voice answered, "No. Policy disagreement. Emperor Ratakonda and the Lord High

194

The Devil's Spawn

Priest could not decide on the split. Normally the church gets ten percent, but I heard church wanted half of the Uneeda gold. I suspect that is why Colonel Gupta is here, to make sure the church gets their share of gold."

Maqbool was too familiar with royal policy fights over power and wealth. His family was still in a precarious position over his grand uncle's attempt forty-two years ago to succeed Ratakonda's father to the imperial throne. He needed to be cautious and remained silent.

"I can't allow that wealth to fall in Zircon hands, which could happen if we lost the fort. Therefore, captain, whatever you are planning must succeed. If your attack fails, there would be barely enough soldiers to secure the fort and gold."

"Then again, if I was successful and routed the Zircons from the valley, the gold could be shipped down to Westport where it could reach Delta."

"For sure we're in agreement that would be the most desirable outcome. First, I want you to call on that scheming Chief Laredo. He is afraid of you. I want you to demand he provides a hundred good warriors to your operation. I don't want him offering to back the Zircons if they agree to let the Lu ranch remain his."

"I don't think there's any chance of the chief and the Zircons joining forces because of the slavery issue," Maqbool said, while wondering where Greg might be.

"Don't be so sure. The chief is a human and only interested in what's best for him, and that ranch is a valuable property. If he will help, I'll provide twenty-five soldiers. With your squad and the chief's warriors you will outnumber the Zircons five-six times in men." The colonel's offer pleased Maqbool.

"Juan Velasquez told me the chief's oldest son, Greg, is missing," Maqbool said, hoping Greg was alive. The oldest son had a

195

lot of influence over the chief, who was unpredictable. "You think something happened to him or he's just off on a raid north of the swamps after Clovis slaves?"

"His family said he is missing, but with those savages it's hard to be certain."

"What about Bergdorf, think his men would help?"

"He's friendly with those Lu women that the chief screwed over, and a Zircon. I would not trust him. Same token, I wouldn't piss him off."

"Alright, I'll talk with the chief."

"Keep in mind, if the Zircon army shows up, the gold is lost, so time is not our friend. I'm pleased you're back, captain, along with Lieutenant Xavier, though we don't have much in the way of cavalry troops for him."

"We'll make do. Xavier has collaborated with the local mercenaries before. Might require some gold, but he'll organize a force of a dozen men for those, ah, unpleasant jobs that occasionally arise."

"Good, well, make the chief deliver those warriors."

Chapter 14

Al wanted to keep the pressure on the Ichneumon command. He asked Bill for use of the Mischief to lob a couple of cannon balls into the fort.

"Tonight," he answered Bill's alarmed question on when. "I want to run out on the lake just outside of rifle range and fire on the Comet and fort. The colonel will look weak if he doesn't fire cannons back at us."

"Damn, if one of the fort's 30-kilogram cannon balls hit, it would sink the Mischief. Remember how close that shot came the

The Devil's Spawn

other day. The little 8-kilogram solid shot or Bär's firecrackers we're firing won't do much to the fort. Why risk the Mischief?"

"It will if Lieutenant Bär manages to fire an incendiary round through the colonel's office window. Besides, you know as well as I those Ichneumons have only fired the fort cannons that once. That was a lucky shot, all the others missed by a kilometer. A few of our little shots will cause chaos in the fort and if any of the fishing boats or Comet are foolish enough to attack, my riflemen and the 40mm crew will manage them."

Around midnight the Mischief was about seven hundred meters off the waterfront by the fish market and a little over a kilometer from the fort's front wall. Each blast of the boat's cannons lit up the riverboat and surrounding lake, so though the night was moonless and dark, the sentries on the castle wall had no difficulty knowing where the cannon balls came from. Bill's Wapiti crew was good, six shots in five minutes. The lieutenant's crew could have fired a hundred rounds in that time, but Al restricted their shots to thirty, half at the Comet and half at the fort. The fort surprised them by firing six shots, with one ball making a giant splash thirty meters off their starboard.

The near miss was a warning not to underestimate your adversary. The crew could hear yelling and see men with torches running about on the fort's walls as small fires started on the Comet and the commander's office.

"Great job, lieutenant, hitting that window. Bill, now take us west along the shore to Velasquez's slave pen," Al ordered, figuring release of the pirate's slaves ought to add to the turmoil and even gather a few volunteers for the militia.

The slave pen location was out of the fort cannon range, so Al figured the Mischief should be safe. The Comet was no threat with cold boilers and three small fires in the pilot cab and engine room that

197

needed to be extinguished. He had brought six of his best men and Sergeant Jones for a landing party. The evening maneuver was risky if disaster struck, but if they pulled off the raid, the Uneeda garrison and pirates would be in an uproar. That would interfere with any plans Colonel Kropp and his new captain had to attack the strongholds.

The earlier cannon fire out on the lake had the three jail guards on alert, confused, and on the wharf yelling at the Mischief not to dock. Al went to the bow and yelled back, "Throw down your arms and stand back, or I'll fire this load of grape." Bill's crew had the brass cannon loaded and aimed at the wharf.

The burly guard making the threats aimed at Al and fired. His shot missed hitting anyone on board. The cannon fired the load of grape sized lead balls and knocked down the three guards. A minute later the boat nudged against the old wooden dock and Al and his men jumped from the boat. The burly guard appeared dead, and the other two had bad wounds and no fight left in them. The crew disarmed them.

"That's quite a shotgun," Jones said, inspecting the havoc caused by the one shot.

Al wanted the men to move fast and ordered, "Clear the wharf, we need to hurry." Jones's men threw the guards in the lake after disarming them. If those bastards manage to save themselves, fine, Al thought, at least his men hadn't shot them in the head. "Bari told me that Velasquez is no fool. He saw where the Mischief headed and will have men on the way to protect his property. We need to move fast before the cavalry arrives."

Jones and his men quickly secured the site and released three Oztec families. A shout brought Al running to the basement from the office where he had been gathering ledgers that listed names and sale information on Velasquez's slavery trade. In two large cages that covered most of the basement several otters were standing up looking at them. The odor of urine and fish was strong as Jones handed him an extra torch to better see. One cage had two young males. The other cage had four females, two pregnant and two appearing to be nursing young pups. Several young pups and all the adult female otters were standing up looking cute and harmless, almost human. He knew better.

A commotion behind him as a thin young girl from one of the Oztec families slipped by his men to enter the basement and crowd between Jones and him.

"Please don't murder them," she implored. "They shot the old one and skinned him. It was horrible," After a breath and a glance to see if she had their attention, the rag-clad girl beseeched him, "Release them, please." Her presence started the otters chattering.

"Who are you?" he asked the grimy thin girl.

"I'm Freda. Please, they will behave. You must release them." That got a sharp laugh from Jones, who, like Al, had thought of that vicious animal they had encountered in the swamp.

Al had met several assertive women in the territories, and he suspected Freda would prove to be another one in a few years. This attractive dark eyed slave girl had a self-confident demeaner that reminded him of Bari Lu.

Before Freda's interruption, he had already realized this setup was just a Uneeda version of a mink farm from back home. The pirate was raising the animals for their furs. He had planned to release the animals just to prevent the pirates from profiting from the pelts when the girl arrived.

"Boss, we need to go," Jones reminded him as he handed him a ring of keys. "The pirates will be here soon."

"Get everybody loaded," Al told Jones, and asked the girl her full name. It was Freda Mint. He could not resist teasing her, saying, "Mint, like the weed?"

She nodded, but she was still genuinely concerned about the otters as she added, "You are going to release them?"

Gathered around the cell door, the adult animals could easily grab his hand when he reached to unlock the cell, and he did not trust them. "If you can talk to them, tell all of them to back away from the doors."

She made a series of purring-like sounds along with hand motions of backing off. The animals did, to Al's amazement. A quick check verified Jones had everyone headed to the Mischief and he sorted through the keys for one that looked like it would fit the old iron door lock. The otters were well clear of the cell door, but still keenly watching them.

"You want to do the honors, Freda?" He handed the smiling girl the key while drawing his revolver. In moments she had both doors open, yet none of the animals rushed the opening.

"Come on Freda, we have a boat to catch," Al said taking her hand, and worried she might forget to save herself. "Tell your friends to run, because bad people are coming." Whether she said did the trick. A moment later a burst of gunfire erupted outside, adding to the urgency of the situation. The animals rushed by them to exit the jail and reached the wharf.

"Wait, you need to free Kit," the girl said, tugging his hand to stop him at the door. "He is locked in the boiler room." She was pointing toward the office building beside the pens where Lieutenant Bär and the rear guard was watching the road as everyone else crowded on the Mischief.

The name was one Al knew. He was not going to pass up a chance to rescue Kit Jacobs. "Thanks, girl, now get on the boat while we free your friend."

She obeyed, and as he was telling the lieutenant about the prisoner, he heard Jones shout, "No damn animals."

The Devil's Spawn

A quick glance toward the Mischief showed the nursing female otters and their pups clustered around Freda as they crowded by the sergeant who shouted, "Girl, those things are dangerous. Tell those damn weasels to jump in the lake." The animals and girl ignored him and pushed on through the milling escaped slaves on the wharf to the gangway.

The boiler room was just a cellar under the office area with an old copper still in one corner that was the reason for the room's name. The place was more a dungeon cell. The basement cut stone walls had numerous iron hooks and eye bolts anchored in them. Several short sections of iron chains attached those cruel neck collars to the eyebolts. The lone room inhabitant wore one of the slave collars and stood on a straw cover section of the concrete floor.

"Help me," the dirty bearded prisoner cried out on seeing Al in his army uniform, "I am a Zircon citizen, Kit Jacobs." He held up the chain to show the padlock that attached the anchor chain to the collar on his neck.

"We are in a rush Herr Jacobs," Al added after had introduced himself. "We don't have any means to cut the collar so we will try to break the chain."

"The fat bastard guarding the place has the keys." Jacobs offered to be helpful as Lieutenant Bär inspected the lock.

Well, hell, Al thought, I hope his body didn't float off. Gunfire outside added to the tension as the corporal with the lieutenant went to search the guard's body. More gunfire and shouting from Jones to get their ass in gear. Then the corporal was back and said, "I was lucky, his body was washed up on the shore." The corporal handed Al a grubby key ring and in moments the prisoner, now free, hastened toward the gangway.

Lieutenant Bär jointed the rear guard to stop the arriving pirates as Al finished chasing the remaining freed slaves milling on the wharf up the gangway on to the Mischief. One of the otter pups had missed the ramp and was on the dock edge whimpering. Al figured the kitten sized-animal was trying to get up its nerve to leap across the three-meter gap between the boat and dock. He stepped toward the pup to see if it would allow him to pick it up. It stood up, hissed, and showed small but still dangerous looking fangs.

"You're going to be like that, save yourself, buddy." Al turned and ran up the ramp behind Bär and grabbed his rifle he had left on board. He then turned and helped hold the arriving pirates at bay as his men dragged in the gangway. Clinging to the end of the gangway like a barnacle was the otter pup. He lost track of the animal after a bullet hit the railing by his hand and he concentrated on shooting any pirates that exposed themselves.

Bill cleared the dock and put some distance between them and the pirates now arriving. Afterwards, Al learned the pirates' gunfire killed one of the passengers and wounded another one, before the demolition charge left by Bär exploded ending the gunfire. As the Mischief settled into crossing the lake back toward the outlet, Al checked on the girl. The otters with her had nursing puppies.

Freda, surrounded by otters, looked wary as Al and Jones approached. She said, "They haven't bit anyone."

"Why didn't they just swim away with the other otters?" Al asked. "Are they pets of yours?"

"The lake pike would eat the pups," she said, then seeing his dubious look, added, "Really, and those cats and monitor lizards living in the ruins hunt them."

Bill came to her defense. "The animals are no trouble," he said leaning out the pilot cabin to check on them.

"You two are probably the only ones on board that believe that," Al said, checking on the other passengers who were keeping well clear of the animals. He dropped the matter, not wanting to quarrel with a young girl and went to check on the wounded men while thinking, forget in the future, that young Mint girl was already a managing female.

As the crowded Mischief approached the riverbank camp by the south stronghold, Bill later told Al the otters had slipped away over the side. Bari was there to greet the rescued slave families, Freda, and Jacobs, along with news.

Lieutenant Maqbool realized his timing was auspicious to make a request for a hundred warriors to help him rout the Zircons out of the valley. On arrival at Chief Laredo's camp, he learned from the warrior that took his horse's rein that the men had found the chief's oldest son alive. Crows feeding on two bodies had alerted the searchers to inspect the backside of a ridge near the north Clear Fork glacier. There they discovered two bodies, and nearby in an old stone hut they found a nearly dead Greg.

Entering the chief's crowded tent, Maqbool spotted a shirtless Greg sietting in a wooden chair by the fire ring with a blanket over his legs. The many facial tattoos he was familiar with assured him the wreck was Greg, his old drinking buddy. His friend managed a weak smile on seeing him.

"Damn captain," Greg said in a weak voice. "I'm glad to see you survived Silver Ridge mountains. Are you ready to help us kick the Zircons out of our land?"

"What happened?" He asked Greg, wondering if that Zircon recon squad was involved. Obviously, someone had shot his friend. One of the chief's older wives was cleaning a serious festering open wound in his left shoulder. Greg's left arm hung useless. The warrior had a gauntness and ghastly wan color of an extremely ill person. As had been Maqbool's experience, the Laredo clan was not big on personal hygiene, so the foul odor in the tent was probably from that, but this stink was a bit sharper than normal. He wondered if Greg's wound had turned gangrenous.

"Those Zircons bushwhacked my son," Chief Laredo snarled. He was sitting behind a table in the rear of the large tent. Red-faced, he slammed the table with an iron mug, spilling its contents and roared, "The Zircons and those sneaky bitches are going to pay."

The chief glared at Maqbool and then gazed slowly and intently around the room, checking his subchiefs and his other son, Zack, who had just entered, for any sign they did not share his loathing and zeal for revenge. The tent audience got the message. Judging from their sudden, screamed outrage and threats against the Lu women and Zircons, along with the waving of their guns and axes, the chief's plan had their enthusiastic support. The man's behavior made Maqbool uneasy. He was hesitant to commit to a campaign led by the chief, and Greg looked rough.

More Agarwal warriors had crowded in the tent fouling the air and crowding Maqbool. He didn't want every yahoo in the territory knowing his plans and asked Chief Laredo to clear the tent so they could discuss a strategy. The chief ignored his request. He had more to say regarding the Zircon shelling of the fort and destruction of the old jail the previous night.

"I heard the fort did not even fire a cannon at the Zircon boat, not one shot," the chief said, standing up to wave his empty mug at a warrior standing by the wooden barrel at the entrance.

"That is not correct. Several cannons fired but missed. The crews lacked practice which is being corrected as we talk."

"Whatever. Your colonel looked pathetic allowing the Zircons to merrily wreck our property and give the slaves wrong ideas. Makes all of us look weak." He threw the mug to the warrior, who easily snatched it from the air. "Fill it up," he told the cup catcher and then asked, "Well, captain, do you agree?"

"You're correct," Maqbool answered. He did agree with the barbarian and added, "Colonel Kropp agrees with you and the cannon men who failed to respond have been disciplined. Before we get to my matter, would you ask your men to give us some privacy." Within a minute only the Laredo men and he were in the tent.

"The colonel has instructed me to attack their stronghold two days from now. If we join forces, you will get your revenge and those women."

As had been his experience dealing with the savage, the chief rehashed his anger, threats, and questions for a bit before Greg, weary of his father's tirade, finally said, "We'll join you and help, but I'll need time to organize." Maqbool understood this to mean time for Greg's wound to heal a bit. "At least a week, will that work for your plan?"

"I will make it work to get you and a hundred of your men." Maqbool, pleased, but worried, got up and walked toward his friend to ask in a quiet voice, "That is a nasty looking wound, are you up to leading your men?"

The warrior gave a weak laugh. "I have been better, but Zack and I will manage. What about your men, I hope you plan to lead the soldiers, not that useless Cortazzo or the colonel?"

"I will command the Ichneumon force. But I am curious how someone managed to ambush a wily hunter like you. Did you or your men kill the sniper?"

"I got careless," Greg said, shaking his head. "It is a story for another time. We will meet you in Uneeda at the start of the river road, one week from today two hours before sunrise. Remember, I want those Lu women, lieutenant. Make sure your men know that and I want them alive."

After the Ichneumon captain rode off, Greg asked his father and Zack to remain. "I need to think this through, for I do not trust Maqbool and the colonel." His father, looking puzzled, started to speak, but Greg held up a hand. "I know what I just agreed to, but I want both empires out of our land. Zack, I would like you to send word to Bergdorf that I want to talk to him without delay."

Al was having coffee and thinking about what a good follow-up to the bombardment of the Uneeda fort might be when Bari and Freda stopped by to talk. "Jose sent word to Freda's tribe that she's here. Chief Mantas, head of her Oztec people, will be here tomorrow."

"Well, good," Al answered and noticing the worried look between the two, asked, "What's the problem?"

"The tribe wants her to be a goat herder. She wants to go to the Jesuit school in Westport and then become a riverboat pilot. Bill's been filling her head with tales of adventure."

Al thought of his goat herding days and did not fault her for not wanting that life. Then he thought of Sisi. No way would he allow a bright girl like Freda to make such a tragic mistake. But how? He had no experience dealing with eight-year old's, especially a female. He would try reason.

"That is a good school, but the school charges a thousand D-marks a semester. Where would you get the fee and what about the cost of room and board? Plus, the student has to be twelve to enroll."

Freda, who had expected a blunt "no way" lit up. "Bill said Knight Industry each year provides scholarships for several war orphans smart enough to get accepted in one of the Jesuit trade schools. I'm smart, I can do long division and read."

And charm Bill and his Mischief crew too, he thought, then asked. "What do you want me to do? Remember you're a minor, a long way from sixteen, and a ward of your tribe and chief."

Bari jumped in. "That's why she needs you to convince her chief to let her stay here with my grandmother and me until she's old enough to try for the school and scholarship." Freda was nodding vigorously in agreement. He was disappointed. He had thought Bari had more sense along with the fact that Freda was four years short of the required age for the school.

"My god, we're in a war zone and could be overwhelmed any day. Our camp is no place for a young girl. An Ichneumon could grab her and force her . . . well, it's no place for a girl."

Freda, with a stricken expression, looked to Bari, who said, "Nonsense, clearly her tribe is not any safer. Remember, she survived three months among Velasquez's pirates."

Al saw Bill by the tent opening. He shouted and motioned for the riverman to join them in the tent. On seeing a tearful Freda and a glaring Bari, Bill hesitated for a moment, then asked what was going on.

Irritated with all of them, Al yelled, "Are you wanting this girl to end up like Sisi, dancing naked on bars for drug money?"

Bill was confused for a moment at the captain's hostile remarks, but after seeing Freda in the tent, he decided it must have something to do with the scholarship. "Is this about the Knight Scholarship?"

"It's about luring a young girl into that pox-ridden cesspool Westport with tales of a free education and adventures."

"You're yelling at the wrong person. Dr. Sebastian is the one that suggested Freda should try for the scholarship. I just offered to let her ride on the Mischief on our next trip to Westport where she could take the Jesuit test."

"The doctor started this?" Al asked. Bill nodded while waving his arms in a "what could I have done" display and edging out of the tent. Bari gave him a harsh look. Realizing the women were angry at him, Al hedged and said, "I'll think on this, Freda, and get back to you. Now we all have work to do."

Chief Mantas and a dozen warriors from the eastern Oztec tribes arrived late that evening at the river road stronghold and requested a meeting for the following morning with the Zircon army commander.

The weather pleasant on this early spring day, Al decided to meet outside by the stronghold's corral. Chief Mantas, a tall thin man, had a friendly manner. In an unusual twist, the chief introduced the warriors in his entourage. For example, according to the chief, Warrior Adze was the strongest ax man in the territory. The man looked the part, massive shoulders on a heavy 190-centimeter frame and holding a double edge ax. Another of his warriors, Black Arrow could bring down flying ducks with arrows. The chief did all the talking, but his men, though silent, seemed relaxed and in good humor. After the chief finished with his fulsome introductions of his warriors, Al briefly introduced his team, Sergeant Jones and Duncan and Lieutenant Bär. He then asked the chief the purpose of his visit.

"Herr Odrick is a neighbor. In the past before the valley went crazy, our tribe used him to broker our livestock. He sent word the Mint girl was here and that I should help you."

"The girl is here, but who are you folks, part of the Agarwal tribe?"

"No. My people are mostly small farmers that own their land. They primarily grow the various cereal grains and fodder in the lands north of the swamps for markets in the Erie Valley. Some families have sufficient land to raise red bison and others herd milk goats and raise horses. The war has disrupted that trade."

"You should help us in our fight with the Ichneumon army." Al would welcome any help he could find. "With the Uneeda River open your people could trade with Westport."

"The marauders hunting slaves are the scourge destroying our trade and families. We are free men and have never owned slaves. I have heard your emperor has outlawed slavery. Is that true?"

"That is correct," Al answered, as he noticed Bari and Freda enter the stronghold.

The Devil's Spawn

"Yesterday, one of Chief Laredo's subchiefs delivered a message. If I help him defeat the Zircon soldiers attacking Uneeda, his men will cease their raids on my lands. He wants me to join his men. The man is a tyrant, untrustworthy."

"You should join your neighbors and help us defeat the Ichneumon garrison. They suffered some serious loss in the recent battles. I expect them to hole up in the fort unless Chief Laredo decides to support them in a new assault."

"We're aware of what happened at Seth. The Ichneumon army and Chief Laredo both need to go. My warriors will help, but they want to be assigned to Herr Odrick's crew." He looked at Duncan with a rifle slung over his shoulder. "And some of those new rifles."

Al felt a great relief. Those Oztec warriors would double the militia and allow him to place a screening force around Uneeda and isolate the garrison. "Thank you, your men will be an immense help. Anyone who joins will be issued a new rifle that he can take home with him after the Ichneumons are gone."

Chief Mantas nodded in agreement, then noticed Bari with the girl waiting by the south end of the corral. He said, "I know that woman," and gestured for her to join the discussion. "Bari Lu and I are old business acquaintances."

Al added, "Freda is the girl with her and whom she wishes to speak to you about."

Chief Mantas sighed after listening to Bari's request and responded, "Those farm families are patriarchal, protective of their women. They will consider unclean any girl or woman who has spent months among slavers and pirates. The unfortunate girl will have a tough time finding acceptance back in our society and a husband." Bari's expression conveyed she didn't agree, prompting the chief to add, "I know it's not right, but it's the truth. Just as in the past Mint females were considered witches by some of the older folks."

Al wondered if that provincial intolerance was behind Freda's wanting to stay with Bari as he asked, "The Mint girl has been helpful and well behaved. I like her. Should I have Freda join the meeting?"

"Sure," the chief said in a hesitant voice. Al figured he was looking for a solution and Bari waved for the girl. Introductions made, the chief then asked Freda what she preferred.

Bari answered for her. "Freda wants to remain with my grandmother and me as my ward. We will give her love and care."

Al had expected something along those lines as Freda said, "Please let me stay with the Lu family."

Al could tell that solution pleased Chief Mantas. After he asked Freda if she was sure, and received an enthusiastic yes, the chief approved Bari Lu becoming Freda Mint's guardian.

Chapter 15

The Devil's Spawn

The riverboat Rouser arrived the morning after Chief Mantas's visit to the Zircon camp and docked across from the Kerry farm. The arrival of any boat was an event. Several farm workers, Al, and Sergeant Duncan walked down to the dock to greet the boat and learn the latest Westport news along with who was among its passengers. The first passenger off the riverboat was a stout, clean shaven middle-aged man with a large bald head, small ears, and dark alert eyes who dressed as a brigadier general. Al recognized him. Count Laumeister had arrived, and he went to greet the man.

The aristocrat received Al's greeting in a perfunctory manner, the man more interested in the Saukko hulk in the river. After studying the abandoned warship for a moment more, the Count asked, "Is that the ship you guys used a naked woman to lure into an ambush?"

"That was some nonsense started by the navy," Al answered, hoping that would squelch the tale. He would be in deep trouble if Bari heard that remark.

"Sounds like the navy," the Count said with a laugh, adding, "They're envious a mere army squad can take out an Ichneumon warship after their failure at Delta." Then in a business-like manner, he instructed Al on what he expected for himself and his two bodyguards.

Nothing too onerous, Al thought. The Count and his men would stay on the Rouser which Al had realized was the old Southern Belle, Amos Reed's infamous floating bordello and casino repainted in the black and gray camo style used by the navy. The aristocrat wanted horses as needed, and when out of camp, several mounted troopers to escort them on his inspections. Contrary to the scuttlebutt about the Count's snobbish behavior he was tolerably sociable with the dock workers, even with Freda who had rowed across the river to see what was going on.

211

David C. Brown

Al recalled General Markel's advice that if Count Laumeister visited the Uneeda front, then chances were the IIS sent him. The general had also cautioned him that one could never be certain that an insolvent scheming highborn like the Count was not there for the gold.

"The day is young," the Count said. "I want to visit the Oztec tribes and learn their attitude toward slavery and Zircon governing of Uneeda after the Ichneumons leave, but today I want to visit Friedrich Bergdorf's mine."

"I'm sure the miner would be happy to meet you here. Save you from risking an encounter with an Ichneumon patrol." The Count's request surprised Al and he wondered if there had been a past connection between them.

"No, I need to see the land and his operation. Is it too late to go today?" The man was full of surprises and was not the usual lazy bureaucrat Al had expected.

By using horses and cutting across the same ridge Bari had first shown Al, they were able to avoid any contact with the Ichneumon patrols around Uneeda and reach the mine quickly. It was a sunny mid-afternoon when Ivan let them into the fenced mine complex and escorted Count Laumeister and Al to Bergdorf's office. Looking around the mine operation as they made their way to the office, the Count appeared intrigued. He also seemed apathetic toward the eight thin men chained together in a line with leg manacles they encountered. The dirt, hair, and whiskers made determining the prisoners' ethnic group difficult, though they appeared a mix of Oztecs and Zircons.

The Count's two bodyguards, aloof thugs, waited in the hallway by the office door while Private Gunner and Corporal Williams visited with Bergdorf's main man, Ivan. Al counted on them

212

to learn the latest gossip around the mine. On entering the dusty mine office and seeing Bergdorf, the Count said in an irritating smug voice, "I'll be damned, you did escape. General Markel thought you were the same Bergdorf that Captain Peiper ran with. I told him no way. My uncle, the emperor, vowed to hang all the coup d'état members."

The mine owner did not appear to Al the least bit concerned with the vexed aristocrat stalking about the office who turned and added, "The IIS claimed to have captured all the plotters. Merlin IRS and IIS had to know about you with their agent, Hans Maxim, working here." The Count made another circle and suddenly stopped. "Duke Soltzendorff's fatal hunting accident, you made a deal with someone. You ratted the duke out to save your ass."

"Please, that's wild speculation and untrue. I am a simple soldier." The miner had loss his casual look. "I was not involved with any attack on my beloved emperor. And yes, I knew Captain Peiper from the Donnelly troubles. I heard he died while disarming those mines involved in the Aram coup attempt on Emperor Schnabel's life. He's considered a hero."

That claim got a scornful snort from the aristocrat.

Al was listening carefully and paid close attention to the interesting conversation. They were referring to that munition train those saboteurs in Aram blew up. Alert, he remembered the details; the explosion was an attempt to assassinate the emperor three years ago. The coup d'état failed. He had been in Myrtle Territory at the time and later heard rumors of a Captain Peiper's involvement in the coup, but had then read the captain died before the IIS could interrogate him. Al now knew why the gold miner asked him about an arrest warrant. Bergdorf had some connection to the Aram coup attempt.

The Count, leaning against the work bench, said, "I wondered at the time about Soltzendorff's accident. Well, enough history. Since you were not involved, then you should have no concerns that the emperor has tasked the IIS with reviewing the IRS and army files on the overthrow attempt." Picking up one of the small transparent glass bowls of gold sand on the table beside the beam scale, he said, "It always amazes me how heavy gold is." Setting the coffee cup-sized bowl back on the table, the Count asked, "Why is your gold not reaching Westport?"

"I suspect Colonel Kropp fears the Zircons will intercept the shipments at Westport."

"Is your mine still producing gold?"

"Not like it used to," the miner answered, then after a glance at Al, added, "Slaves are getting scarce, but I still manage a respectful couple of kilograms each week."

Looking at the Hittite safe in the right corner of the mine office, the Count said, "It has been months since any gold entered Westport. Where is it being stored?"

"You'll have to ask the colonel. I deliver all the gold mined to the fort and get paid in their worthless paper rupees." Al seriously doubted Bergdorf's assertion but said nothing.

"Any thoughts on how much gold is at the fort?"

"Hard to say," Bergdorf answered. "Captain Maqbool just returned from Silver Ridge at the west end of the lake and may have already sent most of the gold out through those high passes."

Al did not believe that. Only a few humans and no Ichneumon he had heard about could survive at an altitude 8,500 meters and that was the height of the lowest of several passes that require crossing to go south toward Delta. Judging from the concerned look that flashed across the Count's demeanor, he was not familiar with those facts.

Besides, Al was confident the Ichneumons would never trust those Oztec porters with their gold and knew Captain Maqbool was in Silver Ridge when Bergdorf and the mine had delivered over hundred kilograms of gold to the fort a couple of weeks ago after the house fire. For whatever reason, the miner was hedging the amount of gold in the fort.

"Is the captain one of the connected Maqbools?" The miner nodded and the Count in a thoughtful tone added, "That is interesting, an Ichneumon prince in this remote place."

"He is not a prince nor an aspirant to the throne. That was his grandfather's brother who the current emperor's father beheaded."

"He is by blood. For sure palace politics is a dangerous game. Are you aware the captain here has the river open to Westport, at least east from the Kerry farm?" Bergdorf shrugged and made a "so what" gesture before opening a cigar box on his desk. "You could avoid the Ichneumons by going around Uneeda like we did to reach here. The navy could deliver your gold then to Westport, so why haven't you?"

"In that office down the hall iare always at least two Ichneumon clerks, guards that watch after the gold as we recover it. If the fort learned the gold was going elsewhere, they would seize the mine and hang me. If the general wants the gold in Westport, which I would love, he needs to invade Uneeda and take the fort."

"A number of us feel the same way, but the general doesn't." Pausing to accept a cigar, the Count added. "His focus is on opening the Erie River by defeating the Ichneumons in Delta. He is of the opinion the army has the gold trapped in Uneeda. I gather you don't share that opinion?"

"I have done business with that sociopath, Colonel Kropp for three years and if he thought General Markel was going to invade Uneeda before Delta fell, he would dump any gold he held in the deep part of the lake. Fortunately, the colonel still thinks the Ichneumons will win."

"If he dropped the gold in the lake, couldn't the navy divers recover it?"

Al had to laugh and said, "Sir, that lake is over a thousand meters deep."

The Count gave him an irritated look and changed the subjects, addressing Bergdorf, asked. "Laredo has many warriors. Why doesn't he help?"

Bergdorf looked at Al, obviously wondering if he wanted to answer the Count. He did and said, "Laredo and his men, supporting the Ichneumons, attacked us during a reconnaissance of the fort's defenses. We repelled them and the Oztecs lost warriors. Two days ago, he," Al pointed at Bergdorf, "told me the chief believed we were involved with his oldest son's disappearance. We were not."

"I have news," the miner said. "Greg is alive, but gravely wounded. Two days ago, he asked me to visit him at their camp. He told me a sniper shot him in Clear Fork and killed the two warriors with him. Greg and the chief blame you."

The Count looking at him, asked if that was true. Al knew no one from his command had been in Clear Fork or shot anyone there. His audience appeared unconvinced and after a moment Bergdorf told them.

"Well captain, Greg had three fired 7.62x65 mm brass cartridges that he said were found in the area where the sniper had fired from. We all know only a select few Zircon soldiers currently have those high-powered rifles. Your man screwed up not taking the brass or finishing the kill. The chief and Greg considered that proof you were behind the attempt to murder him."

"Great!" the Count said turning on Al. "You have managed to piss off the tribe who has enough warriors to help us seize the fort, win this campaign, and free the gold for the emperor."

Learning about the discovered brass Al realized the culprit had to be Bari but snapped, "My men were not involved, otherwise that bastard would be dead. Laredo is untrustworthy, period." Startled by his disrespectful burst of candor and the Count's sudden wrathful look, Al attempted to explain. "Laredo wants General Markel to make him the Uneeda ruler and he does not want slavery eliminated."

"So what? The army's mission, your mission is to take Uneeda from the Ichneumons, which you have failed to do. Refusing help to accomplish your mission because you don't like the man is dereliction of your duties."

"You are wrong, sir. My orders are to stop the Ichneumons and their allies from murdering the farmers along the Uneeda River until the army could deal with the fort. My men are accomplishing that with help from the eastern Oztec tribes and ranchers. They support our emperor's goals such as abolition of slavery. Involving that sociopath Laredo would cost us their support."

Bergdorf looked properly concerned, but Al figured the miner was secretly delighted with the Count's scheme.

"Listen to this naivete," the nobleman shouted. "That is what is wrong with today's young officers. In the old days you used any means available to win. Use Laredo's men and afterward kick him out."

"Better than being gullible," Al snapped. "Did it ever enter your mind Laredo's offer is a plot by Colonel Kropp to infiltrate our ranks with traitors who in the heat of battle will turn on us?"

That suggestion caused the Count to pause. Protecting Bari had been a consideration in his rejection of involving Laredo, but still, what he had just said was true. The pliable Bergdorf said, "I sure would not trust the bastard. He murders any subchief that shows independence."

"Bah, you two think the Zircon army couldn't manage some puffed up local warlord if he started misbehaving." After fuming for a moment, he asked, "Bergdorf, can you arrange a meeting for me with the chief?"

The miner hesitated, looked at Al, then answered, "Greg asked me if there was some other Zircon official he could approach, since the captain tried to murder him. He wants to discuss ways the two sides could eliminate the Ichneumons in Uneeda. I didn't know about you at the time, so yes I should be able to arrange a meeting."

Al now wondered if the chief's oldest son's reported wound was all a plot to bypass him and deal with the Count. For sure he was guilty of under estimating Greg. There was little talk between the Count and him during the trip back to the Kerry Farm. Bergdorf would need a day or two to arrange a meeting with Chief Laredo and his sons.

While the Merlin aristocrat was complicating Al's life, Chief Laredo and his son Greg were in the Uneeda fort irritating Captain Maqbool. The Agarwal Nation chief wanted a meeting with Colonel Kropp, now.

"An opportunity has arrived," the chief declared on entering the fort commander's dark office. The boarded-up window behind the colonel caused him to pause momentary and instead ask, "One of the Zircons' cannon balls?" The commander's annoyed look and muteness made the chief realize it was a sore subject and, suddenly defensive, quickly added, "Count Laumeister is at the Zircon camp. He's after the gold."

Colonel Kropp was out of sorts after an earlier confrontation with Colonel Gupta who had suffered serious burns from the shell that hit the office window and was forced to move to a dungeon cell for safety. Not in the mood for one of the chief's tortuous, longwinded explanations, the commander snapped, "Who the hell is he? How is that an opportunity, everyone is after the damn gold and I'm not giving it to some middling Zircon dignitary."

"Please, colonel, let me finish. That is not my point." The chief looked offended over the dismissive remarks, and after a fleeting pause, turned and addressed Lieutenant Maqbool.

The Devil's Spawn

"You have bragged to my sons about being an assassin who can infiltrate any camp to reach the target and kill it That is what I want, for you to kill Captain Belcher. If he is gone, Count Laumeister will be in charge until the army sends a replacement, which will take weeks, months. I can convince that puffed up swell that I know how to get at the gold and even take the fort. Then, knowing their plans, you can help me ambush the Zircons and free the valley of the bastards."

Captain Maqbool had heard tales of a corrupted aristocrat causing problems for the Zircon army building the Erie Spur railroad. Not a unique problem, he thought of Colonel Gupta. Apparently Count Laumeister was that person, so the chief might have a decent idea. For sure Colonel Kropp had seized on the Chief's idea to avoid a humiliating defeat and loss of the emperor's gold.

The problem Maqbool faced was lack of current intelligent on the Zircon camp. He suspected the bulk of the Zircon force was along the north side of the river valley clustered around the stronghold and road where he had lost so many men. He knew from fishermen's accounts that the Zircons anchored their boats and stored supplies at the Kerry mule farm on the south side of the river valley. By crossing the lake and looping south through the bogs he could come in behind the grasslands and the Kerry farm location. Horses could not manage the bog terrain. He figured the Zircons, not expecting a cavalry attack from that direction, would only lightly guard that approach. Where in the camps Captain Belcher stayed was unknown. He would just have to hunt for the man when he got there.

In the hallway after the meeting where he had agreed to assassinate Belcher, he had to chuckle. Served him right for telling those credulous savages that ranger nonsense. Still, he welcomed the mission. That evening, Maqbool and two trusted men, Corporal Guru and Sergeant Rakesh, crossed Uneeda Lake and hiked into the bogs.

219

While the ill-disposed Count went to his room on Rouser, Bill and Freda stopped Al to hear and settle their dead chicken matter. The riverboat captain kept Ridge Brown hens and a rooster in a coop on the Mischief for fresh eggs. After docking the boat, Al was aware he allowed the birds to range freely about the riverbank and dock area. This morning Bill had discovered the partly eaten carcass of one of his hens. Immediately suspecting the young otter that hung around Freda, he confronted her.

"Otters eat fish. Do not let him put a leg trap by the dead bird. Splash might step on it and be hurt," the girl, holding back tears, said. "It probably was a hawk."

"If that damn weasel is innocent, why are its tracks around the bird?" Bill snapped.

"They're curious animals," she countered. Hands on her hips, she glared at Bill with a defiant look.

Al figured Bill had named the culprit, but having seen the girl's way with animals, in a half serious way asked her, "Did you ask, what's its name, Splash, if he killed Bill's chicken?"

"Er, no. Slash hasn't been around today," Freda answered, with a worried glance toward Bill.

"Don't give me that look, I haven't seen your pet either. You need to tell the pest such behavior won't be tolerated." The riverboat captain, shaking his head in disgust, gathered up the dead bird and walked off.

"I'm sure it was a hawk," she told Bill's back and then after a smile for Al, skipped off toward the Lu tent.

After a day waiting for word from Bergdorf on the meeting with Chief Laredo, and hearing nothing, Count Laumeister was restless and talked of having Rouser take him back to Westport, if the chief would not meet. Al hoped the Count went away. Since things were quiet, Al crossed the river to visit the Lu family. His goal was to get better acquainted with Bari, even entice her to go back to his tent across the river and away from her mother and Freda.

His timing was good. Bari had made a rich chowder of yellow perch, onions, and assorted root vegetables to go with Freda's bread. The girl's flattish delicious bread reminded Al of ciabatta bread in New Hamburg. The Lus' crowded four-by-six-meter tent contained two beds, one for the grandmother and another for Bari and Freda to share. The old wolf was lying on a worn army wool blanket in one corner. They served their meals on a wooden table salvaged from the burned farmhouse. Because of the lack of space, the table was located under another tent with open sides that sat beside the family's tent's entrance and a few meters from a large cast iron stove. More salvage from the Kerry farmhouse, Al reckoned. Frau Kerry still owned the farm but had moved her family to Westport for the duration of the war and had told them to use what they could.

About a dozen meters from the Lu tent, two young otters rested on the small wooden dock that the row boats were tied to. The residents used the small boats to safety cross the river between the camps. Al, to tease Freda, who was wearing an old pale yellow cotton hoodie and new looking jeans, nodded toward the dock, and asked, "Is that the hen killer?"

She was busy cutting the crusty bread but paused to give him a saucy look before answering. "It was a mistake. He didn't know it was Bill's chicken."

"Did you tell Bill? What did he say?"

Sighing as only young girls can when pestered by inquisitive adults she said. "Bill told me as long as it doesn't happen again, he'll forget the matter."

Bari, wearing that gray army style utility jacket and pants she favored announced, "Time to eat." She then placed the heavy four-liter cast iron pot on the table and remover the lid.

Al was still trying to determine if the girl could communicate with animals and asked, "Did Splash agree to leave the chickens alone?"

Freda nodded and her dark intelligent eyes studied him for a moment as she handed the plate of cut bread to Bari and put the knife away. She then whistled and one of the otters, Al didn't know which one, as they both looked identical, ran to Freda, and stood up. She petted its head, then reached into a bucket resting on the ground beside the stove for a large freshwater clam and handed it to the animal.

"Where did you find that clam?" Al asked, amazed at its size. The mollusk's shell was the size of a grapefruit.

"One of the lake fishermen sold it to Bill. Splash, the otters, love them. Opening the clam will occupy them for a while. They use stones to break the shell." Then she said something Al coundn't make out. The animal dashed to him and, clenching the heavy clam with one paw against its torso, stood up holding out its free paw, one with a serious looking set of claws, he noticed. The kitten sized-animals they had freed a month ago were now bobcats and, when it stood, the otter's head nearly reached his belt. Unlike the animal he encountered in the swamp, this otter had a friendly curious temperament.

"Splash promises to ignore the chickens and wants to be friends," the girl said, watching from behind the table.

What a strange place he thought, and shook its hand, paw. The flexible creature twisted around to look back toward Freda and she nodded. After a moment, the otter still standing on its hind legs, took a step by Al to loop back to the dock with its treat.

Suddenly blood splattered Al, then he heard a distant rifle shot. He dove for the ground beside the downed otter. He felt a burning rip across his derriere and a moment later heard another distant gun shot. Then men yelling and guns firing nearby and from across the river.

The Devil's Spawn

Captain Maqbool's anticipated six-hour night hike across the bogs instead proved to be an exhausting twenty hour hike to cross a mere six kilometers. The open areas of the bog consisted of black muck covered with a film of clear chilly water. Not enough water to swim in and the black muck, once disturbed, became like quicksand. Only by staying in the cattails and on clumps of reeds and lily roots had Lieutenant Maqbool and his two men managed to zig zag across the hellish landscape of leaches and mosquitoes. The scrub brush, even those detestable greenbrier vines, were a welcome sight, for they meant solid ground.

The mule farm was about two kilometers east of where Maqbool and his men exited the troublesome bog. They then hacked their way through more than a kilometer of the tangled thorny vine undergrowth that grew under the oak and hickory trees before encountering newly plowed farm fields. Sergeant Rakesh spotted the perimeter guard tower. Being late in the afternoon, the sun was behind them and would interfere with the guard's vision. Even better there was only one man.

Rakesh had his crossbow and chanced a long shot. Luck was with them. The sergeant's first bolt hit the guard. Maqbool raced up the eight-meter-tall tower ladder and threw the thrashing guard off the platform for Corporal Guru to finish the job by cutting the man's gullet. The view from the tower showed a small camp with three of those large drab olive-green army tents Zircon quartermasters used and several smaller gray civilian tents.

Scanning the scene before him he could see the Saukko hulk, the damaged Thumper, and across the river two other riverboats. One looked like the bordello casino riverboat he saw in Delta a few years ago and wondered if the Zircon army provided prostitutes for its soldiers. The large Zircon camp with a dozen tents and a field hospital was on the north side. A large corral with dozens of horses was

223

visible across the river. Proof the original recon squad had grown into a dangerous-sized force. What he saw convinced Maqbool the Zircon army actively supported his nemesis.

Maqbool's problem was he did not know Captain Belcher. Bergdorf told him the Zircon officer was a large, homely man. Until seeing the size of the camps, he had figured he could sort out the officers by observing the troopers' behavior. If he shot several of them in the process of killing the captain, so much the better. As Corporal Guru setup a support for his sniper rifle, Maqbool, using the colonel's 12x55 monocular telescope studied the scene before them.

There was a family near the dock setting out food on a table by one of the gray tents. After studying the woman, he realized she was Bergdorf's livestock buyer, Bari Lu. Probably hiding from Chief Laredo, he figured and then remembered hearing Zack complain that Belcher was friendly with the Lu family. He focused on the man. A hatless big beefy trooper who wore a utilitarian outfit that might be a faded set of Zircon winter camouflage fatigues. If he wore any rank insignia, it was not obvious.

Then he saw something amazing. A young otter ran toward the young girl who had been cutting bread and stood up. After some words and being given a large clam, of all things, the animal went to the man and stood up. Sergeant Rakesh whistled and pointed at three troopers across the far field who appeared to be walking toward the watch tower.

"Do you have a clear shot on the man?" Maqbool asked Corporal Guru who grunted yes. Take it he commanded and with a quick look saw both the otter and man down. The corporal made a second shot at the target before switching his fire at the troopers running toward the tower. It was like a hornet nest exploding. Troopers from across the river started firing at the tower as several troopers, two without shirts rushed out of the tents and started firing at the tower. Guru never had a chance as the fusillade of bullets shredded the platform. He only escaped by letting go of the ladder and dropping the last couple of meters to the ground.

A crying Freda had dashed to help her pet and Al had yanked her to the ground. He was not sure what his status was, only knew his side hurt, and blood and pieces of flesh had splattered him. His men had responded fast, and he figured the sniper was dead or running for cover. He freed the sobbing girl, and they checked the otter. The unconscious animal had a wicked wound to the head and a bleeding paw. Then Bari arrived.

"I'm okay. You need to get the doctor," Al said in response to her query and then told Freda, "Get one of the blankets for your pet."

A half hour later Doctor Sebastian had them patched. Splash now rested in the blanket under the outside table with a sad Freda pampering the comatose animal. The head wound had not penetrated the skull, so there was hope the animal would recover. The consensus was the first bullet hit the clam and severed part of the paw. Pieces of the bullet and shell had hit Al in his right side. The clam shell shattering the dumdum bullet saved Al from a fatal wound. The third bullet had just clipped the right side of his buttock, barely breaking the skin. The doctor removed the minor shrapnel and Bari helped him wash off the bits and pieces of clam and otter. Within an hour of the sniper's shot, Al was at the watch tower with Sergeant Jones looking at the dead sniper.

"The tracks say three men," Jones answered. "Two escaped into the bog. I sent Corporal Williams with four men to hunt them."

Al had earlier checked the bog to see how accessible the mule farm was from that direction. He had decided not very. "I fear the bog will even defeat Williams's talent for tracking. I hope he is cautious. Anyone who crossed that swamp is no one to take lightly."

"Damn right, the gang was out to assassinate you," Jones said.

225

"Or Count Laumeister," Al said. Jones shook his head in disagreement as Al added, "The men know the sniper wounded me, just not how bad. I am going to stay out of sight. I want you to spread the word I am dying, and Bill has taken me to Westport. I want to see who comes calling, especially for the Count."

Count Laumeister, in wishful moments, had envisaged being in charge and winning the fort. He would then ask the emperor for half of the ten percent reward for captured Ichneumon gold. The sudden and intense gunfire across the river had alarmed him and he ran to the stronghold. Half an hour later he learned Captain Belcher had been the assassin's target. The captain had survived, but rumor was his wounds required Westport medical help.

The news cheered him. Lady Luck had smiled on him after abandoning him over the last couple of years. Still, he knew around the men the moment required a concerned worried demeanor on his part. First, he needed to check on Captain Belcher and with Lieutenant Bär and First Sergeant Duncan he crossed the river to the Lu tent. They met the captain and Sergeant Jones returning from the watch tower.

"You look a long way from dying," the Count, smiling told Belcher. His hopes of taking charge appeared stillborn. He asked what had happened.

The Devil's Spawn

Chapter 16

Captain Cortazzo's man, who hung out at the Uneeda docks, was the first to hear the Zircon captain went to Westport for medical help. He passed the information to the police captain, who in turn told Colonel Kropp who did know of Captain Maqbool's mission. The captain had not reported in, and the colonel prayed his best officer had survived the mission. He told Cortazzo to send word to Chief Laredo that he needed to meet the Count.

Kropp's plan, though he was careful to imply Chief Laredo had thought up the scheme, was based on a widely believed tale that an old abandoned storm sewer ran under the fort. He knew the Zircons had investigated the sewer but had not followed up with any action. Kropp figured Captain Belcher realized they lacked the men to secure the entrance into the sewer while a snapper crew constructed the mine under the fort's wall.

The chief's job was to convince the Count that his warriors would supply the means to protect the Zircon miners and would then help in the assault of the fort after the mine breeched the fort walls.

After the Zircons entered the sewer, the Agarwal warriors and his men would attack and trap the Zircons in the culvert. Not a very imaginative plan, but Kropp knew the Zircons liked using mines and Count Laumeister wanted the gold.

Lieutenant Maqbool's success in wounding the Zircon captain and word that Count Laumeister had assumed command excited Chief Laredo. He was ready to do his part to defeat the Zircons, but, a cautious man, he sent his sons to the first meeting with the Count.

Zack worried his father's information might be wrong and Captain Belcher's men would arrest him. But being a dutiful son, he did what his father and older brother requested and found out he had worried over nothing. Count Laumeister had learned of the chief's proposal earlier from Bergdorf. The aristocrat welcomed Zack as a dear comrade who had come to help him rid the valley of those evil Ichneumons. Zack sent word to Greg who then joined the meeting in a tent behind the stronghold.

"What accounts for your fathers change of heart?" the Count asked the chief's oldest son, who he figured was in charge even if the man looked seriously ill. The aristocrat, after a glance at Lieutenant Bär, who had just entered the meeting, added, "Two weeks ago, you joined the Ichneumon attack against our men. Now I understand your father wants to help us beat the Ichneumons, so what changed?"

"That unfortunate action resulted from our men pursuing renegade tribal members and mistaking the Zircons for them. My father wants what is best for the Agarwal Nation and is willing to overlook your attempt to murder me," an irritable and fatigued Greg answered.

"I have been assured no Zircon soldier was involved." The Count's remark got a snort of disbelief from both Laredo sons.

The Devil's Spawn

Shaking his head, Greg asked, "My father needs to know if what you plan has any chance of successedingl. He cannot afford to make enemies of the Ichneumons."

After an annoyed look at the two Laredo sons, the Count spoke. "I seriously doubt you or your father have the expertise to judge a Zircon army battle plan. However, since you are here, Lieutenant Bär will explain the part of the army's plan that concern your men so that you may pass the information to your father."

Greg colored a bit, clearly angered by the remarks, but said nothing and after a moment the lieutenant spoke.

"The entrance to the storm sewer we plan to use is less than four hundred meters from the north wall of the fort. Fortunately, none of the fort's cannons pointed in that direction, but we can all agree the Ichneumons will discover our mining attempt and attack." Bär's audience nodded in agreement as he continued.

"The difficulty is having to carry the explosives four hundred meters while crawling through a narrow pipe to the planned mine location under the north fort wall. Even using twenty of our troopers to convey the boxes of explosives to the location will take hours. During that period, half of our most effective fighters in the valley will be in the tunnel."

"That is why the army needs your father's help," the Count said to Greg.

The plan the lieutenant outlined was a gift to the Laredo tribe if Belcher was stupid enough to follow it. Greg wondered who had thought up the harebrained scheme. Once the Zircons were in the sewer, killing them would be easy. He needed to encourage the foolish plan. "That is a good plan if my father will supply sufficient men to discourage Colonel Kropp from attacking and stop them if they do."

About then, Bari Lu, dressed in a clean white linen shift dress entered the tent with glasses of red wine on a large tray. As she served

229

each of them a glass, Greg studied her. He had to admit she was not a bad looking bitch and that probably accounted for the Zircons allowing her to hideout in their camp. Handing him a delicate small wine glass, she looked directly at him, a fearless perusal with a hint of satisfaction that had him wondering. Could she have been the one who crippled him? His stoicism and injuries restrained his response to a nod acknowledgment. One day at a time, he thought. First help the Ichneumons run the Zircons out of the valley, then deal with the bitch and get his answers. She left after passing out the wine, which Greg did not drink.

Zack then addressed their father's key concern. "Have you discussed with General Markel the appointment of my father as Uneeda's chief?"

"Yes," the Count lied. The army would have the fort and gold before the chief learned he would be lucky to avoid prison if Captain Belcher had his way. Instead, he said. "General Markel was pleased to learn of your father's willingness to serve the people. You do understand the gold we recover in the fort belongs to the emperor?"

"All of it?" Zack asked, thinking that was no way for partners to operate, even though he knew his father planned to ambush the Zircons while they were in the sewer.

"Resolving that and those other questions," the Count said while glancing at the lieutenant, "requires your father since you cannot answer them. He needs to meet with me and explain his plans for Uneeda after the evil bastards are gone." The aristocrat paused. Greg wondered if the man realized that last demand might queer the deal, but the aristocrat then added a worse demand. "The last item for your father is which of you will be the hostage to guarantee your warriors do not turn tail."

Captain Maqbool escaped the bog and Zircon pursuers because Sergeant Rakesh volunteered to remain behind and ambush them. Reporting in, he was disappointed to learn from Colonel Kropp that Corporal Guru's shot had only wounded Captain Belcher.

"Two good men died and all that was accomplished was wounding the bastard," Maqbool muttered.

"What's that?" the colonel asked. Maqbool just shook his head and after a moment Kropp said, "Cheer up, captain, it worked. Count Laumeister is in charge and Chief Laredo is meeting with the aristocrat tomorrow to finalize the sharing of our gold."

His boss chuckled over that and then added, "Remember, no Ichneumons can be seen talking with the Agarwal warriors or the Laredo men. The Zircon spies will be watching for anything suspicious."

Maqbool thought the Zircons are idiots to trust the chief. But though skeptical, he hoped they did, for the Ichneumon hold on Uneeda was becoming precarious. The last mission had cost him two of his best men.

Captain Belcher and Herr Odrick with four troopers had left the camp several hours before the Count's meeting with the Laredo sons. He figured the chief had sent his sons to assess whether he could safely attend a meeting in the Zircon camp. Al expected the meeting would achieve nothing but left Lieutenant Bär with instructions to watch the Count. If the aristocrat tried to commit them to some foolishness with Laredo, he should respectfully decline to act on it.

Al, whose recent wounds in his butt and ribs were aggravated by the joshing from the saddle, was wondering by the end of the first day, when some chemist on Erden would invent a better pain pill to replace that nasty black willow extract the army used for minor pains. The purpose of his trip to Chief Mantas's ranch was to ask the Eastern Oztec Nation for their assistance in securing Uneeda and routing the Ichneumon army. The chief had already provided half a dozen men, but Al needed more. He also wanted Mantas's permission to propose him to General Markel as the leader of the new Uneeda council that would govern the new territory. Late in the evening of the second day, they reached Mantas's log home.

The next day, after a large breakfast provided by the chief, Al explained Chief Laredo's offer to switch sides and his concerns. "I don't trust the chief. His primary income is from selling his captives as slaves. And he is a tyrant."

"It is worse than that," Mantas said. "The main buyers of Laredo's slaves are the Ichneumons and Bergdorf's mine. Why would he attack his buyers?"

The chief's response cheered Al, for it confirmed his initial opinion that the Eastern Oztec chief was a decent human being. "Well," he said. "That is true, but Bergdorf is friendly, talks against putting the chief in charge, and of supporting our effort."

"Just because he is another Zircon, don't think he is a friend," the chief snapped. "A malicious predator hides behind that amiable persona. Bergdorf's cruel and heartless treatment of his workers requires a steady supply of slaves to replace the dead ones to keep his blood gold operation running. His mining method is not practical without those helpless captives that Laredo and his henchmen provide." Al knew that and realized the miner's pleasant demeanor had clouded his judgment. Mantas had another matter to discuss.

"For the record I and my people consider Bergdorf's gold to belong to the families that lost sons and daughters to the mine's slavers."

Al shrugged, "I don't have a problem with that." He figured the emperor would settle that matter when the time came and changed topic. "I was hoping you could enlighten me on just how formidable a force Laredo has. Do you view him a threat to your nation?"

"The Western Oztec Nation out number us about two to one." Al figured his concerns must have shown, for the chief added, "The

232

numbers are misleading because fewer than half the western subchiefs wants anything to do with Laredo." That was news to Al, and he asked Mantas to explained.

"The subchiefs that support Laredo are the ones that raid us and the other western tribes for captives and booty. I figure he has about two hundred warriors that will answer his call."

"That is an impressive force. Why do you suppose he has not used them to help the Ichneumons?"

"The real war leader of the group was Greg Laredo. He had about seven or eight subchiefs that would do anything he requested. I don't know how you managed to accomplish killing that monster, but thankfully you did."

Al suspected Bari had shot Greg and preferred Laredo's vengeance be directed at him and not the Lu women. Shaking his head, he explained, "Unfortunately, the sniper was not successful. Two days ago, Greg attended a meeting with the Count and though I heard he was crippled by the sniper, the man is still very much alive and dangerous."

"That is an unlucky break for us," the chief said with a frustrated sigh before continuing. "Chief Laredo is dependent on Greg's band of murderous subchiefs who, like sergeants to your army, control the men. I think if something happened to Greg and the chief, I could unite the nations and end raids as well as slavery." That answered Al's question on whether Mantas was willing to serve as the new territory's chief.

No surprise, Chief Laredo had an informant in Chief Mantas's tribe who passed on news of his meeting with the Zircons. The rumored purpose of the meeting was a request for warriors to aid the Zircon attack on Uneeda. Laredo had expected the Zircons to reach out to the Eastern Oztec Nation for men and that did not worry him. The easterners were a bunch of farmers that never could protect themselves from raids by his men.

What did worry Laredo was Mantas's talk of uniting the dissatisfied Western Oztec subchiefs with his Eastern council of subchiefs. If the Zircons turned to that farmer, Mantas, as the Oztec nations leader, his dream of ruling the territory might not come to fruition, and that was unacceptable. The Ichneumons and he needed to defeat Belcher's small force then he could eliminate that upstart Chief Mantas. Later when the Zircons finally moved on the Ichneumons, he could make a deal with General Markel to betray the fort.

For the Ichneumons to defeat Belcher's force, he needed to convince the captain he had their back when they entered the sewer to mine the fort wall. By trapping part of the Zircon force in the sewer, the fort's garrison should have no problem eliminating the rest of Belcher's recon squad. He liked the plan, but Greg, though he also liked the plan, thought the Zircon captain was not serious. The man was just letting that aristocrat entertain himself with dreams of recovering gold for the emperor while Belcher tried to find more allies. But that hostage requirement now had his father convinced the Zircons were serious.

Unlike his son, the chief believed that in the Zircon empire, aristocrats like Count Laumeister held the real power, made the decisions. If he could convince him the Laredo tribe would protect their miners, the Count would order the captain to implement the plan.

Agreeing on the location for their meeting required a day of exchanging notes. The Zircon army did not want to risk seizure of their aristocrat as a hostage by the Ichneumons and would not consider any location but their stronghold. The chief still blamed the attempt on his son's life on Captain Belcher and he worried the Count's insistence on a one-on-one meeting with no witnesses might allow the Zircons to seize him as a hostage. Greg resolved the matter by explaining to his father that if he were not willing to trust the Zircons enough to meet the Count in the North River Stronghold, why would the Zircons ever trust them to protect their men while in the culvert? The chief agreed to meet at the Zircon stronghold.

The small number of Zircon soldiers guarding the large gray tent erected just outside the stronghold cheered Chief Laredo. His warriors outnumbered the Zircons three to one around the tent where Count Laumeister waited with the engineer Lieutenant Bär. The lack of refreshments other than tea and coffee set the pragmatic tenor of the meeting. The Zircon aristocrat started the meeting by asking the army officer with him to explain the planned mining of the culvert and the need for sufficient warriors to protect the miners from the expected counterattack from the fort.

"Why not use your own troops for that?" the chief asked the Count.

"The goal of the mine is to breech the fort's wall and that requires having a forlorn hope squad ready to exploit the opening. I need trained soldiers for that murderous initial assault."

That information gave the chief pause. The whole scheme he had cooked up with the fort commander involved not allowing the wall to be breeched while trapping half the Zircon soldiers in the sewer and joining the Ichneumon counterattack on the remaining Zircon force. News of a special assault squad waiting nearby for the wall rupture alarmed him. If those enemy soldiers realized his men were killing their comrades in the sewer, they could respond against his warriors before the fort's soldiers could come to his aid. The count unaware of his concern asked if he had any other questions for the engineer. He shook his head and the lieutenant left.

After that and a break to pour a fresh cup of coffee, the Count said, "Your oldest son explained what you expect for assisting in the defeat of those evil bastards. General Markel has agreed to appoint

235

you ruler of Uneeda until the people have an opportunity to form a government." The Count's smirk after sprouting that last part of foolishness convinced the chief the aristocrat shared his disdain for allowing the common folks to manage their own affairs.

"Greg said you will claim the gold found in the fort," the chief countered, figuring the Count's main interest was who ended up with the gold.

"For the emperor," the Count quickly answered. Misreading the chief's look, he added, "Who knows how much will be discovered?"

The chief thought, no way this peacock will ever touch any of that gold unless he supported Laredo tribe's claim to Uneeda, and he changed the subject.

"What about that ranch my tribe seized? Is that an issue?" He knew that was a serious matter with that damn Belcher.

"That is the type of issues best settled by the new administration that will run Uneeda," the Count responded

His remark made the chief smile and the meeting broke up with the agreement the Zircons would pick the day for the assault and provide two-day notice to his son, Greg, who would coordinate with Captain Belcher's replacement. Later that evening the chief realized the Count never mentioned the hostage.

Al did not share Chief Laredo's low opinion of the eastern Oztecs's fighting ability. Their problem was they lacked the military training and discipline required during an organized assault against an entrenched enemy or to survive an ambush. They were hunters, who if properly armed with a good rifle and positioned behind a barricade could be an effective force. Whether they would respond favorably to Zircon army discipline he would soon learn. Mantas's twenty warriors that returned with Al to the Zircon camp he assigned to Sergeant Duncan and his men for training and supplies.

The Devil's Spawn

While Duncan got busy incorporating the new recruits into the army, Al went looking for Lieutenant Bär to learn how the meeting between the chief and Count ended. He wanted to know where matters stood. Instead, Sergeant Gunther and Corporal Ackerman found him. The stout middle-aged sergeant caught Al's attention with shout from the dock area. A sternwheeler had quietly arrived while he was looking for Lieutenant Bär. He recognized it, the Clovis Belle, an old paddle wheel river boat that had two coal barges. Heavy canvas tarps covered both barges to shield the nature of their cargo and, even better, the general had apparently sent another squad of troopers with the cargo.

He went to greet his friends whom he had first encountered during the assault on Hickory Ridge three years ago. For a month, Al, the corporal, and Sergeant Gunther had commanded the enemy's abandoned battery of heavy mortars that had later allowed General Markel to successfully with stand repeated attempts by the Ichneumon army to recapture the critical fort. Hickory Ridge controlled the Upper Erie River Valley and the critical resupply rail connection across the East Mountains to the main ocean port at New Hamburg.

A cheerful Sergeant Gunther waited for him at the wooden wharf with a half dozen men. After introductions the sergeant, pointing toward the barges, said, "I have three siege mortars and plenty of shells. You get me and my crew to within a couple of kilometers of the fort and I'll turn it into dust."

That was no idle boast, Al knew. The problem was the mortar weight made moving and maneuvering the powerful weapon difficult. Its maximum effective bombardment range of a couple of kilometers required placing the weapon close to the target exposing the crew to sudden raids and cannon fire. Still, they offered a better solution than crawling through a sewer guarded by untrustworthy allies.

Al called his key people together for a war council. Sergeant Jones and Duncan, Corporal Williams and Ackerman, Bill Walker, captain of the Mischief, Lieutenant Bär, the rancher Herr Odrick, Jose, Dr. Sebastian, and Bari Lu gathered behind the north stronghold for the meeting. The discussion concerned the enemy's next move. Al opened the meeting.

"I've been fighting those devils long enough to know Ichneumons like Captain Maqbool will attack. The real question is whether his colonel will allow him ten men or 120 men for a decisive attack in force on our stronghold. Jose's spy tells him Chief Laredo has pledged a hundred warriors to help the Ichneumon army."

Bill, sounding disappointed, said, "I thought the chief was on our side."

"The chief's only concern is himself. I abandoned the idea of mining the old sewer after Duncan and I inspected the sewer. I used the Count's meetings with the Laredo chiefs to gain time to organize the ranchers and Eastern Oztecs. I also hoped the promised support in heavy weapons would arrive before the Ichneumons lost patience in their attempt to lure us into the sewer." Then, pointing at Gunther, he added in a loud jubilant voice, "And by god, Sergeant Gunther and his mortars arrived this morning."

The men cheered his news as the Count and Captain Reed joined the meeting. He learned the late arrivals had heard him say he did not plan to mine the fort wall or enter the sewer.

"The chief will join the Ichneumons," the astonished aristocrat charged. "We'll be outnumbered and overrun. You'll lose Uneeda."

"Yes, we will be outnumbered. Our spies say Chief Laredo's warriors and Ichneumons are planning an attack with two hundred men. I figure most, if not all, the Agarwal warriors and the thirty or so of Maqbool's men will mount a massive cavalry attack trying to turn about our north flank to get behind our redan by the river road to block our retreat and seize our boats. Not sure if they'll bring cannons and the Comet into the battle."

Sergeant Duncan spoke up. "You're asking a lot to expect twenty men to stop a charge of two hundred horses. And a couple of cannons would make quick work of reducing the redan to a pile of dirt and scattered timbers."

With a confident nod and smile to the worried Duncan, Al said, "The sergeant raises good points. He's right. If we try to defend the redan, the bastards will overwhelm us. So, we won't. I will meet with each of you in private after the meeting to explain your part in the plan."

Greg Laredo met with Maqbool at the entrance to the sewer. "Captain Reed said the Zircon captain blocked my father's deal with Count Laumeister." After a laugh Greg added, "Never thought they were that stupid. So, what's your plan?"

Maqbool knew about the heavy mortars and realized they had to strike before the Zircons managed to position those weapons within range of the fort. "Assemble all our forces and attack the Zircon camp, kill them, and seize or burn their boats."

"Why should my father get involved?"

He wanted to snap, "To save his sorry-ass life," but instead answered, "Chief Mantas. If the Zircon army wins, the Laredo tribe is out and the Eastern Oztec tribe will rule the Agarwal Nation. But you know that, so let us not waste each other's time. Can you meet me in two days with a hundred mounted warriors ready to kill Zircons?"

Two day later, about two hours before sunrise, Maqbool and Lieutenant Xavier with fifty mounted Ichneumon soldiers between them, joined the milling mass of a 120 Agarwal riders at the river road intersection. The size of the Laredo group of warriors cheered

239

the Ichneumon officers. With any bit of luck, Maqbool thought, we should send those Zircons to hell. In locating and reaching Chief Laredo and his son Zack, he encountered several of their warriors who seemed drunk. Nothing unusual in that, he thought. He didn't approve of the practice, but he knew many soldiers liked a shot of liquid courage before a battle.

"I want to form up men now to make our charge at first light on the redan. I'll form up my men on the north side of the road if you still plan on taking the center and river side."

About then one of the subchiefs rode over with a dripping battered tin bucket full of foaming liquid and a grimy ceramic cup. "Chief, this is good cider." He offered a briming cup-full to Laredo, who accepted it and drank it in one long drink.

"Damn that is good stuff," the chief said, wiping his mouth with his arm. "Try some captain, it'll settle your nervousness."

Captain Maqbool demurred. He was not drinking a strange liquid from that filthy cup. Instead, he asked what was going on and learned the first Laredo warriors to arrive had encountered a farmer at the water-trough. The Oztec farmer had a single horse drawn wagon loaded with several wooden barrels. Barrels full of tasty hard cider, two of which Laredo's subchiefs had appropriated before allowing the man to leave for the fish market. In the melee to unload the heavy barrels they broke a wheel on the wagon, forcing the farmer to leave the broken wagon across the street from the watering trough. After receiving assurances from the subchiefs the rest of his cargo would be safe, the farmer had unhitched the horse and ridden into Uneeda to find a blacksmith and help.

Barrels, Maqbool thought, something is not right, then learned after finishing off the first barrels, they had opened the remaining cider barrels and yelled for their friends to share the windfall. Looking at the crowd of horses and unruly men around the old guard house and watering point, an irritated Maqbool remembered the Saukko mine and yelled.

"This is no time for a party, chief. It could be some Zircon trick, poison. The men need to be formed up . . ."

The guard house exploded. Rock fragments, pieces of lumber, and roofing slate rained down around him. All the explosion debris missed him and Zack, but pieces hit the chief, knocking him off his horse. The man who had the cider bucket was lying on the ground not moving, with an arm-sized shard of wood jutting from his back. The chief was on his feet holding his arm and asking what happened.

"I'd say a Zircon mine exploded. Are you okay?" Maqbool asked the chief, looking about to verify the blast had not scattered his troopers.

"I'll live," the chief answered, adding, "Greg, Zack, you two need to take charge and tell the subchiefs to organize their warriors. They need to kill Zircons. The wounded can wait."

While the chief obtained a horse, Maqbool rode over and made a quick check of the blast site. Most of the men near the barrels were dead or so severely injured they soon would be dead. The chief, now mounted, joined him.

"My left arm is broken, and I need to find a doctor." Maqbool advised him, "Go to the fort." The chief added, "I want vengeance. There are at least ninety of my men still available. With your troopers, we outnumber the Prussians." The chief's attitude cheered Maqbool. A moment later his anxious son, Zack, joined them near the still smoking blast zone and in a fretful voice, asked, "Are you Ichneumons still willing to charge?"

"Us? . . . I have been waiting on you . . ." "Clowns," he almost shouted, but he needed these savages. After a moment to calm himself, he added in an unruffled voice, "Yes, my men are ready. Your father and I are waiting on you to form up your men. We need to hit the redan together, now, before the sun clears the horizon and blinds us."

But events did not wait on them. Rifle fire near the east side of the blast zone alerted them that several Zircon cavalry men had approached the intersection. Maqbool realized what was occurring and shouted, "Those hateful bastards are shooting our men trying to untangle the unharmed horses from the dead and crippled animals. Lieutenant Xavier, go deal with those sons of bitches. Zack, get your ass in gear, we need to end this."

Al's preference was nibbling away the enemy's strength in a series of small sudden attacks and withdrawals while avoiding major engagements. His strategy ought to succeed against an Ichneumon garrison that had no hope of receiving reinforcements. Captain Maqbool's arrival had changed the dynamics. The officer had recognized that the Ichneumon garrison's best chance of defeating Al's men was to join with the hundreds of the capable Agarwal mounted warriors out for Zircon blood. Today's contest would be a bloody slugfest that Al and his men had to win.

Small groups of Agarwal warriors had been arriving all night. The dark interfered with obtaining an accurate count, but a hundred plus seemed reasonable. The number of Ichneumons present was known because Al had one of his troopers hid near the fort's gate and counted the soldiers riding out. Fifty was the number, so Colonel Kropp was making a major commitment of his remaining strength to clear the valley of Zircons who did not plan to oblige him.

Lieutenant Bär and his snappers' mine had taken a bit out of the Laredo gang. Al told the lieutenant as they watched the dust settle from the satisfying explosion, "You did well. Now I want you and your men to ride back and help defend the stronghold. I have Odrick and three of his men who volunteered to remain to help me."

The Devil's Spawn

Al and the ranchers had then ridden ahead and stopped just east of the blast area where they waited for the warriors to rush in to help survivors. Only a few men ventured into the area, the explosion had made the warriors cautions. Cries of the maimed men and animals broke the unnatural silence following the blast. Then Al heard an Ichneumon whistle and realized their cavalry was moving toward the river road, leaving the wounded Agarwal warriors for others to deal with.

"Take three carefully aimed rifle shots," Al reminded his men as the enemy horsemen came into view. "Make them count, you won't have better shots today. Then run for the stronghold. Keep your revolver handy, don't waste time trying to use a rifle while galloping on a horse." The Ichneumon cavalry, formed up three abreast, was advancing toward the river intersection, clearly not expecting Zircons so nearby.

Their fusillade unseated the three front ranks of the enemy, testimony to the excellent marksmanship of the ranchers. Thinning the enemy's numbers was one goal. The main purpose for taking the risk was to entice the Ichneumons to make a furious charge down River Road. Al's and the ranchers were successful. But luck is a fickle thing. At the two-kilometer marker they ran into another group of Laredo warriors who had cut through the north woods to reach the river road, planning on traveling up it to Uneeda, and instead had encountered Lieutenant Bär's men. The surviving warriors held their fire. Al figured they were not sure who the new riders coming from Uneeda were. To add confusion he shouted, "Have you seen any Zircons?"

A moment later the group met and Al, along with his men, fired their revolvers at can't miss range. A couple of the warriors recovered fast enough to get off several shots that hit one of the ranch hands. All the warriors were down, but Odrick had stopped to check on his man. Al shouted, "Don't stop, ride."

The Ichneumon cavalry had used the melee delay to close the distance to where they started chancing rifle shots. Whether it was Al's command or the dangerously near misses of rifle bullets, Odrick abandoned his fallen worker and joined their gallop toward the stronghold. The goal was to get the pursuing cavalry into the ambush zone two more kilometers down the road where that hedgerow Al had carried Bari's grandmother to was located. The bushy berm was located on the river side of the hundred-meter-wide bean fields that ran parallel along the river road for a kilometer. The new stronghold was several hundred meters after that on a low ridge. Scattered in the hedgerow, waiting for the pursuing enemy, were twenty riflemen and Bari. Sergeant Jones and Corporal Williams were there to supervise the placement of the volunteers. They would trigger the ambush. Sergeant Duncan with twelve mounted troopers waited north of the stronghold to stop any attempt to flank the stronghold.

The horizon was lightening. Good, Al thought, now the Ichneumons would lose their night vision advantage. Looking about he realized they were in the ambush zone. He hoped his men did not mistake them for the enemy.

Next thought Al had was what happened to his mount. The animal was down and sliding across the road with him in the air headed for the ditch. A moment later he landed hard, headfirst in a muddy ditch. He needed a moment to recover his wits. Next, he realized a horse with a rider had stopped on the road above him while other riders raced by. Not good, it had to be an Ichneumon and Al had lost his revolver. Then a single distant shot rang out and the rider was falling from his horse.

Al scrambled to his hands and knees to hunt for his revolver as intense gunfire started. Horses with riders and horses without riders were flying about as someone nearby shouted to charge the hedgerow, kill the bastards. The enemy soldier who had planned to shoot him landed dead in the ditch beside him still clinching his revolver, which

Al pried from his hand. The man was an Ichneumon officer, but now mounted Laredo warriors were riding across the ditch to join the assault on the hedgerow. Avoiding the hoofs of five-hundred-kilogram horses landing around him alerted one of the warriors to the fact he was not dead. The rider stabbed him with a lance as Al shot him. His revolver shot was lost among the ongoing gun fire from and at the hedgerow.

The spear pierced Al's foot. Then the dead rider's body fell against the protruding spear shaft twisting the spear free while tearing an excruciating rip in Al's right foot. The pain was fearsome as he tried to keep the wound clear of the mud while not to attracting attention. A dozen warriors milled about near the ditch side of the bean field, having second thoughts about joining the Ichneumon charge as the gunfire from the hedgerow had stayed steady. Then one of the warriors in the group near where Al lay in the ditch fell from his horse. That triggered an exodus of mounted men from the field and more dangerous hoofs hitting about him.

Bari had one of the few scoped rifles among the volunteers waiting in the hedgerow for the enemy. Using her rifle optics, she spotted the captain. He was the third horseman in the bait group. By swinging her rifle toward Uneeda, she could see the lead riders of Ichneumon cavalry chasing Captain Belcher and Odrick's men. A couple of hundred meters separated the two groups, too far apart for the Ichneumons firing their rifles to have much chance of hitting the Zircons. Then she watched the captain's horse snap sideways and collapse, flinging its rider into the ditch. The type of accident that often broke a rider's neck or back, not to mention her friend now lay in the ambush zone and the enemy would be on him in moments.

"Oh god, the captain is down," Bari cried, turning toward Corporal Williams who was a few meters east of her in the hedgerow. He held a finger to his lip to be silent. The agreed plan was the

245

corporal would tell them when to trigger the ambush by firing his rifle. "What if they see him in the ditch?" she whispered.

"He'll be okay," the corporal answered, then addressed the others. "Everyone holds your fire, let them enter deeper into the zone, stay calm."

As he spoke, one of the Ichneumon riders stopped where the captain lay. Bari, watching through her scope, saw the rider aim his revolver at the ditch. She shot and Williams yelled, "What the hell woman, now the bastards know our location . . ."

Then the hedgerow erupted as twenty rifles fired. Only part of the enemy cavalry had entered the ambush zone. The Ichneumons recognized what was occurring and turned and charged across the bean field toward the hedgerow to scatter and kill their ambushers.

Bari figured later she accounted for five of the hits, but those ranchers and stray volunteers made her proud. None of them ran and all made effective use of those bolt action, magazine-fed rifles the captain had supplied. Laredo's warriors had arrived late for the Ichneumon assault on the hedgerow. Then when the defenders' unwavering aimed rifle fire shattered their and the Ichneumon cavalry assault, littering the bean field with dead and wounded men and horses, the Laredo men abandoned the assault and rode north. She hoped they ran into Duncan's men.

Doctor Sebastian told Al not to whine. "If that spear had hit your lower spine instead of your foot, you might be dead."

"Lucky me. Your stitching, it feels like you're using hemp rope for the suture material."

For sure he would not be hiking for a while. Regardless, the bean field battle had dealt a serious blow to the Ichneumon garrison. He had eighteen identification medallions recovered from dead Ichneumon soldiers left on the field. One tag was for a commissioned officer, Lieutenant Xavier. According to Sergeant Duncan, several of the Ichneumons who had escaped appeared wounded. And he remembered the initial exchange of gunfire at the road intersection; several of those cavalry riders fell off their mount like they were dead or seriously injured. Adding up the numbers, Al figured the Ichneumon garrison had lost a couple of dozen soldiers. Laredo's warriors had taken a serious hit too. The chief had lost sixteen men in the bean field and, another five in their encounter with Duncan, along with an unknown number killed in the spring house blast.

The morning fighting had been costly for the Zircon soldiers and Uneeda ranchers, with five Zircon soldiers dead along with seven of the volunteers and twelve others of Al's men wounded. His men had held the field against what Al suspected was the Ichneumons' last offensive action. He hoped Colonel Kropp would wait in the fort for relief from Delta. Chief Laredo would retreat to the Lu farm to lick his wounds, but soon be back and up to some mischief. He needed to take the fort.

Chapter 17

Bergdorf paid their camp a visit the morning after the bean field confrontation. Probably to spy and learn how the Prussians had fared. Count Laumeister was with the miner and going on about how they had kicked some serious ass yesterday. After a miserable night and a painful time using the latrine, Al was in no mood for visitors or idle gossip. How to exploit their success and finish off the Ichneumon garrison was his focus. Thinking the miner might have some useful information, Al invited him into the large army tent located in a grove of white pines behind the hospital tent near where the Mischief and Thumper docked on the north shore.

"Uneeda folks are asking how a squad of soldiers managed to trounce a force of hundreds of warriors and Ichneumons." Seeing Al's held up hand and head shake, Bergdorf change topic. "Don't want to talk about it, okay. The other reason for my visit is Chief Laredo asked me to tell you he's willing to join forces with you to defeat the Ichneumons and would like a meeting." The Count was nodding his head in agreement with the idea. Al figured Bergdorf had run the idea by him first as the Count added,

"That's great, we need the chief."

"I'm not impressed with Laredo's warriors," Al said as Bergdorf looked for a place to sit. "I did not trust the chief before and after yesterday, will never."

"Your foot might not agree," the miner said in a jolly way and remained standing.

The pair were annoying Al with their jovial air. "You need to be careful promoting traitorous schemes. Spies get hanged in war time."

The miner jerked his head back, startled, and after a moment in a subdued voice said, "I was trying to be helpful."

"Really? Many good people, Agarwal warriors included, died yesterday because of that greedy fool. If he is ready to vacate the Lu farm and stop slave raids, then I might spare his life."

"Don't throw away this opportunity," the Count said throwing up his hands. "You need him. With the chief's support, you can starve the garrison into surrendering. Think of the gold in that fort, you would be a hero. Hell, the general would make you a colonel."

The Devil's Spawn

"And Laredo, would be there wanting credit and petitioning to be named head of the Uneeda Territory. Our men are not dying to replace one monster with another one. Now leave, I have work to do." The shocked look on the aristocrat's face at his dismissal almost made Al forget his sore foot.

The next day there was an early morning meeting at the Uneeda garrison. Colonel Kropp had just ripped Captain Cortazzo over his failure to integrate the survivors of Lieutenant Xavier cavalry troop into the police force.

"The days of cavalry charges are over. If that Zircon bastard knew how dreadful things were, he'd be at the fort's gates. Get those men organized to guard the fort and town," the colonel yelled. Captain Cortazzo fled. The colonel wondered to himself how that fool ever made captain. A minute later, Captain Maqbool entered and reported. Unlike the police captain, the captain was an effective officer.

"Learn any more on the Zircons casualties?"

"Nothing solid, Bergdorf paid them a visit with Laredo's offer and asked around. He said the militia number is growing and all the people he usually saw at such get togethers were there. Captain Belcher was wounded but in charge."

Kropp asked how Laredo's offer went over.

"Belcher threatened to hang him if he brought anymore dumb ideas to him," Maqbool said with a frown. "He listed the conditions Belcher wanted to spare the chief's life."

"So, it didn't go well. If I'd only known the man had a soft spot for the Lu women." The colonel shook his head in disgust, then got up and refilled his teacup, adding., "Some hot tea, captain?"

"A cup would be good. I'll pay our chief a visit this afternoon, get his read, but I don't think the Zircons will trust him."

249

David C. Brown

"I agree, so let's talk about something that might happen," the colonel said replacing the pot on the desk. "I fear the Zircons may succeed in taking this fort. I will stay and fight to the end, should that happen. I have a different mission for you, prevent the Zircons from seizing our gold."

"I'm not sure what you're asking. The Zircons have the river closed unless we can capture the stronghold. As you asked, I went to Silver Ridge to check on caravans across the high passes. The only route that might lead to Delta requires crossing two passes, both over 8,500 meters elevation. Our men can't manage such high altitude, only a few Oztecs can. And they're all bandits. Are you thinking of burying the gold out in the forest?"

"How would the location be kept secret?" the colonel asked, while rolling a small iron cannonball back and forth on his desk. Maqbool recognized it as one of those iron balls the Zircon boat had shot into the fort last week.

"Short of killing everyone afterward who helped with the relocation, you wouldn't."

"That's about how I see it. If one person got away, in time the Zircons would have the gold. Our choices are beat the Zircons or dump the gold in the deep part of the lake where no one could recover it."

"We're not beaten yet. Until the Zircons can bring the fort under mortar fire, they can't take the fort. Captain Cortazzo needs to patrol the area around the fort where a mortar could be placed."

"Tell him what you want," the commander said. Maqbool's comments had brighten his mood and he asked, "Do you know a Captain Reed?"

"I know of the Rouser. He's the captain of that sternwheeler."

"Bergdorf told me the man's a pirate and can be bought. Could you use him to reach Belcher?" the colonel asked.

The Devil's Spawn

Maqbool rubbed the back of his neck as he considered the information. "Trying to assassinate Belcher in camp is a suicide mission. Guys like Reed wouldn't be interested in that, but he might be interested in kidnapping the young Lu woman, who we could then use for bait to lure our nemesis into a trap."

Al, on reflection, decided Chief Laredo's offer to switch sides was not a repeat of his earlier attempt the lure the Zircons into dropping their guard, but signified the weasel feared he had backed the wrong side. That suggested the Ichneumons had suffered serious losses. The hang up was that no human, Bergdorf included, knew for sure what remained of the Ichneumon garrison's will and ability to resist. The Uneeda fort was no longer a sanctuary. It was about to become a trap thanks to Sergeant Gunther's mortars. The man had refitted the coal barge to hold two mortars and wanted to use the Mischief to push the barge into position.

Time for the final push, Al decided, and he went to Sergeant Gunther, who had been studying the fort layout.

"Good news boss," the sergeant greeted him. Al knew the old NCO had little use for military conventions. "I discovered the fort's front wall and the platform the cannons are mounted on blocks the cannons from being able to shell vessels with in a hundred meters of the shore. If you put soldiers in those buildings between the fort and lake shore to repel riflemen from the fort, my crew will be safe parked just offshore behind those buildings. Well, at least long enough to destroy the front wall and main gate. Might even get lucky and hit the fort's magazine."

To Al's pleasant surprise Duncan, Lieutenant Bär, and Bill all liked Gunther's plan and put it into play. Al's wound handicapped him, but with a horse he'd manage.

Three hours before sunrise tomorrow the Mischief would push the gun platform into position and anchor it, then run by the

251

dock area and sink the Comet before moving out of rifle fire range. Lieutenant Bär's crew would use the two 40mm guns to support Duncan and Gunther's men. Al's main worry was the hospital and camp would be lightly guarded when Duncan's crew left for the Uneeda assault. Then Captain Reed, who had rejected past attempts to use the empty rooms on his riverboat for care of the wounded, reconsidered and offered the use of Rouser's rooms and even to haul the gravely wounded to the Westport hospital.

Bari liked that idea of evacuating the wounded to Westport and offered to go with them. Captain Reed would embark after the medics delivered the wounded to his riverboat. That lessened Al's concerns about the enemy raiders slipping by him and slaughtering everyone at the camp hospital while they attacked the fort tomorrow. The Mischief would deal with tomorrow's casualties from the fort assault.

Al intended to end this fight today and had left only two of Chief Mantas' warriors to guard the camp and backup Lieutenant Duffield and his three men. The lieutenant had a serious leg wound but chose to remain. Bari went with the wounded on Reed's riverboat.

An hour before sunrise Al and thirty of his and Odrick's men quietly infiltrated the buildings along the shoreline. Sergeant Williams, whom Al had promoted, had gone ahead to silence the two Ichneumons who were patrolling the beach area. Then Al heard the Mischief.

The Ichneumon soldiers on the fort's front wall had too. With their much better night vision, the guards had spotted the steamboat out on the lake and started sounding an alarm bell. Then within moments, to Al's astonishment, the fort fired a cannon at the Mischief with its mortar barge. He had been setting up a sniper nest with another trooper at one of the upper story window openings across from the fort's front gate. He dashed through the building's trashed

252

up hallways to the lake side window to check on the Mischief and heard a second cannon fire. He was in time to witness the iron ball ripping off the upper part of the boat's smokestack and land with a large splash fifty meters out in the lake beyond the boat. The Ichneumon gunners had become organized he realized.

The Mischief's 40mm gun crew fired several shots toward the fort's cannons before the shore building blocked the gun's view of the fort. Then Bill's crew was busy unhooking the mortar barge as it pushed it into position a dozen meters from the rocky lake shore. The cannons fired again. Their iron shot mading impressive but harmless fountains of water out in the lake past the barge, proving Sergeant Gunther's prediction that the fort's layout and front wall prevented the cannons from being able to fire at that spot.

After parking Gunther's mortar barge in position, Bill kept the Mischief close to the shore as it ran toward the fish market to stay blind to the fort's cannons. The 40mm crew used the opportunity to set fire the Comet and Velasquez's wharf area. Bill's maneuver worked, the cannons stopped, and Al rushed back to the front window in time to see a swarm of Ichneumon soldiers pouring out of the fort. The enemy clearly knew of the mortars and correctly understood the barge's purpose.

"Don't let them reach the lake," Al yelled, and went to check on his other men.

A blast of light and noise followed a moment later by an intense explosion announced the start of the bombardment. Gunther's crew quickly settled into a shot every minute, which within a brief time reduced the front wall and gate to smoking rubble. During that time Al and his men engaged in a murderous room-to-room fight with a squad of Ichneumons that had rushed into the building. Their intent was reaching locations where they could use rifle fire to kill the mortar crew the cannons could not reach. Al would not allow that, and a violent fight raged through out the lake front buildings.

While that bloody room-to-room fight was occurring Sergeant Gunther had switched aim to lop bombs into the tower and main building area. About a half hour after the start of the bombardment, one of the mortar shells triggered a powerful explosion that resulted in a shower of debris and the toppling of the fort's central tower. The main magazine exploding, Al reckoned, after the debris ceased falling, some pieces even landed in the lake near the barge. He limped to the building roof for a better view of the fort and where he could see Gunther. The east horizon was red, the sun would be up in few more minutes. The interior of the fort was a burning wreck. The battle for protecting the mortar crew ended shortly after when the Ichneumon captain went down, and his two surviving soldiers surrendered.

Al's men had beaten the Uneeda Ichneumons, but the fort rubble would offer plenty of hiding places for any enemy soldiers still alive and wanting to fight. The Zircon attack had breached the fort and shattered the Ichneumon garrison, but Al worried if he had enough men to finish the conquest of Uneeda Territory. Hostile forces surrounding the Zircons would attack if they sensed a weakness. The Laredo gang and the Velasquez band of pirates were all threats. And then there was the rumored gold hoard in that pile of rubble that would attract dangerous men. That meant he now needed the fort. To stop more destruction, he fired two red flares, signals for the mortar crew to stop shelling and for the Mischief to return. They were not secure yet, but in a much better position than their enemy.

By eleven o'clock the Zircon soldiers were in control of the fort. Fourteen Ichneumon prisoners awaited their fate in the shade along the fort's east wall. The troopers had secured the prisoners using the slave neck collars and chain found in the stable. Several officers were among the prisoners, a colonel, captain, and a lieutenant. Al had expected around one hundred of the enemy, so either there were a lot of bodies hiding, buried in the rubble, or escaped. The rubble from the collapsed tower and the magazine crater debris had buried the entrance to the fort's underground storage and dungeon area. Burning debris littered the area. A layer of yellowish dust and ash covered every surface and coated the men.

Al's wound kept him from going with Duncan to place the Zircon flag on top of the rubble pile that had been fort's main tower. Lieutenant Bär and his crew were busy placing one of the 40mm guns in a redoubt hastily constructed in the rubble pile that had been the lake side wall and main gate. The magazine explosion had damaged the fort's west wall, but it still stood. The north wall by the old school and the east wall were undamaged and Zircon soldiers now patrolled the parapets. The gold was safe for the moment.

The next item on Al's list was having Gunner move his two mortars into the fort while assigning men to organize a search of all the nooks and crannies for surviving enemy soldiers and slaves. Once he was convinced his men had the place secured, the camp at the mule farm would temporarily be reestablished within the fort. Then there was the question of what to do with the prisoners. Herr Odrick's one request of Al when he agreed to lead the militia was that the officers involved in the Seth massacre face justice.

"Who is the senior officer?" Al asked the group of prisoners.

The oldest Ichneumon wearily grunted, "I am, Colonel Kropp, the Uneeda commander." The cut and bandaged exhausted prisoner remained seated against the wall. After a defiant look, he added, "Since you bastards always shoot prisoners, how about getting on with it and spare me your gloating."

"Is Colonel Gupta present?" Several of the prisoners shook their head without making eye contact. The colonel, shaking his head in a weary manner answered.

"He's buried somewhere in the rubble."

"How about Lieutenant Halona?" No one spoke, but a few of the prisoners looked toward the man dressed in a tattered officer's blouse. Al asked the man if he was the lieutenant, and he wearily nodded his head. "Sergeant Williams escort that prisoner to Herr Odrick."

After the sergeant unchained and dragged Halona unwillingly to his feet and marched him off, Al asked for Captain Maqbool. The solider with whom he had been in a vicious, no hold barred fight in the shoreline brick building spoke. "I agree with my commander, spare us your bullshit and finish the job."

"All at the proper time. Now you folks are going to help with clearing the entrance into the storage rooms and dungeon."

The Mischief returned from taking the morning's wounded to the camp's hospital at the mule farm. The first person off the riverboat was Count Laumeister.

"Congratulations, captain, you managed the impossible. I sent a request by way of Captain Reed's ravens to Colonel Haddad informing him of your victory. I also explained the need for auditors and an armed navy ship to take possession of the gold hoard we expect to find here." By then they had reached the fort and the aristocrat paused to look about. "My god, you destroyed the fort. Look at that crater, is the gold safe? Have your men found the gold?"

"No. Our focus is repairing the fort sufficiently to offer a safe place from which to operate and finish flushing out hidden Ichneumons." Several muffled gunshots from the rubble of the west stables indicated the enemy was still fighting and a danger. Al pointed toward the whisps of black smoke coming from the rubble, where he thought the entrance to the dungeon was located. "Those deep smoldering fires and not knowing what other munitions were stored in those underground rooms mean the search won't start until the fires burn out."

The Devil's Spawn

Captain Reed had to be involved, Bari realized. Knockout drops of some sort were in that cup of tea they had shared in the Rouser pilot house while waiting for the crew to unload several small crates of freight at Seth. They had been on their return from delivering the Zircon soldiers wounded in the Uneeda battle to Westport's military hospital. The navy riverboat, The Ray, had gone on with the army's accountants who would oversee the gold bullion transfer at the Ichneumon fort.

Someone had wrapped her in a tarp and tied it on a mule. Based on the overheard conversations, her kidnappers were several Laredo warriors. If her abduction was Chief Laredo's attempt to have a bargaining chip with Captain Belcher, she might live. If this was Greg Laredo's doings, a horrible fate awaited her. And what of Freda, did she escape?

Al was delighted when one of those new navy riverboats arrived in Uneeda and Captain Max Groesbeck, General Markel's senior quartermaster accountant, disembarked. He knew the captain from the Erie Railroad Spur project and that the man had a sterling reputation for integrity. Count Laumeister was proper but not friendly in welcoming Max. In the brief meeting they agreed the work of recovering the gold bars in storage would start in the morning. After the accountant left to find quarters for his crew the Count asked Al to remain.

"Bergdorf is kicking up a fuss over the no-slave law. He is threatening to close the mine and turn loose a hundred former slaves. Chief Laredo says he will kill any ex-slave that enters his land. Now your pal Chief Mantas has taken over to the Uneeda courthouse and police station. He acts like he is the boss, not the army. Laredo had expected the job."

"Yeah, well fxxk the son of a bitch. If he doesn't behave, I'll arrest him." Al glanced toward the prisoners working on clearing rubble. At least that seemed to be working, but what to do with those Ichneumons was unresolved. Most people wanted them dead.

"There will be a civil war between Oztec tribes if you and the army don't take control," The Count said, forgetting he was the one making promises to that bastard.

"Laredo should be thankful he is not in jail. His sons and warriors fought with the Ichneumons. As far as I am concerned, he is the enemy. Why do you care what that backstabbing weasel wants?"

The Count got defensive and held up his hands. "Whoa, man, I know the chief is treacherous, but we don't need a new war. And why let any Oztecs run Uneeda? The Zircon army should run this territory until the emperor can appoint a new council."

"Well, keep in mind Oztecs make up most of the territory's population. I asked our ally Chief Mantas, to take charge of the Uneeda civilian government and police. He knows most of the subchiefs and he knows the first council will be appointed by the emperor."

The aristocrat grudgingly acknowledged Al's plan made sense. He agreed to visit Bergdorf and ask him not to make any drastic changes until the army had Uneeda settled, and they could talk.

The slothfulness of Captain Reed's men searching for her saved Freda. She had been playing with the two ravens caged on top of the Rouser's pilot house when she heard the captain tell Jake, his main man, to find the brat and drown her. She had never liked the sly man but figured she had misunderstood. He could not be serious. Bari would never allow that.

The commotion from the arrival of several Laredo warriors with their zig zag face tattoos at the Seth wharf caused her to pause in going to find Bari. Captain Reed had hustled down the stairs from the pilot house to greet the warriors. Two crew members carrying a wrapped bundle emerged from the cabin section of the boat where the room she and Bari shared was located. The sight alarmed Freda.

The older warrior handed the captain a small leather bag that he opened to examine the contents. After a moment, he said. "Tell Greg to enjoy his wildcat."

Over the next couple of minutes, Freda watched and listened as the warriors and crew members worked at loading and securing the squirming bundle on a mule. As the warriors rode off, she heard the captain order his men to find the girl, her. What to do? She needed to find Captain Belcher. He would know how to save Bari. While Freda considered her options, the riverboat headed up the river. She knew the boat was the fastest means to reach Uneeda, and she settled down behind the cage. If the search reached here, she could always jump and swim to the shore. She would rather chance being someone's dinner than let those hateful people catch her.

The search never amounted to much, at least no one ever came to check the ravens. The following morning, she awoke to see the approaching Uneeda dock and a grinning Jake looming over her. Freda never hesitated. She leaped up as the man grabbed at her shirt which thankfully just ripped, freeing her to dive off. Unfortunately, the jerk ripping the shirt caused her to clip the handrail on the lower deck as she fell and caused her to land close to the boat. If the pilot had not stopped the paddle wheel to slow the boat's approach to the dock at the fish market, it would have smashed her.

Several of the crew started shooting and yelling at her, but she was a strong swimmer and the sternwheel structure blocked them from getting a clear shot. The shooting attracted soldiers from the fort, and she headed for them.

Al, expecting the arrival of the Rouser in Uneeda, had showered and put on a clean uniform to greet the returning Bari and Freda. The swimmer and rifle shots attracted his attention and he jogged over to where the swimmer would arrive. The guard on the riverboat who had shot at the swimmer had stopped after the soldiers yelled at him. A wet shivering Freda emerged from the lake yelling for him. He ran to the girl and hugged her. Instead of answering his questions she told him the captain had sold Bari to some Laredo warriors at Seth.

After taking a moment to digest Freda's startling news, he ordered Sergeant Jones who had joined him at the lake shore, to bring Reed to the fort. Freda wanted to go with the soldiers.

"No, you're the key witness. Besides, you need dry clothing," Al explained. They walked to his command tent in the fort, where she could dry off while he waited for Jones to return.

The Count who had been watching the excavation of the dungeon entrance and dreaming of wealth spotted two soldiers and Captain Reed enter the tent Belcher was using for an office. Curious, he walked over to join the meeting.

"Freda," an angry Belcher said to him on entering the tent while pointing at the young girl he had seen about the camps, "says this piece of shit sold Bari Lu to Laredo warriors."

Dismay swept through Count Laumeister as Captain Reed shook his head in denial. What had that greedy fool done? He was not privy to Penton's plans, but suspected Reed's riverboat was a critical part of whatever the criminal had planned with the gold shipment.

"Bergdorf's buyer stayed in Westport to help with the wounded," Reed answered in an exasperated voice. The man was a cool customer. He appeared amused by and dismissive of the girl's tale. "The guard thought the girl was some thieving Oztec stowaway when she ran."

"What was wrapped in the bundle you sold the warriors?" Belcher radiated violence but asked Reed in a quiet voice.

The Devil's Spawn

"That's what she's crying about?" Reed chuckled and flipped his hand in a dismissive manner. "What nonsense, the bundle was a large ice bear skin that Chief Laredo ordered I deliver. Hell, you know those valuable furs need protection, same as I'm sure you did with those silver otter skins you sold."

That Oztec girl had a stricken look. He wondered if he had a similar look. Reed, no fool, had produced a credible story, though Al did not believe his ice bear tale.

Those damn silver otter pelts, Al thought, but said, "I can't check your story now, but I know Bari planned on returning and Freda here wouldn't have boarded your shitty boat unless Bari was with her. Don't attempt to leave until I verify where Bari is."

"You can't stop me on some brat's nonsense. You don't have the authority."

"I have cannons. Do yourself a favor and let Rouser's boilers go cold, else I'll put guards on board and you in jail."

Captain Reed left with the Count, whose angry whispered remarks and behavior suggested he was concerned and believed the girl's claim. Al figured it was not over Bari's welfare, but some scheme they had to grab the gold that the Count feared might be compromised by a search for the missing woman.

Bari's abduction was due to either Reed and the schemers after the gold wanting a hold on him or Greg Laredo's desire for revenge. The involvement of the Laredo warriors made the crippled warrior his main suspect. The twisted man had decided Bari was the one who shot him, and this was his retaliation. Al was not sure where to start and went to Chief Mantas' office to seek his assistance in discovering Greg Laredo's location.

Al tried not to think what that cruel pervert human might do to her. Instead, on the walk over he attempted to justify the silver otter business. He knew Reed's comment had diminished his standing with Freda, though she said she understood.

Chapter 18

Bari, barely conscious from the lack of water and air, cried out when the spiteful kidnappers dumped her on the ground from the mule. She had lost track of time. At least two days, maybe three, she thought, as her kidnappers roughly unrolled her from the tarp. Dehydrated, she was desperate for water and crawled to the ditch near where the warriors had dumped her. The men laughed and joked about her feeble efforts. The bastards had kept her wrapped up in the tarp for the entire trip and denied her breaks. She was disgustingly soiled. Two days wrapped in her own filth accounted for not yet being gang raped.

Two of the men used their boots to shove her into the creek. Laughing, they told her to wash off, she stunk. Someone had stripped her. The icy water was reviving her, but the guards were watching her. A few glances around showed her she was in the center of a small Oztec camp of a dozen warriors. After a couple of minutes, the burly guard decided she was clean enough and dragged her over to a large oak. There he hung her by her arms from a large tree limb, leaving most of her weight still supported by her feet. Such a pretty morning to die, she thought.

Greg Laredo hobbled out of a tent and jointed the several warriors staring at her. Those animals' plan was clear to her as Greg spoke.

"Your Zircon boy couldn't kill me and now you and he are going to pay for trying to murder me."

The man looked awful. He had aged years since that day at the cabin. If only she had gone and finished the job. "Belcher's men didn't shoot you. I did."

Greg chuckled. "What nonsense, the sniper was no woman. You cannot save your lover boy. I'm going to kill him when he tries to rescue you. My men can have you tonight and I'll burn what's left of you tomorrow, bitch."

"What's the matter, chief, can't manage me, have to let your men do it?" By then hate had driven all fear from her mind and she added, "I always heard you were a limp dick, impotent bastard."

With a mean laugh, he said. "Unfortunately for you, my men aren't." That got several shouts of agreement from the men watching her as Greg, shaking his head, added, "Oh, just so you know, afterward I'll find your grandmother and that little girl and chop them up for my hogs to eat."

Her arms were numb, her throat so dry speaking was painful. She was not the only person suffering. Greg's warriors had a man spread eagle by the smaller fire pit where one of the men was pulling out red-hot embers and placing them on the man's belly. His shrieks were horrible. A half hour later the warrior who had put the embers on the tied-down man came toward her with a clay cup of water and held it for her to drink. Afterward she thanked him. He nodded and in a normal voice explained.

"I didn't want you to die before I get my turn. Sex with a corpse is no fun."

Chief Mantas had his hands full establishing law and order in Uneeda but made time for Feda and Al. "Chief Laredo must have panicked when the fort fell, knowing you would support Bari over his claim on the Lu ranch. The grandmother will be in danger."

"I've already placed her under guard. Where would Greg take Bari?"

"Since they grabbed her at Seth, I'd say Greg is using his old slave hunting camp near the Clovis territory. It's a two-day trip northeast form here. Ride through the night, you can be there by early afternoon tomorrow. My warrior Black Arrow knows the way and his skills with a bow might be handy."

Chief Mantas' helpful attitude cheered Al, but now he owed the chief.

Max Groesbeck did not want Al riding off. "Any moment the crew will uncover the room with the gold. You're the only man here that I trust. The Count is a crook, the navy captain of the Ray has a history of trouble managing petty cash, and Captain Reed is a bandit. You can't leave."

"Max, I have no choice, but I have a solution to your concerns. Give me a half hour."

Al wanted to take Duncan and Williams with him and leave Lieutenant Duffield and Kurt Bär in charge while he was gone. All the men knew and like Bari. They approved of him attempting to rescue her. Al justified his plan.

"That excavation the Ichneumon prisoners are digging has become a death trap. The tunnel could collapse at any moment."

"Solve what to do with the prisoners," Kurt said, then adding on seeing his look, "I'm joking. What's your plan?"

"I want you to place charges and collapse the narrow tunnel. Afterward, the excavation can progress with the proper side slope and not endanger the workers. Do it now, no delay, pull the men out."

"Oh man, the Count will throw a fit," Kurt said with a laugh. "Right now, right?" Al nodded and fifteen minutes later three small explosions caved the tunnel in with a cloud of dust, burying the partly exposed entrance to the dungeon again. He could hear Kurt explaining to the cursing Count the need for proper slopes to protect the workers. Groesbeck just shook his head while agreeing that reaching the gold would require several more days of digging. Captain Maqbool and his crew of prisoners looked perplexed.

Chief Mantas' information had been correct and Black Arrow's guidance dead on. Greg Laredo's camp for launching slave raids was before them. It was a modest affair of a half dozen Oztec tents constructed from old tarps and cured skins form bison and goats. Two rock-ringed fire pits were located on the southside of the tents near a large oak tree and a small spring fed stream. The creek sustained Odrick's north range pond several kilometers to the southeast. Several warriors were gathering wood and constructing what appeared to be a large bonfire. Adding to the camp's evil ambiance was a dead man staked spread eagle on the ground by one of the firepits with the smoking remains of fire on his belly.

Greg's men had suspended a nude Bari by her arms from the oak tree by the creek. The horror of the scene two hundred meters below him clashed with the good news that she was alive. How to save his friend now he had found her without getting her killed he had not resolved. Those fourteen horses and two mules in the corral behind the tents suggested there were at least ten more warriors in the tents.

The situation called for a distraction. Preferably one that did not suggest an imminent attack but would still take the guards' attention off Bari. The tall grass around the camp was dry as tinder. After a quick discussion with Black Arrow, the two warriors with him left to start several small grassfires several hundred meters up wind from the corral and camp. While waiting for Bari's kidnappers to notice grassfire, Duncan and Williams with the two soldiers conferred on which of Greg's warriors they would target for their first shot. The purpose was to avoid two of them shooting the same man in the critical initial strike. That is when Al would gallop to Bari, cut the rope, and hopefully race off with her. If not, they would take shelter by the oak and join the riflemen in shooting Greg's men.

Patience was not Al's strong point, but he forced himself and his men to wait for the grassfires to develop and their smoke to be noticeable in the camp. Two of the guards splitting logs and stacking the pieces in the large fire-pit paused to study the distance fire. After some talk among themselves, one of them went to the largest tent and entered. Less than a minute later several other men and the guards exited the tent and walked around back by the horse corral for a better view of the distant brush fire. One of them was Greg who, after a quick glance toward the grassfire, turned and scanned the ridge Al's men waited on, hidden. He was clearly suspicious.

The Devil's Spawn

Al was on his horse behind the ridge crest, and by standing in the stirrups he could see Greg through the golden rod and tall grasses that grew alone the ridge. He saw the man pull his revolver and limp toward Bari while shouting some unclear order that caused several of the warriors by the corral to start saddling their horses and four other warriors to exit the tent and look toward the ridge. Greg had decided to vacate the camp and kill Bari, or he planned to haul her to another location where he could torture her undisturbed.

The warriors were milling about putting their new orders into effect. Most if not all the Laredo warriors were outside the tents, perfect for Al's men to take down. He hesitated because Bari would be in the middle of the bullet storm, but Greg stopping in front of Bari and aiming his revolver at her decided the issue. Williams and Duncan would both have the madman in their sights. Al gave the order to fire and charged for Bari.

The Zircon gunfire had knocked Greg to his knees. A moment later he tried raising his revolver to shoot Bari, but by then Al and the roan horse had reached the campground. Yelling Greg's name caused him to turn and fire at him. Hitting a large horse and rider galloping straight at you required strong nerves. More rifle bullets hitting him and his warriors falling shot around him did not help Greg's aim as Al's horse ran right over him. Al had cleared the stirrups and landed on his feet. He gave the man a vicious slice with his razor-sharp sword as he ran the dozen meters to Bari and sliced the rope. He caught her and dived behind the oak.

Bari was alive, breathing, but unresponsive as he freed her hands, which had an alarming blackish gray appearance. Al feared he might have been too late as he checked for threats. Seeing none, he stood up and saw the few surviving Laredo warriors were fleeing north on foot toward the fire smoke to escape. Greg was dead along with several of his warriors around the firepit. He waited by Bari for his men who were just now cautiously entering the camp.

The instant Al's men secured the camp, his next order of business was making Bari comfortable and then taking her to Doctor Sebastian and her family. No, he realized she needed some sort of clothing or wrap first and thought of his bedding tied behind the saddle on the dead horse.

"Is Freda, okay?" she whispered as he returned with the blanket.

Her question cheered Al and gave him hope his love would recover and he could set about convincing her to marry him, "Yes, she is the one that told us what happen."

The return to Uneeda required an extra half day. Al rigged a travois frame to carry Bari since a wagon was not available, and injuries to her hands and shoulder joints precluded riding a horse. He had thought about riding ahead to Uneeda and arresting Captain Reed for his involvement in Bari's kidnapping but decided to remain with her until she was aboard the Mischief and under the care of Doctor Sebastian and Freda.

Sergeant Jones was the first one to greet Al and his crew on their arrival at the Zircon camp. The sergeant pulled Al to the side and told him that Captain Reed and his riverboat, Rouser, had embarked the evening before for Westport with Chief Laredo aboard. Realizing the villain had made good his escape, Al decided to spend the night on the Mischief with Bari. The next morning, he checked on her. Her hands appeared to be recovering other than for a couple of fingers that might require amputation to avoid gangrene. Afterward he rode to Uneeda where he found Captain Groesbeck and Count Laumeister in upbeat moods. The laborers had uncovered the bottom dungeon cell door.

"The blast had damaged the door," the accountant said. "Your man Bär is down there setting a charge to blow the door. Ought to know what gold is there shortly."

268

The Devil's Spawn

The Ichneumon prisoners, Zircon soldiers, and officers all milled about waiting near the excavation. Captain Bär and his men emerged yelling "Fire in the hole." A moment later a blast occurred. As they waited for the dust and explosion fumes to dissipate, the Count asked Al his intentions concerning Chief Laredo and Captain Reed.

"Not decided, I had assumed he fled with your pal Reed. We'll talk later."

"No," the aristocrat snapped after checking no one was close enough to hear. He continued, "I want this matter settled now. Reed works for powerful people in Guderian and Myrtle Territories who will cause all of us grief if you try to arrest Reed before having the general's blessing. You got her back and killed Greg, don't start a new uproar."

"Chief Laredo may have run, but he'll be back to try reestablishing his band of marauders and cause all of us problems," Al argued while scraping the ground with his boot to check the thickness of the tan-colored dust that covered every surface in the fort.

"So deal with him then but forget Reed," the Count said, before turning to point toward the Ichneumon prisoners waiting in the shade under the east wall. "Why have they not been shot?"

The man's concern for Reed suggested he must still need him for some scheme. Why the aristocrat wanted the prisoners shot was not clear.

"General Markel told us, his frontline officers, that he wanted the murdering of enemy prisoners to stop. He hopes to exchange them for our captured men. I think it's a sane policy."

Grimacing and shaking his head the Count disputed that. "The Ichneumons will never do that. They always shoot our men."

"Someone has to make the first move," Al said, knowing it was a lost cause trying to convince this narcissistic bastard that not murdering prisoners of war was a sensible military strategy.

"Well, I, Captain Corliss, and most Uneeda residents don't agree. I want them gone. I spoke with Chief Mantas about the killers, and he agrees with me. He wants them out of Uneeda and offered to have his subchief Black Arrow take them north to work on drainage projects. At least they would be earning their keep until Markel realizes his plan won't work."

"Very well, then, I'll make arrangements with the chief." About then Bär wave all clear and Al told the conniving aristocrat, "Let's see if there is any gold."

They entered the excavation to look in the cell. The fumes from the explosives couldn't compete with the smell from three decomposed bodies of Ichneumon soldiers in the rubble covering the floor and gold ingots. After picking up an ingot to verify it was gold, Al told everyone to leave the cell and excavation except for the accountant's men. A quick check of the several cells that had not collapsed found eighteen dead men and women. Many of the bodies were in advanced decomposition, a few skeletons, which suggested some of the prisoners had been dead a while before the assault. The discoveries stoked the hatred of Ichneumons in the people who saw the sight. To keep things calm, Al had Duncan post a guard force at the cell entrance while his men removed all civilians from the fort and locked the place down. The Count stayed with Captain Groesbeck to help weigh the gold bars.

With the treasure secure Al went to Chief Mantas' office in the police station to report on Bari's successful rescue and to thank him for his help. The grey stone two-story police building was a smaller version of the fort; a two-meter-high yellow brick wall surrounding the hundred-meter by hundred-meter square lot with the office building toward the southwest corner and facing the waterfront.

The Zircon's mortar bombardment had spared the police station except for damage from several 40 mm shells used to rout snipers in the stables, a large two-story dark weathered wooden building whose ground floor served as the stable for the police horses. Its upper floor, though missing several sections of its front wall and roof, now served as the barrack for Mantas' policemen. The structure was located along the north side of the lot. Several Oztec-style conical tents stood along the east wall and near the main gate.

With the compound's three gates wide open and bustling with men, women, and noisy children of all the races, except for Ichneumons, the place was more like an Oztec market than a police station. The evil forbidden ambiance of the Ichneumon era was gone. The Count had told him the new police chief had taken over the large back office on the first floor reached by a hallway from the front desk and booking office. Al did not see any holding cells as he waited for the desk clerk to notify Chief Mantas he was there and wondered if the building had a basement, and if the cells were down there. Unoccupied he hoped.

The chief wore one of the Ichneumon police uniforms that had the golden serpent shoulder patches removed and replaced with the red Zircon Iron Cross patches. He greeted Al at the office door with a smile.

"I was delighted to hear the rescue went well and Bari is on the mend." Then in a robust voice, Mantas continued with, "Black Arrow said you ended Greg Laredo's reign of terror." A usually somber and serious man, he surprised Al by grabbing and vigorously shaking his hand. "You did the valley a great service killing that son of a bitch. The Eastern Oztecs thank you."

After acknowledging the chief's kind words and giving Black Arrow and his warriors credit, Al looked around for a chair while saying, "Count Laumeister told me you had concerns about the Ichneumon prisoners."

The chief had started to glance out the window and snapped his attention back to Al. After a noticeable pause, followed by a slight shake of his head, he answered, "I do, but it is complicated. People that two weeks ago were happy to do business with Colonel Kropp's garrison now claim to be afraid of those few surviving Ichneumons. Just how many prisoners are there?"

"Fourteen Ichneumon soldiers were captured, eight had survived their wounds and grueling labor to repair the fort's walls and excavate the dungeon. Colonel Kropp was one of the surviving officers, but then he cut his wrists and died, leaving Captain Maqbool as the surviving Ichneumon officer."

"Hardly the threat to the community that your Count and some of the Uneeda residents worry about. I suggested the army loan the prisoners out to work on the water collection works the eastern tribes are doing with Odrick's men until General Markel tells you what to do with them. That would get them out of Uneeda, out of sight, out of mind."

"Our goal is to end slavery," Al said shaking his head at the chief's suggestion.

"Well, I'm confident the prisoners would prefer that to being lined up and shot. But here's the complication, Juan Velasquez contacted Black Arrow and told him that Reed docked at Seth waiting on the navy warship to escort him to Westport. Apparently, Bergdorf hired the Rouser to transport his gold catch and they supposedly fear traveling alone through the swamp." That nonsense had Al shaking his head in disagreement as the chief added, "For sure, news of your return spooked Reed and caused him to embark before the Zircon Ray."

"Are Bergdorf and his men with Reed?"

The Devil's Spawn

"I figure Bergdorf is going to stick close to his gold and he's not a man to travel without his guards. However, word is he did leave his main henchman, Ivan, to guard the mine and slaves until their legal status is resolved."

"He's wasting his time. General Markel will never allow Bergdorf to use slaves going forward."

"Would you help right a wrong, if it didn't require you breaking the law?" Al nodded curious to hear what hairbrained scheme the chief had in mind.

"Juan offered my man five-thousand D-marks if he would deliver those eight Ichneumon prisoners to Reed at Seth instead of taking them to Odrick's project." The chief appeared amused at Al's startled look.

With the defeat of the Ichneumon army in Uneeda valley, Al had figured a navy warship could safely transport the gold to Westport. River pirates would never attempt to hijack a navy warship, tempting though a three-ton shipment of the emperor's gold might be. They knew the emperor, army and navy would never stop hunting them. The real gangsters like Reed and Penton with their henchmen, as Al suspected Captain Corliss and possibly Count Laumeister to be, would try such a brazen robbery only if they had a dupe, a fall guy, to pin the crime on. Who could be better than an Ichneumon army unit?

"Wow," The audacity of the move gave Al pause for a moment. "Do you think those fools are planning to hijack the Zircon Ray?"

"What would General Markel and you think on discovering the burned-out hulk of Captain Corliss's warship in the swamp and a half-dozen dead Ichneumon soldiers littered about the wreck?"

"I need to sound the alert."

Please don't, I have a better plan."

Chapter 19

"Bergdorf told me you were one of the sane Ichneumons," Al said to the grimy prisoner, Captain Maqbool, whom Black Arrow had unchained and brought to his tent. The chief remained to guard the prisoner after seating him on a chair across the table from Al.

"By that, the miner meant you didn't believe the Sun God bullshit and the need to kill humans. Of course, being a sane person, you would agree, so I will not ask you if that is correct. I think it might be, so instead of executing you and your men I have a proposal."

"I'm all ears," the weary prisoner said with a faint laugh, looking around the tent before focusing back on Al, who then elaborated.

"That riverboat, Rouser, I believe you know the one I'm referring to." Maqbool nodded. "It's parked near where you will be tomorrow evening. It could be your ticket to the Erie River."

"What might that ticket cost?" the prisoner asked, clearly interested, and scooting forward on the chair.

"Probably your life, but here's the offer. My orders are to turn all Ichneumon prisoners over to Chief Black Arrow. He's the warrior who brought you here." Al motioned with a hand toward the warrior and then continued. "His men will march you and your men north to work on drainage works tomorrow. However, if you are agreeable,

The Devil's Spawn

Captain Reed has offered to buy the lot of you for five thousand D-marks."

"Dang, five thousand, we're not worth much, are we?" Maqbool remarked with a brittle laugh. "Why would that procurer want us? I'd kill the bastard the first opportunity that I had."

"Well, I suspect he really just wants your bodies for the police to find so whatever scheme he has planned to hijack the gold shipment appears to be the work of Ichneumons."

After a brief incredulous stare, the prisoner with a shake of his head, asked, "You're serious, the navy warship? How can you know this?"

Freda interrupted the meeting by entering with a pitcher of chilled pear cider and three glasses. She served them while the prisoner and she studied each other. She left without comment. Maqbool, after a moment asked. "Is she the girl from Juan's otter pen?"

Al nodded, thinking after a sip of Freda's cider, pears do make a good drink, then got to business. "What you need to know is Bergdorf is believed to have delivered one hundred and fifty kilograms of gold dust to the riverboat Rouser for delivery to Westport. The chief here would like that gold for his tribe, payment for the families who lost men in the recent battles and died as slaves mining the gold. The Zircon army will not be involved in this unlawful attack. I am involved only because I owe the chief for his help in rescuing Bari. The key point for you and your men is Black Arrow has no use for the boat but thought you might."

Maqbool was not a slow person. "He wants our help when the Oztecs hijack the boat?" Al and the warrior chief both nodded, and the prisoner answered, "Hell, yes, I like the plan."

"The only ones aboard are thugs, Reed's crew. All I ask is Captain Reed not survive the attack. Now here is my suggestion for seizing the Rouser intact."

275

By sunrise, the next morning Al figured everyone in Uneeda territory knew the army found 287 ingots of gold in the fort, about three tons of gold worth two-hundred million D-marks. Count Laumeister wanted the warship Ray to immediately haul all the gold to Westport. Captain Groesbeck wanted to split the hoard into three shipments to minimize loss in the event of a hijacking attempt. They compromised. The Zircon Ray would load only half the gold on the first trip. Count Laumeister and the warship would embark for Westport early tomorrow morning.

Herr Odrick reported to Al the riverboat Rouser remained docked upriver from Seth. Al passed the information on to Black Arrow. Early that afternoon twenty-five of Chief Mantas warriors marched the eight prisoners away from the fort along with a mule that was carrying supplies. The Count, with Al, watched the prisoners and their guards leave, and asked,

"Why are there so many guards?"

"The fighting is over. I figure most of the Oztec warriors are just tagging along to return home," Al answered while praying the attack went as planned and there was no blowback, for powerful people were about to have their plans thwarted.

The Count laughed, "You should have shot them, now the Uneeda folks who are watching the march probably think you sold the Ichneumons to the Oztecs. The locals will figure your talk about outlawing slavey is just more Zircon Empire hypocrisy." Al had no comment.

The next morning the Zircon Ray left with 144 ingots of gold, along with Count Laumeister and Captain Groesbeck for Westport. Al spent the rest of his day supervising repairs to the fort and waiting for news on Black Arrow. Around noon Chief Mantas visited the fort to inspect the repairs.

"I see you're not taking any chances with the remaining ingots walking off," the chief commented, assessing the new iron door set in a thick stone wall that sealed the entrance into the cell. "I have other news," Mantas added, turning and walking back into the sunlight. "Let's us find a quiet corner."

Taking a deep breath and looking around the area, the chief said, "The ambush didn't go as cleanly as we hoped. Black Arrow was hit twice, and Bergdorf escaped, or at least his body wasn't found." To Al's question, he answered, "Black Arrow will recover. Captain Reed is dead. The Ichneumons made good their escape on the Rouser. What we need to wait on is to learn if Rouser managed to stay ahead of the Zircon Ray. Arrow said Maqbool had only a three-hour head start on the warship."

Shaking his head, Al said, "Bergdorf on the loose is a bad break. Maqbool should be okay, he also has a sixty-kilometer head start. Did the rest of it pan out?" The chief nodded. "What about the site, any evidence left, bodies?"

"No, Arrow put Reed and his crew's corpses back on the riverboat and asked Maqbool to leave his three dead soldiers also on board to be discovered after he abandons the Rouser above Westport. It will help the authorities to understand what happened."

"Well let's hope the river got Bergdorf."

Eight days later the Zircon Ray arrived back at Uneeda for the rest of the gold shipment along with news and Colonel Caprivi, General Markel's adjutant. The warship on its trip downriver had discovered the smoking hulk of the Rouser about fifteen kilometers above Westport. No one was sure what had occurred other than the boiler had exploded. Based on the bodies recovered, Chief Laredo, several of his Oztec warriors, and four Ichneumon soldiers along with

Captain Reed's headless body and six of the riverboat crew members, the navy believed Laredo and some of his Ichneumon allies had hijacked the boat and Bergdorf's gold. Since the miner and his gold were both missing, what happened remained a mystery.

Colonel Caprivi, who went to Al's office in the fort as soon as he got free of Chief Mantas, for once had good news. "General Markel sends his congratulations on a job well done and your promotion to major." The promotion pleased Al, though he had hoped for a lieutenant colonel slot.

"The general is not overly concerned that gangsters like Reed come to bad endings," the colonel said. "But the loss of a riverboat to rogue Ichneumon soldiers has him concerned. Your new assignment is to eliminate the rogue Ichneumon soldiers and pirates along with the slavery trade in the Uneeda territory."

Those orders the new Major Belcher could get his heart into.

www.ingramcontent.com/pod-product-compliance
Lightning Source LLC
Chambersburg PA
CBHW060859250626
47159CB00008B/2809